The Hollywood Murder Mystery

A Clay Brooke Mystery

By Herbert Crooker

Originally published in 1930

The Hollywood Murder Mystery

Published by Resurrected Press

This classic book was handcrafted by Resurrected Press. Resurrected Press is dedicated to bringing high quality classic books back to the readers who enjoy them. These are not scanned versions of the originals, but, rather, quality checked and edited books meant to be enjoyed!

Please visit ResurrectedPress.com to view our entire catalogue!

For updates on future releases, LIKE us on Facebook:
http://www.Facebook.com/ResurrectedPress

ISBN 13: 978-1-943403-15-8

Printed in the United States of America

RESURRECTED PRESS BOOKS IN
ERIC LEVISON'S
DR. EDWARD LESTER MYSTERY SERIES

Hidden Eyes

Eyewitness

Ashes of Evidence

RESURRECTED PRESS BOOKS FROM *THE ETHEL THOMAS DETECTIVE STORY* SERIES BY CORTLAND FITZSIMMON'S

The Whispering Window

The Moving Finger

Mystery at Hidden Harbor

The Evil Men Do

RESURRECTED PRESS BOOKS FROM *THE JAMES "BONNIE" DUNDEE MYSTERY* SERIES BY ANNE AUSTIN

The Black Pigeon

The Avenging Parrot

Murder Backstairs

Murder at Bridge

One Drop of Blood

Murdered, But Not Dead

RESURRECTED PRESS CLASSIC MYSTERY CATALOGUE

Journeys into Mystery
Travel and Mystery in a More Elegant Time

The Edwardian Detectives
Literary Sleuths of the Edwardian Era

Gems of Mystery
Lost Jewels from a More Elegant Age

Anne Austin
One Drop of Blood
The Black Pigeon
Murder at Bridge
Murder Backstairs

E. C. Bentley
Trent's Last Case: The Woman in Black

Ernest Bramah
Max Carrados Resurrected:
The Detective Stories of Max Carrados

Agatha Christie
The Secret Adversary
The Mysterious Affair at Styles

Octavus Roy Cohen
Midnight

Freeman Wills Croft
The Ponson Case
The Pit Prop Syndicate

J. S. Fletcher

The Herapath Property
The Rayner-Slade Amalgamation
The Chestermarke Instinct
The Paradise Mystery
Dead Men's Money
The Middle of Things
Ravensdene Court
Scarhaven Keep
The Orange-Yellow Diamond
The Middle Temple Murder
The Tallyrand Maxim
The Borough Treasurer
In the Mayor's Parlour
The Saftey Pin

R. Austin Freeman

The Mystery of 31 New Inn from the Dr. Thorndyke Series
John Thorndyke's Cases from the Dr. Thorndyke Series
The Red Thumb Mark from The Dr. Thorndyke Series
The Eye of Osiris from The Dr. Thorndyke Series
A Silent Witness from the Dr. John Thorndyke Series
The Cat's Eye from the Dr. John Thorndyke Series
Helen Vardon's Confession: A Dr. John Thorndyke Story
As a Thief in the Night: A Dr. John Thorndyke Story
Mr. Pottermack's Oversight: A Dr. John Thorndyke Story
Dr. Thorndyke Intervenes: A Dr. John Thorndyke Story
The Singing Bone: The Adventures of Dr. Thorndyke
The Stoneware Monkey: A Dr. John Thorndyke Story
The Great Portrait Mystery, and Other Stories: A Collection of Dr. John Thorndyke and Other Stories
The Penrose Mystery: A Dr. John Thorndyke Story

The Uttermost Farthing: A Savant's Vendetta

Arthur Griffiths
The Passenger From Calais
The Rome Express

Fergus Hume
The Mystery of a Hansom Cab
The Green Mummy
The Silent House
The Secret Passage

Edgar Jepson
The Loudwater Mystery

A. E. W. Mason
At the Villa Rose

A. A. Milne
The Red House Mystery

Baroness Emma Orczy
The Old Man in the Corner

Edgar Allan Poe
The Detective Stories of Edgar Allan Poe

Arthur J. Rees
The Hampstead Mystery
The Shrieking Pit
The Hand In The Dark
The Moon Rock
The Mystery of the Downs

Mary Roberts Rinehart
Sight Unseen and The Confession

Dorothy L. Sayers

Whose Body?

Sir William Magnay
The Hunt Ball Mystery

Mabel and Paul Thorne
The Sheridan Road Mystery

Louis Tracy
The Strange Case of Mortimer Fenley
The Albert Gate Mystery
The Bartlett Mystery
The Postmaster's Daughter
The House of Peril
The Sandling Case: What Would You Have Done?

Charles Edmonds Walk
The Paternoster Ruby

John R. Watson
The Mystery of the Downs
The Hampstead Mystery

Edgar Wallace
The Daffodil Mystery
The Crimson Circle

Carolyn Wells
Vicky Van
The Man Who Fell Through the Earth
In the Onyx Lobby
Raspberry Jam
The Clue
The Room with the Tassels
The Vanishing of Betty Varian
The Mystery Girl
The White Alley
The Curved Blades

FOREWORD

The Hollywood Murder Mystery is set in the unique world of Hollywood in the period between the first motion picture and the end of Prohibition, a time of wild parties, speak-easies, and stars and starlets. Southern California film industry at the time was awash with movie money as successful actors, directors and producers became overnight millionaires who sought to spend their money as quickly and as publicly as they had made it.

When an up and coming starlet is found murdered at one of the studios, it becomes the task of detective Clay Brooke to solve her murder. In typical Hollywood fashion, Brooke is in California to work on a screen play. The studios were as willing pay writers as actors, and the huge amounts of money they were willing to spend attracted such literary luminaries as Dashiell Hammett, F. Scot Fitzgerald, and William Faulkner.

Hollywood, itself, with its money, extravagances, and rivalries, was to become fertile ground for writers of detective fiction, most notably by Raymond Chandler and Raoul Whitfield. And given the public's demand at the time for mystery novels, it's not surprising that many a screen-writer turned their hand to the genre. Given the old adage, "write what you know," it is only natural that some of them turned to their own industry as subject matter.

It's unclear how closely Herbert Crooker was associated with the film industry, lesser known screen-writers rarely got credit for their work. Yet, from his detailed knowledge of the locale and his familiarity with the behind the camera workings of a studio it is obvious that he must have spent some time in the business. It is known that he was involved in the serialization of one movie serial for printing in newspapers as early as 1923, and he is also credited as writer and producer of the short film "I'll Tell the World" in 1939. One can only assume that he was involved in other capacities in the interim.

Today, *The Hollywood Murder Mystery* is as much of interest for its portrayal of the early movie industry as it is for the murder mystery it contains. It is with pleasure that Resurrected Press releases this new edition of this forgotten novel.

About the Author

Herbert Crooker, the author of *the Hollywood Murder Mystery,* also wrote *The Crime in Washington Mews* (1931) featuring the same detective, Clay Brooke. Other mysteries by him include *The Sweet Cheat* (1931) and *Man About Broadway* (1946). During his early career, he wrote stories for magazines such as *New Yorker* as well as the newspaper serialization *The Timber Queen* which was adapted from a movie serial. He is also credited as the writer and producer of the 1939 short film "I'll Tell the World."

Greg Fowlkes
Editor-In-Chief
Resurrected Press
www.ResurrectedPress.com

TABLE OF CONTENTS

I. The Telephone Rings

When Clay Brooke and I set out for Claire Demoset's garden party, in the fashionable Beverly Hills section of Hollywood, we looked forward to an afternoon of perfect enjoyment. There was nothing to mar the serenity of the occasion—nothing to foreshadow the succession of terrorizing events that so soon were to plunge the film colony into abysmal chaos.

Of one thing I was certain—that Brooke looked forward to seeing Claire Demoset. I had been considering my friend's symptoms since his first meeting with the glamorous beauty of the films, and with the authority of a scenario expert who had "done things" in the way of supplying love interest where plots ran tepid, I put Brooke's feelings down as the real thing, almost from the first. When I would question him quizzically as to his intentions toward the lady, he would fix his humorous blue eyes on me and reply in a manner which was always disarming.

"Gregory, old fellow," he would say, "there have been a great many beautiful women in my life—in a nice way, of course! Some of them have interested me more than others. In fact, Miss Demoset comes under this category, if it will make you any happier to know it. But, if the truth be told, Gregory Black, I am a philanderer at heart."

It was odd that Clay Brooke, one of America's foremost criminologists; whom I had never seen until a few weeks ago, should be confiding his inmost thoughts and feelings to me—odd that we should have struck up such a close friendship in so short a time. But there it was! And what was more, Brooke was sharing my bungalow.

It had all come about through his dislike of the ostentation of Hollywood's best hotel, where a suite had been reserved for him by my producing organization, which had summoned him to assist me in the creation of a series of underworld pictures. At that time he confessed that he thoroughly enjoyed the novelty of his contacts with the people of the film world, but that he hankered for privacy when the day's work was done.

When I invited him to share my quarters, he accepted unhesitatingly. That it was an excellent move, I was certain; for, our first collaboration was already giving promise of being something different in the way of underworld "thrillers". His intensive study of crime and the criminal—which was his hobby, or his pet vice, as he called it—fitted him admirably for the work.

I judged Clay Brooke to be a man in his late thirties. He had a fine head, and his dark hair was graying slightly, lending the distinction of maturity to his firm features and his youthful bearing. The few, almost imperceptible, wrinkles about his eyes deepened when he smiled, and his smile was almost perpetual. His whimsical sense of humor, together with his modesty and unobtrusiveness, heightened his pronounced charm of personality. Nature had been generous to him; life had been kind to him; and he reflected both gifts in everything he did.

His coming to Hollywood to do film work, Brooke treated as a lark. It was amazing the degree of fun he could get out of everything. He had been lionized by the social set of filmdom. The fact is, there were whisperings that his connection with films was being used as a blind, that there was something, much deeper, connected with his sudden arrival. Perhaps that was only gossip; although I knew that the criminologist had been spending considerable time with District Attorney John Rawson. Brooke told me that the man's legal mind stimulated him, and I was satisfied to accept that as the reason for the friendship.

On this particular day, Brooke and I decided to knock off work and attend Claire's party; and, with the stimulation we'd bring back from it, resume the complications of our screen play. There was no particular reason why Claire Demoset should give a party, so far as anybody knew, except that she had just completed work on her latest picture and would have a few days' leisure before facing the cameras again. But after all, minor excuses in Hollywood are good enough for gay festivities without the major ones of a legal holiday, somebody's wedding, or, perhaps, a divorce.

"Well, are you ready?" Brooke asked, peering into my room. Then, when he saw me eyeing his spotless white flannels, he added, "I won't be committing a breach of etiquette if I wear these, will I? I simply detest plus fours, you know—don't even wear 'em on the golf course. The beastly stockings make my legs itch."

"Not all of us wear knickerbockers," I laughed. "There are occasional gentlemen in Hollywood who prefer white flannels. To keep you company, I'll add to their number."

"Well, let's get going!" he admonished good-naturedly. "It's not exactly the thing to keep a hostess waiting—especially such a beautiful one!"

Fifteen minutes later we were in my coupe humming along the boulevard in the direction of Beverly Hills. On the way, Brooke was silent, living in thoughts that I could almost guess and which I had no wish to interrupt. It was only when I made the turn in the road toward the gravel drive which led to the star's magnificent estate that I called out, "Here we are!" and startled my friend back, to the time and the place.

Claire Demoset's house, which was splendidly set at some distance from the street and drive, was a gem of Spanish architecture. On the four acres of the place there were a swimming pool of generous dimensions, two tennis courts—one of grass and one of cement—a guest-house, garage, and servants' quarters.

"A model estate in miniature," Brooke observed in enthusiastic admiration, "a spot worthy of its exquisite owner."

As we left the car in the parking space, music came to us from the rear of the house and we lost no time joining those at the scene of gaiety.

"Enchanting!" exclaimed Brooke.

My gaze involuntarily followed his. Claire Demoset was coming toward us. No wonder he had found so much enchantment in the scene!

"Oh, I'm so glad you've come!" she cried. "And you, too, Greg! I'm sure you both know everybody here, and even if you don't it doesn't matter. Now, please tell me what you want to do! If you want to take a swim—there's the pool! If you want to dance— there's the tennis court and the best music in captivity! If you—"

"Please—please!" Brooke exclaimed in mock bewilderment. "I'd be ever so happy if you'd just permit me to walk around and feast my eyes on the abundance of concentrated beauty assembled here."

Claire laughed, for he looked pointedly at her while he spoke.

"I'm glad you like—everything." She broke off, with a sweeping gesture which seemed to take in "everything".

"Like it!" echoed Brooke. "I'm simply enchanted!"

"Oh, but I've something new to show you— something in the way of beauty which you haven't seen yet. No, don't let him interrupt me, Greg." She turned to me in pretended appeal. "And as a reward I'll show her to you, too!"

"What is this tremendous mystery?" Brooke laughed.

Just then a girl flitted by.

"There!" exclaimed our hostess. "There she is now!" Then before we could interpose she called, "Berylyn!"

The girl turned. She was a perfect blonde type with a mass of tawny hair and a figure lithe and supple. As she approached, Claire hastened to tell us that she was a new picture star just come from the Follies. Then, smilingly, she presented her.

"Miss Bovary is going to make my afternoon a huge success," she finished. "You'll see!"

"I can see it already," Brooke said gallantly.

"Your friends are flatterers," Berylyn Bovary said with a pleased little laugh, turning to Claire.

"Heavens! I hope not!" exclaimed Claire, pretending consternation. "That would rob me of all the pleasure I've had from everything they've ever said to me!" She looked at Clay Brooke as she spoke.

"Then you must give me the opportunity to reassure you," he smiled.

"What opportunity do you want?" Claire asked, wide-eyed.

"First, the proper setting—such as a secluded nook. I'm sure you've one of those things nearby." Then, taking Claire's arm, he said to the blonde girl and me, "You will excuse us? I'm leaving you in good hands, Miss Bovary."

Without waiting for them to disappear, I turned my attention to my companion. She appeared to be deep in thought. "Something disquieting," I said to myself. A cold look came into her lovely gray eyes. Then, becoming aware of my presence as suddenly as she had forgotten me, she smiled disarmingly.

"I—I was thinking of Claire," she said. "A flaming beauty, isn't she?" But there was a sinister undercurrent in her tone.

"She *is* flaming," I returned. "A lovely creature."

"Oh, yes," she conceded. "Her reddish blonde hair is quite the rage, I understand—goes so well with blue eyes, too." She laughed mockingly, and beautiful as she was in her sophisticated way, at that moment she looked almost repulsive. "Envy," I said to myself.

She broke off suddenly, and a look of terror crept into her eyes. I followed her gaze to see what it was that had startled her so strangely, but could only glimpse the passing figure of a man. Berylyn Bovary glanced quickly about; then, before I knew it, she was gone without a word.

What could have been the reason for her agitation, I wondered, for her abrupt departure without a word of explanation or apology. Well, she certainly wasn't wasting any love on our hostess. Couldn't matter much to Claire, In any event. She was the most beautiful star in Hollywood—riding on the crest of the wave of popularity, no matter what Berylyn Bovary thought or felt.

Suddenly I wondered what had become of Clay Brooke. Then I remembered the secluded nook he had hoped to find, and I wished that I might secure just such a place for serious reflection. I walked past the pool where a gathering of film celebrities were having the time of their joyous young lives, and continued along a path which wound up at a lovely arbor. Presently my attention was drawn to a stone bench almost entirely surrounded by heavy, thick foliage. It beckoned invitingly and I sat down to the comfort of its seclusion and lighted a cigaret.

As I tossed the match away, I heard voices coming from the dense shrubbery behind me—voices raised in dispute—a man's voice and a woman's. And the woman's voice unmistakably belonged to Berylyn Bovary.

"I tell you—I've had enough of this!" the man stormed. "This is going to be a show-down the finish!"

"No! No!" she begged. "Can't you be reasonable? If you'll only wait—"

"I won't wait! Tonight—do you hear me!"

This was an opportunity for me to steal away. It didn't seem right for me to be listening. But, somehow, I felt myself rooted to the spot. Perhaps, too, I ought to stay, I told myself—offer to help her, if necessary.

"Very well, then—tonight!" she agreed in her desperation. "I'll be through at the studio about seven o'clock—I'll see you then. But for God's sake, go now!"

Evidently he departed, for there was quiet again. Then came a sound as if the girl was weeping. I decided to make my presence known; but, before I could stir, the sobs turned into a crescendo of hysterical laughter.

I had had about enough of it. The whole thing was beginning to get on my nerves. I determined to seize the opportunity and find my way to pleasanter distractions. But I had hardly risen from my concealed position when I realized the need of resuming it again. Footsteps, and the low conversation of a couple coming from the direction in which I was about to beat my retreat, reached my ears. I scarcely felt equal to facing any one at the moment.

Were my auditory nerves, now taut and tense, playing me a trick? I was sure that I recognized Claire Demoset's voice—strained, somewhat, but her voice, nevertheless—and it was Berylyn Bovary about whom she was talking.

"I suppose I should be surprised, but I'm not," she was saying. "According to what I've heard, this is not the first home Berylyn has wrecked."

"Well, it'll be her last!" came bitterly from the man. I did not recognize his voice, nor could I see his face. As they came closer I was in fear of discovery, for a moment, lest they enter the arbor to continue their talk.

"Don't spare her!" Claire was saying vehemently. "She deserves no mercy!"

"She'll get none from me!" returned her companion grimly. "If you—"

Just then, Berylyn Bovary, who had evidently recovered her composure enough to rejoin the party, came upon them. I wondered if she had heard anything of their conversation, but if she had, she gave no sign. Calmly she called, "Oh, hello, Claire!" and came toward them.

As the young man turned I could see his face—an unfamiliar one to me. He was looking questioningly at

Claire, who in the surprise of the incident was inarticulate. The blonde girl appeared to be enjoying the situation, and coming closer, she went on, with a little laugh, "Hunting for another little secluded nook, Claire? Delightful grounds you have—seem to be secluded spots 'most everywhere."

Claire Demoset flashed a significant glance at her escort. Then:

"Miss Bovary, may I present Mr. Gilbert—Charles Gilbert's son?"

I saw the blonde girl start at the mention of the name, but she recovered her poise and flashed a captivating smile at him as she acknowledged the introduction.

"Mr. Gilbert has requested an introduction to you," Claire said meaningly. "He wanted to meet the girl that— in whom his father is so greatly interested." There was the glitter of battle in Claire's eyes as she spoke. For a long moment the Bovary girl returned her gaze insolently.

"I should like to have a few words alone with Miss Bovary," young Gilbert cut in; then turning to the blonde girl, he added, "if I may?"

Affecting the sort of smile she gave him earlier, Berylyn Bovary said evenly, "Certainly, but not just now. I've promised Miss Demoset I'd dance for her guests and it's very nearly time."

"When, then?" he asked tensely.

She appeared to be considering the question; then, as if she were extracting some humor from her decision, she said, "Oh, any time at the Eclaire Studio. I'm making a test there later this afternoon. You might drop in if you happen to be passing—say around seven? Perhaps Miss Demoset will bring you?" And continuing to smile, she blew a kiss in their direction, and a moment later she was gone.

Claire Demoset and the young man watched her in silence until she disappeared from view. "Bad and brazen," was Claire's comment.

"But she can't get away with it, you know!" he exclaimed. "Hollywood is too small to hold a woman of that sort and—my—my—mother—"

But they had gone and the rest was lost. I could not control a low whistle of amazement, as I made my way back to the crowd, when I reflected on all I'd seen and heard. Certainly I had not bargained on that sort of entertainment when I'd accepted Claire's invitation. Then I remembered Clay Brooke, and the idea came to me to hunt him up and tell him of the strange events; but then I decided I would let them keep till later.

"Well—well, old fellow!" I looked up and beheld the criminologist smiling at me. "You've appeared from your retirement just in time. Claire is about to start the fire-works. I'm wagering it's going to be a bull fight! Let's get a good place on the lawn where we can see everything."

Just then we saw Claire beckoning to us from the other side of the cement tennis court and we hastened to join her. I looked for traces of her recent agitation, but she seemed serene. As we found seats, the drummer of the orchestra struck his cymbals for attention and a hush followed, most of the guests drawing their chairs closer to the edge of the court. The drummer then rose and made an announcement which we were unable to understand.

The band suddenly began the strange rhythm of a tango, and the next moment Berylyn Bovary and a dark young man appeared, and ran to the center of the tennis court. A storm of applause greeted them as they clasped hands and bowed—"Tribute," I reflected, "to the girl's startling beauty." Then they faced each other and began to dance.

It was an exciting picture. They were a handsome couple as they glided and dipped to the syncopation of the *Argentine*, while the array of surrounding beauty watched in intense admiration. The Bovary girl's blonde beauty, with her mass of tawny tresses tossing in the sunlight, was accentuated by the dark good looks of her partner, who had the appearance of a Spaniard, from his sleek, glossy hair, to his white teeth and well-chiseled features.

"She's a handsome wench," Brooke remarked to Claire Demoset, watching them admiringly. "But who's the—who is her partner?"

"I didn't get the name—it's rather a strange one. You see, when I 'phoned Miss Bovary and invited her, she offered to help me entertain my guests—that is, if I would permit her to bring the young man—the one she's dancing with."

At that moment the dance ended, and another storm of applause greeted the dancers. Then the strains of an old-fashioned waltz came from the other side of the tennis court. And as the girl and her dancing-partner began their graceful interpretation of it, Claire Demoset settled, back in her chair and sighed happily. Her party was a success. She had discovered something new—fresh talent for jaded Hollywood.

Just then, I heard a man's voice behind me.

"Oh, she isn't so hot!" he was saying. "You don't know her as I do. She's a trouble-maker—that one. But she isn't going to make any in the picture of hers that I'm directing—not if I can help it. She'll get hers some day if she don't watch her step."

"Is the sheik with her, her leading man?" came a girl's voice.

"Him!" The man laughed rather unpleasantly. "He's—nothing! And he's going to get his, too. Wait and you'll see, baby." There was a pause for a moment. Then: "You know old man Gilbert—the Charles Gilbert? Well, he's the sucker who's financing her picture—and all the rest."

For some reason I glanced at Clay Brooke and saw that he, too, had overheard the conversation. He smiled oddly in my direction, then turned to Claire. "Who are those two people behind us?" he asked in a low tone.

Claire darted a glance over her shoulder. Then: "I don't know them, but I believe the man is a director—the sort that makes 'quickies', pictures made on a shoe-string. I didn't invite them to the party—they must have crashed."

"Crashed?" Brooke repeated blankly. "Then they are aviators?"

Claire laughed and was about to reply when the waltz ended. I could see Brooke's eyes following the radiant head of the Bovary girl as she bowed and smiled while the applause continued. There was such a touch of childish delight in her manner over the pleasure of her reception from the onlookers that it was difficult for me to believe that the strange scenes I had overheard were true. Suddenly the orchestra blazed into a fox-trot, and everyone swarmed onto the cement court for dancing.

It was shortly after six when we returned to my bungalow. Brooke was jubilant over the party, first discussing the charm of Claire Demoset, then the blonde beauty of the Bovary girl whose dancing seemed to have quite captivated him.

"I very nearly escorted the lady home," he said. "In fact, I would have, but she departed early. Claire said she had to report to the studio to make a camera test. Damned annoying, the uncertain hours of your working girls!"

"Not thinking of transferring your affections, are you?" I asked.

Brooke threw back his head and laughed. "My affections are a source of trouble to you, aren't they, Greg? No, I can't say that I am." He became serious for a moment. "But—I can't explain it—there's something about the blonde girl that intrigues, in a way that almost troubles me—something rather disquieting, almost eerie. Frankly, I'm worried, but I can't for the life of me explain why. Great Heavens!" he laughed again. "Can it be that I'm getting psychic—at my age!"

I had been debating with myself whether to tell Brooke of the strange scenes I had witnessed during the afternoon, and his last remark induced me to unfold everything. But as I was about to speak, dinner was announced and my Japanese servant hung over us.

When we had finished, and Brooke had discarded his coat for the greater comfort of his smoking jacket, we retired to my study. He had so many new ideas for our scenario that there was nothing for me to do but to fall into his spirit of work. We had finished one Sequence, and were about to take up the next, when the shrill ringing of the telephone broke against the stillness of the night. Startled, we both jumped at the sudden sound.

"I'll answer it," Brooke said. "It's probably the District Attorney. He said something about calling me to arrange a foursome of golf."

Presently, I could hear his staccato ejaculations coming from the hallway where he had gone to answer the telephone. In a few minutes he returned, the glitter of suppressed excitement in his eyes.

"Can you stand a shock, Greg?" he asked, coming close to me.

"Was it the District Attorney?"

"Yes—but not about golf!"

There was a strange expression in his eyes, now. Something in his tone gripped me.

"What—"

"Murder!" Brooke stepped back to watch the effect of his announcement on me.

For a long moment I was stupefied. The incidents of the afternoon, of which Brooke knew nothing, came crowding in on me in a confused jumble. Then, the thing that stood out clearly, more clearly than anything else at the moment, was the sinister expression in the Bovary girl's eyes when she spoke of Claire Demoset after Brooke had walked off with the screen star. Yes, that was it. The women must have quarreled, and in a jealous rage, the dancer had killed Claire. I stared at Brooke who stood off regarding me queerly, and I thought that he had grown peculiarly pale. Then, at length, I managed to blurt out:

"Not—not Claire Demoset!"

"Good God—no!" There was a note of relief in his tone, with something akin to terror at the suggestion.

"The murder took place at the Eclaire Studio," he went on more evenly.

"And the victim? Out with it, man!"

"The Bovary girl—"

"Miss Bovary!" I broke in, startled.

"Yes," Brooke said quietly. "The blonde dancer. Uncanny, isn't it?"

"Berylyn Bovary—dead—! Killed, you say—?" I asked again, looking at him in blank incredulity.

"Berylyn Bovary," he repeated, almost solemnly this time. "The District Attorney wants me to run up and look the ground over. Suppose you come along? Don't like to leave you here alone," he smiled. "You look all shot to pieces."

If I looked "all shot to pieces", as Brooke had suggested, I certainly felt it; for now a thought took hold of me even more ghastly than the earlier one, and try as I would, I couldn't shake it off.

"I'll be ready in a minute," Brooke was saying as he made for his room. "Just have to change my coat."

II. The Murder

In the brief interval, while I was alone, all of the wild, incongruous events of the afternoon flashed before my eyes with kaleidoscopic rapidity. The incidents I had overheard at Claire Demoset's garden party seemed as utterly mad and inexplicable as the tea party presided over by the Mad Hatter in *Alice in Wonderland*, with the exception that there was no drowsy dormouse.

As the events rushed through my mind again they were more incredible than ever. I remembered Claire's rather proprietary air when she presented us to the Bovary girl; then the strange dispute I had overheard between Berylyn and the man whom I was unable to identify. Who was the fellow, anyway? And had he kept that seven o'clock studio appointment with the dancer?

I recalled the colorful tango performed by Berylyn Bovary and the dark young stranger. What part did he play in the drama? Then, like a flash, Claire Demoset's relentless words to young Gilbert recurred to me. "Don't show her any mercy!" she had said. And again I tried to shut out the dread thought that had come to me before. But I couldn't, somehow. Was it possible that the film queen could be implicated in the murder?

"Well, are you coming along, Greg?" Brooke asked, returning. "It's a chance to watch the unraveling of a crime from behind the scenes, you know."

"Yes—" I agreed, without any conscious volition on my part.

"Good!" returned Brooke with something of forced enthusiasm. He was doing his utmost, I could see, to lift me out of the strange mood that had taken possession of me. "Besides," he went on genially, "now, I can return the compliment! You have been so kind as to show me how a miniature steamship can be sunk in a tub of water and look like the real thing—now I can attempt to show you how the solution of a crime is worked out from the beginning, and the guilty party brought to justice."

Within a few minutes we were in my car, speeding toward the Eclaire Studio, which was one of the smaller ones on Sunset Boulevard. While I was wondering if I should tell Brooke of the events of the afternoon, the criminologist was gazing ahead into the darkness. Finally he drew out his watch and looked at it. As the street lights flashed by I could see that it was about eight o'clock.

"Who is—or was, this Berylyn Bovary?" Brooke suddenly asked. "I don't believe I ever heard of her before this afternoon."

"To tell the truth, I don't know much more about her than you do. I remember that Claire mentioned that she had been in the *Follies.*"

"Yes—one of those girls who glorifies herself into getting a movie contract. H'm! Remember the fellow who sat behind us on the lawn? He hinted rather scandalous information concerning Bovary's connections with a Mr. Charles Gilbert. Let's see, the fellow behind us was to direct Bovary, wasn't he? Greg, do you happen to know this Gilbert?"

"I know *of* him—but I've never met him. He's a very wealthy man. He's always been interested in motion pictures."

"And pretty girls who want to play in them, no doubt," Brooke finished for me.

I was about to mention the rather startling fact that young Gilbert was probably mixed up in the affair, but I hesitated. It might bring Claire Demoset into the ugly mess, and I saw no need of doing that. I decided to wait. Brooke drew out his lighter and lighted a fresh cigaret. Then he sank back into silence until we reached the bright-light section of Hollywood.

"Hello, what's this!" he said, peering ahead. "Look at the crowd that's gathered, already! Mr. and Mrs. Morbid and all the little Morbids are here in advance of us, so this must be the place. Better park around here, somewhere, hadn't we?"

I pulled up to the curb and stopped a short distance from the studio entrance. Then I followed Brooke toward the scene of the murder. He pushed his way through the excited throng and approached the door, while I hurried to keep up with him.

"Hey! Where d'you think you're goin'!" demanded a burly police officer who was posted at the entrance.

"The District Attorney expects me—Clay Brooke is my name—"

"Oh, yes!" answered the officer conciliatorily. "Mr. Rawson is inside with the others—right up them stairs, Mr. Brooke, and then keep goin'."

We entered the studio, passed through the dimly-lighted waiting room, with its empty benches usually swarming with "extras", and started up the short flight of stairs which led to the studio stage. When we reached the top, Brooke paused and gazed with admiration at a Chinese street "set" which was on our left.

"Shanghai, as I live!" he ejaculated. "You people can do amazing things, Greg. Sinister-looking in this light, isn't it? Takes me back six years. I was trailing a chap who thought he was a master-mind, and if my memory isn't playing me tricks, I got him on just such a street as this one. If he hadn't used a certain make of typewriter and writing-paper with an unusual watermark, he'd still be master-minding.

Brooke wandered through the Chinese "set," gazing at it curiously. He seemed to be in no hurry to find the District Attorney, so fascinated had he become by the oriental scene. Where doorways were open, he peered inside and chuckled at the small "back-drop" that gave the effect of an interior.

"It's all very interesting, Greg." Then, like a flash, his interest was deflected to something on the floor.

"Hello—what's this!" he exclaimed, stooping to pick up a dainty white kid glove which he held up, presently, and dangled it triumphantly in his hand.

"Belonged to a lady," he remarked, "a lady with a tiny hand. Now, what was she doing here—and in this bizarre spot."

Then he sniffed it and a startled expression came into his eyes. He was about to say something, but changed his mind, and, crushing the glove in his hand, he stuffed it into his pocket. "Let's get on," he said quickly, affecting a lightness of manner which he was far from feeling, I judged. "I see another minion of the law directly ahead. That must be where the polishing-off took place."

We continued onward and passed two other "sets" which stood on our left. The flickering glare of the single arc-light, which furnished the only illumination on the studio stage, threw eerie shadows and brought out all of the crude points of the scenic-painter's art. One set was a small corner of an office, replete with the usual furnishings; the other, at the extreme end of the stage, was a lavishly furnished interior. It was evident" that work had recently been going on, for the lights were still standing facing the living-room "set". We passed a door labeled "Office" on our right; then we came to another, where a police officer regarded us.

"I'm to see Mr. Rawson," Brooke announced. "Kindly inform him that Clay Brooke is here."

The stern expression on the officer's face changed to one of almost welcome. "You can go right in, sir," he said. "Mr. Rawson is waiting for you." He opened the door and we both entered.

The scene that met our eyes is common to any one connected with the motion-picture studio or the theater. It was an ordinary dressing-room, with a dressing-table, mirror, and lights in one corner, and a small wash-bowl with running water in the other. The room had only one window, which was closed, and on the right of it stood a couch. In another corner was a clothes wardrobe with the door half open. A number of chairs completed the furnishings. I glanced about in vain for signs of the victim. The occupants of the room turned expectantly as we entered.

I immediately recognized John Rawson, the District Attorney, prominent politically in Los Angeles. I judged him to be about fifty years of age. He was of middle height and well built. His hair was gray; and he had a rather colorless complexion, and a firm profile. His forehead was prominent, and his face was clean-shaven. His eyes were unusually small and round, with an expression in them which was both searching and disquieting.

"Glad you came, Brooke," he said, stepping forward 'to shake hands with the criminologist. "Ugly crime here," he frowned darkly, "may have to ask for your help in the case."

Then turning to the others, he added, "This, Brooke, is Brimmer, the studio manager; this is Inspector McGregory; this is Carling, captain of detectives; and this is Taylor, private detective for a group of the studios."

Brooke bowed pleasantly as he shook hands with each one of them. Then he introduced me all around.

Paul Brimmer, the studio manager, I had known since the days when he was a property boy on the Superfilm "lot." He was. slender, with the droop in his narrow shoulders of the day-and-night toiler, and his smooth-shaven face wore the pallor of an indoor existence under studio lights. There was a perpetual, forbidding squint in his eyes, and above them rose a tall brow, almost abnormal in height, crowned by a mass of black curly hair—not the sort of person with whom one could be friendly.

Inspector McGregory and Detective Captain Carling I had never seen before. McGregory defied detective tradition by wearing a golf cap. He was a slight, wiry individual, with watery eyes that gave the impression of looking past you. Carling, who was to be associated with us on the case, was of benevolent aspect and portly build, a fatherly sort of man. A Panama hat rested on his close-cropped head and a pair of small bright eyes looked out keenly on the world from beneath bushy eyebrows. Taylor, the studio detective, was a nondescript type, short and stocky, with an absurd-looking, close-cropped mustache beneath his snub nose. His large blue eyes, with perpetually startled expression, seemed to dart glances in all directions. His general appearance was that of a comedy character in a play, endeavoring with all his soul to ape his superiors!

"It's an ugly crime, Brooke, an ugly crime," John Rawson repeated, when formalities were over. "I'm glad you were so prompt in getting here. Got here only a few moments ago myself, and outside of questioning a number of people I haven't had an opportunity to make much of an investigation. I wish you would look the ground over well before the experts arrive and start messing things around."

"Why, Rawson—this is, indeed, flattery!" Brooke smiled. "Now, what—er—what sort of a room is this, if I may ask?"

"This is the dressing-room the victim used. But first let me tell you all I know of the case. I've questioned the night watchman and Miss Bovary's maid briefly. I learned most of the facts of value from Taylor, here, the studio detective. Seems that Miss Bovary came to the studio late this afternoon to have some camera tests taken in the gowns for her film production. Quite the usual custom before the actual filming commences, according to Taylor."

He paused and glanced at the studio detective who confirmed his statement by bobbing his head rapidly.

"Miss Bovary had completed the necessary tests and had retired to this room. This was about seven o'clock. The studio staff—that is, the director, cameraman, and electricians, had left the studio, and Miss Bovary's personal maid had stepped out to get some aspirin for the star. She says that Miss Bovary had complained of a headache. Shortly after seven, Mr. Charles Gilbert—I'll tell you more of him in a moment—arrived at the studio to take Miss Bovary out—dinner and the theater. He spoke to the night watchman upon entering, waited inside for some minutes, and when the maid returned both of them entered this room and found the body of Miss Bovary in that small wardrobe in the corner."

Our eyes turned automatically in the direction of the half-open door of the wardrobe which the District Attorney indicated.

"You can see," Rawson continued, "that at the time the crime was committed, the studio crew had left, the victim's maid was out for a moment, and the night watchman was at his post. Then Mr. Gilbert arrived, followed by the maid, and discovered the crime. Puzzle, eh, Brooke?"

"Er—yes. But tell me more about this fellow, Charles Gilbert?"

"Mr. Gilbert is a man well past middle age. I would say he is striking-looking, well-preserved, and always well-groomed. He is said to be worth several million, and he is married and has a son. As to his relations with the victim—if that's what you're driving at—I can tell you nothing. I understand that he financially assisted in the production of a number of motion pictures, and it is altogether probable that he was interested in this picture Miss Bovary was to star in, although that is speculation on my part. Mr. Gilbert's pretty cut up over what happened and has offered to assist me in every way possible. I didn't think it advisable to hold him because of his social standing, but I'm having him watched. There was also a woman here who came in after Gilbert did— the movie star, Claire Demoset."

The color came and went on Brooke's face, and he quickly lighted a cigaret to conceal his nervousness.

"What did she want?" he asked calmly.

"Says she just dropped in to see the Bovary girl," Rawson replied. "Awfully hard hit, though, when she heard the news. Had a terrible case of hysterics. I hustled her out and sent her home. But she'll be needed at the inquest."

Brooke nodded with well-simulated casualness. But his hand went involuntarily to the pocket into which I had seen him put the glove he had found. There was something protective in the movement, I couldn't help thinking.

"We are inclined to believe the motive of the crime to be robbery," Rawson went on. "The victim possessed a remarkable collection of costly jewels. She wore some of them to the studio and they're missing. Besides, Taylor has seen a suspicious-looking man hanging around ever since Miss Bovary started work here; and the victim's maid, Margaret Hagney, has corroborated Taylor's statement and given a very similar description of the man."

"H'm—that's interesting," Brooke remarked. "Now—now may I have a look at the body? I promise not to disturb anything."

"Assuredly," replied the District Attorney. "Haven't moved anything yet, myself. Best to leave things as they are until my staff of experts arrive." He approached the wardrobe in the corner of the room and pushed back the door slightly.

There, in a mass of disorder, lay the crumpled form of Berylyn Bovary in an unnatural, twisted position. Her head was dropped forward and her blonde hair was disheveled and matted with blood. I could see a number of ugly bruises on her neck on either side of the collar bone, and the torn condition of her gown gave testimony of an ineffectual struggle with her assailant.

"You can see, Clay," Rawson said quietly, "that I have left the scene of the crime as I found it."

"Curious," said Brooke, bending forward and examining the victim, "curious that the murderer should trouble to thrust the body in this place. H'm—those marks on the neck are peculiar—don't look like finger-marks, Rawson. But, it appears as if she has been strangled. That's an ugly wound on her head. Must have been struck by some blunt object. Anybody find a blunt object lying about? Her clothes are pretty badly torn, but that's what would be expected. A mighty strenuous affair this was, and she put up a game fight for life. Hang it all, I can't quite understand those marks on her neck! Let's have a look at the hands—the hands of the victim are most important. Yes, there are sure signs of a struggle—look at the way that stone in her ring has indented the flesh. And by the way, Rawson, why didn't the murderer take that ring, if a theft of. jewels was the motive? Probably was in a hurry to make a getaway, eh? Better make a note of it just the same. Now the finger-nails. No, not much can be discovered there without the aid of a microscope. Well, we'd better wait for the autopsy surgeon and see what his official statement will bring forth.

"Now let's look around and see if we can find our blunt object," Clay Brooke said rising to his feet. He examined the floor with a sweeping glance, peered under the couch, and then walked over to the dressing-table. Something attracted his eye. Then with an ejaculation of impatience, he hurried back to the wardrobe and examined it as best he could without moving the body.

"Carling," he said suddenly, turning to the captain of detectives, "haven't you been able to find some kind of a blunt object around here? That's right—you haven't been here much longer than I have. How about you, Taylor? And there really should be at least one drop of blood on the floor. Curious, isn't it? Now the murderer couldn't possibly have used one of these chairs. Still, let's have a look at them and see if there are any signs of blood."

"Nothing here, sir," Carling announced. "Clean as a whistle."

"Or a hound's tooth," Brooke added. "Well, our weapon couldn't have been thrown out of the window, because the window is shut and locked. It must have been that he took it with him. But on the other hand, he was probably devilish anxious to get rid of it. Well, we'll find it in the next fifteen minutes, I'll wager. I see the lady had company some time this evening."

"What's that, sir?" asked Inspector McGregory.

"Two different brands of cigarets have been smoked, according to the ash-tray on the dressing-table. The butt of only one of them shows signs of lip rouge. Elemental of course, but it offers a hint. I fancy the maid can explain that to us. How about finger-prints?"

"The finger-print experts are on the way," said the District Attorney, "as well as the photographer. And it's about time Dr. Jeffreys arrived."

"Who's he?" Brooke demanded.

"Jeffreys?—why, he's the county autopsy surgeon."

"Oh, to be sure!" the criminologist said with a laugh. "My mind is so set upon finding that blunt object that I can't think of anything else. I'll step outside for a few minutes, if you don't mind, and regard that street of old Shanghai. I'd like to look the ground over. You know the studio pretty well, don't you, Taylor? Maybe you can act as my official guide. Want to come along, Gregory?"

Clay Brooke and I followed as the studio detective stepped out of the scene of the tragedy and toward the studio stage. John Rawson and his men decided to remain behind and wait for their colleagues to arrive.

"This here, in front of us, is the main stage," began our guide. "The interior 'set' where the camera is set up is where they were taking the tests of Miss Bovary. That's all a blank wall way over there."

"And what's this door next to the dressing-room door?"

"That's the office of the studio."

"H'm, locked, I suppose," Brooke remarked. "I should think that Brimmer, the studio manager, would want to take a look in there."

"Yeh—you'd think so. Now right over there, behind that Chinese street 'set', is the room they call the 'prop' room. They keep all sorts of costumes, paraphernalia, antiques, and so on, in there."

"Antiques?" Brooke repeated with sudden interest. "I'll have to have a look in there as soon as we finish our tour."

Finally we came to the landing at the top of the stairs.

"That window ahead of us," Taylor volunteered, "was shut all evening. In fact, I believe it's always shut."

"You don't say!" said Brooke. "A whim of the movie industry, I suppose? But it could have been opened from the inside and slammed shut from the outside."

"Yes, sir, I suppose it could," replied the studio detective. "Now at the bottom of these stairs—that's where you came in—is the information booth and casting window. There's also a lot of benches for 'airedales' to sit on and wait for jobs."

"Airedales?" repeated the criminologist in a puzzled manner.

"Yeh—'airedales' is studio lingo for 'extra' people. You know, the long-bearded kind."

"Oh, I see! Beards and everything—but not a single blunt object. Where do those stairs lead to?" Brooke pointed to a wooden staircase beside the window. At the bottom was a gate which was padlocked.

"That leads to more dressing-rooms on a small wing above—directly over the office and the dressing-room Miss Bovary had."

"I see—well, let's get back to Rawson. I have an idea that there's something back there I overlooked."

As we returned to the scene of the crime, Clay Brooke's eyes searched the floor. Then it seemed as though an idea suddenly came to him, for his pace quickened and he hastily opened the door of the dressing-room and requested the District Attorney and his men to step out.

"Well, Brooke, what do you think of it?" Rawson asked.

"A very pretty murder, very nice indeed," said the criminologist. "However, I'll have to reserve what theories I may have until I've questioned a number of people." Then turning suddenly to the policeman on duty, he asked, "Officer, since you've been stationed here, no one has passed you or been around this door with the exception of ourselves?"

"Oh, no, sir!"

Then the criminologist squatted down on his haunches and regarded the floor intently. His eyes traveled slowly from the dressing-room door, to the door which led to the studio office.

"Anybody here got a flashlight?" he called.

"I have, sir," came the wondering reply from Carling.

"Kindly play it on the floor and move it slowly between those doors."

The captain of detectives did as Brooke instructed, while the rest of us watched curiously. Finally Brooke rose and turned to the studio manager.

"I suppose this office is locked?" he asked.

"Oh, yes! We always keep it locked when we close in the afternoon."

"I see," Brooke replied, a peculiar smile on his face. "Well, gentlemen, I believe I still have a few of those fifteen minutes to find my precious blunt object. The murder, without a doubt, was committed in that office. A pair of heel tracks can be clearly seen on the floor, indicating that the victim was dragged from the other side of that door to its present position in the dressing-room. Now, Taylor, will you oblige me by opening that door—I think you'll find that it is unlocked."

The studio detective looked at the criminologist with a puzzled expression and gingerly took hold of the knob of the door, turned it, and slowly swung it open.

III. A Pair of Gloves

We all stood in silence, for a moment, staring into the dark room. Clay Brooke looked inquiringly at the District Attorney.

"I really think, Rawson," he said with a strange smile, "that inasmuch as you out-rank each one of us, you should be first to enter."

The District Attorney glanced sharply at the criminologist, then led the way into the room which served as an office to the studio. Carling followed, while Brimmer, the studio manager, groped for the switch and snapped on the light. The office furniture consisted of a number of desks, the usual swivel chairs—one of them being upset—and a bench for visitors. In the farthest right-hand corner from the door stood a regulation safe. The office had only one window, and it was closed.

Clay Brooke stepped rapidly to the center of the room, his eyes seeking the floor and the vicinity of the nearest desk.

"Here it is!" he cried gleefully, stepping forward and pushing a waste-basket aside with his foot. A large notary seal was disclosed.

"Here's my precious blunt object! But we mustn't touch it until the finger-print experts have a look. Give me your flashlight again, Carling." And squatting on his haunches, the criminologist flashed the bright ray on his discovery.

"Sure enough!" he exclaimed. "This's what did the trick! And a nasty weapon it is, indeed. There's tell-tale blood on it, too. H'm! I presume in his haste the murderer heaved it in the direction of the waste-basket with the odd idea that the janitor would dump it out with the waste paper in the morning. Dear, dear! What optimistic imaginations maddened minds have! And what long chances they take! I'll wager he left splendid finger-print specimens in the pressure used when he struck the fatal blow."

Clay Brooke was now in excellent spirits. He rose from his squatting position and rapidly paced the length of the room, seeking each corner with sharp glances.

"H'm! We ought to be able to find something else! Rawson, would you believe it when I tell you that I once got the necessary clue to assure conviction when I stumbled on an elusive collar button? Yes, a low-down, undignified, comedy collar button. This is strange—no blood-stains on the floor!"

He again glanced the length of the room and then walked rapidly to the overturned chair.

"Ah! Here we have it!" he exclaimed with an expression of chagrin. "Now why didn't I look here first! And how about you, Carling—and you, Taylor? Dear me! I'm like one of those blundering fictionary detectives who sometimes turns out to be the guilty man and certainly deserves all he gets! Let's see what might have happened, Rawson, following your theory of a jewel robbery.

"Now then—somehow or other—perhaps by the window, and perhaps he slipped in while the filming was going on—our crook got into the lady's dressing-room. He must have known the geography of the studio, which is borne out by Taylor, who has seen a suspicious character hanging around. Anyway, he crooked the jewels and then he heard his victim approaching. Perhaps he stood behind the door when she came in, or possibly he hid in the wardrobe. Anyway, he must have slipped out without her seeing him—she might have been washing the makeup out of her eyes. She probably got a glimpse of him going out the door, and another glance told her that her jewels were gone. Right here she should have screamed— something I understand blondes usually do, and a very sensible act it is in a situation like this.

"Well, our crook probably started for the street, then spied the night watchman. He took a chance and ducked into this office which happened to be unlocked. I wonder why it wasn't locked? Oh, well, we'll come back to that later. Anyway, let's imagine him in this office. His victim doubtless heard the door shut, entered, and rushed at him. Then there was a struggle. He probably backed her up against that desk—I hope he got his face scratched, because that'll be a great help to us—and he grabbed the nearest thing handy which happened to be the notary seal. He tapped her over the head with it, doubtless much harder than he intended, and she dropped, upsetting the chair. The blood-stains on the inside of the back of it bear me out—and no stains on the floor! Then he dragged her into the dressing-room for some strange reason, and thrust her into the wardrobe closet where we found her. Thank you very much, ladies and gentlemen! Next week we will present 'East Lynne' with an all-star cast."

"And you think that is what happened?" the District Attorney asked, ignoring his friend's levity.

"Well, it sounds fairly logical," replied Brooke. "I'd at least look for a man with a scratched face. Your capitalist friend, Gilbert, appeared with an unruffled countenance, I hope?"

"Good heavens!" John Rawson exploded. "You don't suspect him!"

"Of course not, my dear fellow! What would he want with the lady's jewels! He was probably about to present her with another pretty gewgaw, and more's the pity that she didn't get it."

"There's one thing I'd like you to explain to me, sir," Carling put in. "How in the devil did this man get in and out of the place with so many people about?"

"We mustn't forget the mysterious stranger," Brooke said with a smile. "He had been getting the lay of the land, you know."

"I've noticed him for several days," the studio detective volunteered, "but, of course, I had no idea what he was up to."

The criminologist appeared not to hear Taylor's remark. He was gazing intently at the safe, at the other end of the room.

"Oh, Mr. Brimmer," he called, turning to the studio manager, "suppose we have a look at that safe. Anything to speak of in it?"

An expression of alarm came over the studio manager's face.

"Why, yes!" he said. "There happens to be a large sum of money in it. We've got to meet a heavy payroll tomorrow—several hundred 'extras', among other items. Shall I open it?"

"By all means," assented Brooke. "We may find another motive for the crime—interrupted robbery."

Clay Brooke watched Brimmer closely as he approached the safe, fingered the dial, and finally threw the heavy door open. The studio manager then made a rapid investigation, drawing out a metal strong-box which he unlocked.

"Thank God, everything seems to be here!" he said, with deep relief.

"Good! Better lock it up again. By the way, Brimmer, where have you been the last hour and a half?"

"Mr. Brimmer has a perfect alibi," the District Attorney smiled. "He has been at his home and I had great difficulty getting him here because of a dinner party his wife is giving tonight."

Brooke nodded, satisfied.

A sharp knock at the door came. The District Attorney gestured Carling to open it. The police officer on duty looked in.

"Dr. Jeffreys is here, sir," he said.

"Good! Come on, Brooke, we'll see what the Doc has to say." Then turning to the policeman, he added,

"I want you to watch this door and the other one. Admit no one without written permission from me."

"Yes, sir."

When we returned to the star's dressing-room, we found a sprightly little man who proved to be Dr. Jeffreys. The District Attorney introduced him around, laying special emphasis upon the name of Clay Brooke.

"Oh, yes!" said the autopsy surgeon with a smile. "Rawson has told me about you. We were to play golf in the morning. H'm—I suppose this ugly mess will keep us too busy. And when we've got this out of the way the rainy season will set in, unless," he added with a sly wink, "the Los Angeles Chamber of Commerce tries to prevent it, if only to save their pride. Well, it's always something, Mr. Brooke, always something. Now, where is the unfortunate young woman?"

The District Attorney indicated the wardrobe in the corner.

"Brooke has very clearly proven to us," he added, "that the victim met her death in the next room, the studio office, and was dragged in here and thrust into that closet."

"H'm," murmured Dr. Jeffreys. "Not a pleasing task for a murderer to perform, I'd say. I don't see why he didn't leave her where he did the job."

"But, you see, he liked this room," Brooke said, rubbing his chin in an amused manner. "He pinched her jewels in here, you know, and this room is really the scene of his original crime. Puzzling, isn't it?"

The District Attorney regarded the criminologist curiously, as if wondering what Brooke was driving at. Carling and Taylor also gazed at Brooke as if to fathom his thoughts.

"All murders are puzzling," sniffed the autopsy surgeon. "But let's get to this unpleasant duty." And stepping quickly, to the wardrobe, he began a rapid examination of the crumpled form.

"This—ahem!" he said after a moment, "is a rather impossible spot to make a thorough examination. Would you two gentlemen"—he indicated Taylor and me—"mind lending your strong arms and help me lift the victim onto that couch?"

Taylor looked at the medical examiner with an expression which clearly showed his distaste, and I must confess that I felt sickened at the idea of complying with the request. I looked in the direction of Clay Brooke and saw an almost imperceptible smile playing about his lips; so, I fought off my reluctance and stepped forward, followed by the studio detective.

"Thank you, gentlemen," Dr. Jeffreys said, after the body had been laid flat upon the couch, "this will enable me to get a detailed necropsy."

While the examination was being made, Clay Brooke stepped quietly to the wardrobe and peered in. An exclamation escaped him, which brought the District Attorney and the captain of detectives to his side.

"Look, gentlemen!" he said, pointing to a corner of the small closet. "There's a bit of evidence for your archives— a-pair of tortoise-shell glasses! And very worth finding, too! I'll wager that when the lady's arm dropped forward it knocked them from the nose of the assassin, and in his haste he left them. I suggest that Carling take them and visit all local opticians to see what he can discover. Also, leave a memorandum to watch for future customers— especially a party with a scratched face."

Carling picked up the glasses and examined them. Then he attempted to put them on.

"This guy has a smaller head than mine," said the detective captain.

"And consequently, fewer brain cells," Brooke smiled.

Carling looked at the criminologist sharply, then turned to the District Attorney. "Shall I take charge of these, sir?" he asked.

"Yes, indeed! Follow Mr. Brooke's suggestion and then hand your report over to me."

"Well, gentlemen," said Dr. Jeffreys, turning and facing us, apparently finished with his examination, "I'll be running along now. Great heavens—it's almost nine o'clock! Regarding this unfortunate young woman, she met her death about two hours ago—pretty close to seven o'clock. It's hardly a case of strangulation, although there are marks to show that she received plenty of rough treatment around the neck and throat. The wound on her head is what finished her, and it's a mighty ugly one. There are also a few minor bruises which were probably caused by falling. The victim evidently put up a good fight for life, as can be seen by the bruises on the arms and wrists."

"Beg pardon, sir," said the officer on duty, opening the door and peering in, "the finger-print experts are here."

"Tell them we'll see them directly," said the District Attorney.

"Oh, Dr. Jeffreys," Brooke cut in, "did you notice anything peculiar about the marks on the neck? Frankly, they puzzle me."

"H'm!" said the surgeon, returning to the form of the deceased. "No, they don't resemble the usual finger-print. I'd say possibly—"

"That the murderer wore gloves?" Brooke finished. "You can barely make out the criss-cross of the seams on the finger-tips."

"I think you're right," murmured Dr. Jeffreys. "If that's the case, and the murderer wore gloves, I hardly think you will need your finger-print sleuths. Is there anything else, Rawson? If not, I'll run along and 'phone for an ambulance to call for the girl's body at once. I'll have a post-mortem prepared by morning and arrange with the coroner for the inquest. Good night, gentlemen." Dr. Jeffreys nodded to us, and hurried out.

"Yes, he wore gloves, all right," Brooke said, half to himself. "Anyway, we've got the fellow's glasses, and I jolly well hope he's near-sighted."

"Shall we see what our finger-print hounds can discover?" Carling asked.

The District Attorney nodded and we followed him from the dressing-room into the studio where two men were waiting, one of them carrying a large camera case and a folding tripod. They proved to be Detective Sergeant McDonald, and Hollis, the latter being official photographer of the Homicide Squad.

"McDonald," Rawson began, "it is, unfortunately, our theory that the murderer wore gloves. Nevertheless, I want you to go over everything thoroughly. Take a look at the things on the dressing-table in this dressing-room and then I'll tell you what's next of importance."

The detective sergeant stepped into the dressing-room followed by Hollis and approached the dressing-table. Screwing a jeweler's microscopic glass in his eye, and flashing his pocket light on the different objects, he examined each one of them thoroughly.

"Nothing here," he said after a time. "Just what you might find on any lady's hand-furniture. Smattering of powder, grease-paint and finger-prints but all very lady-like."

"Take a look at that wardrobe," suggested Carling, with a glance at Clay Brooke as if for approval. "That's where the body was found."

McDonald approached the wardrobe and again went through his investigation. He examined the edges of both doors, inside and out.

"Nope, nothing here," he finally announced. "Guess people use their elbows to open doors these days."

"Now, I want you to step into the office, next door," Rawson said. "We've found the weapon the murderer used and it's our one hope of success by the finger-print route."

"Then here's to success!" McDonald said grimly, as he followed the District Attorney and Brooke out of the dressing-room and into the office. The criminologist stepped proudly to the waste-basket.

"Here, Sergeant," he said, pointing to the notary seal. "Here's the jolly little object that did the deed! I'm one that's praying for you to find a finger-print."

"All right," said McDonald, getting down on his knees. "How about holding my light for me, Hollis?" The photographer took the flashlight the detective-sergeant offered and snapped its ray on the murderous implement. McDonald, face downward, began his investigation. He managed to edge the seal away from the wall a little and then studied all sides of it with the 'utmost care, directing Hollis with the light as he did so.

"Can't seem to make out anything except blood on the base of it," he said after a minute or so. "Anyway, I'm going to give it the powder." He took out a small object resembling a hand-bellows and blew a thin layer of yellow dust around the handle and sides of the seal. Then he took the light from Hollis, held it close to the strange weapon and blew off the coating of powder. Again he screwed the magnifying glass into his eye and carefully scrutinized the heavy object. After a moment he grunted and rose to his feet.

"This bozo wore gloves, all right, Mr. Rawson," he announced. "There's not a sign of a finger-print."

"That's too bad!" Brooke sighed. "Well, at least we've got a dandy pair of spectacles."

"How about the door-knobs, Mr. Rawson?" McDonald cut in. "Shall I give them the once-over?"

"By all means," Brooke said. "But only the inside one. We've all been toying with the outside one, and goodness knows, none of us wants to be locked up."

McDonald went through the examination with his usual thoroughness, but he could discover nothing. He shrugged his shoulders and thrust his paraphernalia back into his pocket. At that moment there came a knock on the door. It was the officer on duty.

"Beg pardon, Mr. Rawson," he said, "but a coupla internes 've come with an ambulance for th' corpse of th' deceased."

"All right. Carling, will you show them into the dressing-room and supervise their work. And you'd better have a man go along to the morgue with them."

"I guess there's nothing more for us to do here, sir," McDonald said, after Carling had left the room. "This bird seems to have kept his fingers to himself. Suppose I take the weapon back with me and give it the double-O again?"

"Good," Rawson said approvingly. "If anything comes up I'll send for you."

The detective-sergeant wrapped the seal carefully in a silk handkerchief and then followed the photographer from the room. The District Attorney turned to Clay Brooke with an expression of deep despair.

"Looks pretty hopeless, doesn't it, Clay?" he said.

"Hopeless? I should say not! Think of all the things that are going to come to light when you begin to question your witnesses! I'll wager we can learn something from the maid about the gentleman who smoked a cigaret with the victim. Then Charles Gilbert may disclose any number of interesting facts; to say nothing of the night watchman, who must have made some kind of an observation. Besides, we have a pair of tortoise-shell glasses, and you mustn't forget that a murderer in an odious case which occurred not so long ago in Chicago was apprehended mainly by a pair of glasses which were found at the scene of the crime."

"I wish I had your optimism," Rawson answered with a sad smile. "As—"

The District Attorney was interrupted by another knock on the door.

"Isn't this getting to be a busy place?" Brooke remarked pleasantly.

"What is it?" Rawson demanded.

The police officer again poked his head into the room.

"Leahy wants to see you, sir. He says he's found something."

"Tell him to come in."

"God bless Leahy—! Who is he?" Brooke put in.

"One of our inspectors," the District Attorney answered. "He's been looking over the ground on the outside of the studio—outside of the various windows."

The door swung open and a huge thick-set man entered. He looked at us curiously and then approached John Rawson.

"I found these outside, sir," he said. "They were near the closed window that's at the top of the stair landing."

He held in his hand a pair of cotton gloves—one of them showing a crimson blood-stain.

IV. The Stolen Cab

Clay Brooke was the first to recover himself. "Exhibit Number Two," he said, smiling genially at the District Attorney. "I'm afraid I've predicted that things would happen soon enough."

"Where did you say you found those, Leahy?" Rawson asked.

"Right outside the window, sir—the window that's at the landing, at the head of the stairs."

"Any footprints?" Taylor asked.

Leahy gave the studio detective a withering glance. "Footprints!" he snorted. "There's enough footprints out there to fit all the 'extras' they used when they filmed *The Big Parade!*"

"But are there any fresh ones?" Brooke demanded.

"Fresh ones?" Leahy glanced in the direction of the District Attorney. Then: "Well, sir, it's difficult to tell by our lights. There's such a conglomeration of them that they've got me. Naturally, I looked for deep ones —deep heel prints—because the murderer had to make a jump from the window ledge. Even figurin' that way it's hard to find anything satisfactory."

The door of the dressing-room suddenly swung open and Carling entered.

"I've got them hospital interns off with the body," he reported. "Hullo! What's this?"

"Cotton gloves," smiled Clay Brooke. "Cotton gloves with blood on them. Doesn't that warm the cockles of your heart, Carling?"

"H'm," grunted the detective-captain, examining Leahy's find. "Them are the things that put a crimp in McDonald's work—regular painters' or carpenters' gloves.

I don't think they'll help us much. Too common around here."

"I suppose it's your theory," Brooke remarked, "that the blood dropped on them when the wearer was carrying the body to the wardrobe?"

"That's what I'd say," Carling agreed. "There's so much blood been spilt on the back of the chair that I doubt if the murderer got any on himself, except mebbe when he dragged the body into the dressing-room."

"Well," cut in the District Attorney impatiently, "let's get down to business. It's getting late."

"Yes, sir," Carling nodded. "We're holding the witnesses outside. How about putting 'em through a preliminary questioning?"

"Too bad you sent Charles Gilbert home," Brooke remarked with a sidelong glance at Rawson. "I'd be interested in hearing his story."

"We can get him any time," Rawson said defiantly, "the same as we can Claire Demoset. I'm just holding the maid, the night watchman, the director and his crew. Suppose we have the night watchman first, Carling."

"Leahy," Carling said, turning to the detective, "go out and have Inspector Edwards send Barney in. Tell him to hold the rest until we send for them. I'll take them gloves from you."

"Okay, chief," Leahy replied, reluctantly handing over his discovery and leaving the room.

"Oh, by the way, Brimmer," the District Attorney said turning to the studio manager, "you might as well run along. We won't need you any more. When I want you, I'll send for you."

"Thank you, sir."

"May I suggest," Clay Brooke ventured, after Brimmer had left, "that we carry on this investigation in the dressing-room? There are more places in there for one to sit and be comfortable."

"A good suggestion, Brooke," Rawson commented with a smile. "I'm glad you joined us tonight. You have so many bright ideas."

So we moved into the next room, Brooke, Taylor, and myself seating ourselves on the couch, while the District Attorney selected a chair. Carling stationed himself at the door to watch for the first witness.

"He's coming," he said after a minute or so.

We raised our eyes expectantly as a large man with a good-natured face entered the room. He looked at each one of us and then ran his coat sleeve nervously across his mouth.

"Kind of an unpleasant evening, gents," he remarked.

"Your name is Barney, is it not?" demanded the District Attorney.

"Yes, your honor, Barney Dougherty. I'm the night watchman."

"So I understand," Rawson drily replied. "And never mind calling me 'your honor'. I am hardly a 'judge."

"Yes, sir," said Barney, gulping in a confused manner.

"Tell me what happened this evening between a quarter to seven and a quarter after seven."

"Well, you see, sir, I kinda keep watch all along here, but tonight I happened to be outside this studio door most of the time. I'll try to tell you all I remember. Now that you happen to mention quarter to seven, I think it was about that time that a man went in the studio. The 'phone rang and—"

"A man!" snapped Carling. "Who was he?"

"I dunno," was Barney's disappointing reply. "I hardly noticed him. You see, a 'phone in one of the booths rang just as he came in. It was the wrong number as usual and during the argument I forgot about him."

"Can't you remember what he looked like?" Rawson asked.

"Yes, sir," Barney smiled faintly. "I remember he was a young feller, and pretty well-dressed. I only happen to remember that because I just barely saw him and I seen he wasn't a workman."

"Did you see him come out?" Brooke asked.

"Not that I know of. No, I guess I would have noticed him if he'd come out. I usually kinda look around to see who's comin' and I don't seem to recollect anyone comin' out at all. No stranger, anyway."

"What happened next?" the District Attorney asked.

"Well, sir," Barney continued, "I remember hearing a town clock striking seven because I always listen fer it to strike, and it was a few minutes after that that Miss Hagney come out and—"

"Who is Miss Hagney?" Rawson demanded.

"Miss—Miss Margaret Hagney, sir. She's the maid — Miss Bovary's maid. Well, she come out and said she was goin' fer some aspirin fer Miss Bovary. The studio crew come out at the same time and went over to the corner lunch-room to get something to eat. Let's see now—Oh, I remember it now, sir! Wagner—he was directing the tests—Wagner stood there a moment and said he'd better go back and get his coat as he was goin' to the fights. Naturally, I was wishin' I could go with him and—"

"Did you see him come out again?" Brooke asked.

"No, sir; I didn't, because I went on an errand fer Miss Hagney. She asked me if I'd mind goin' fer a sandwich fer Miss Bovary. So I said 'sure', and I went. It was—"

"Is it the usual custom for you to leave the door to get sandwiches?" the District Attorney demanded.

"Oh, yes, sir!" Barney replied, shifting uncomfortably from one foot to the other. "I often do it. Actors and actresses is always yellin' fer sandwiches, sir."

"How far did you go—and when did you return?"

"Only down the block to the delicatessen. Of course, it takes a little time fer the Greek to make a sandwich. Somebody was ahead of me, too. Well, I got the sandwich and come back."

"Was Margaret Hagney waiting for you?"

"No, sir. She hadn't come back yet. She told me to wait fer her at the door, so I waited."

"What happened next?"

"Nothing much, sir. Oh, yes! While I was waiting, Mr. Gilbert come along and talked with me a minute or two. He wanted to know if they were through working inside, and I told him I thought so. Well, he naturally went in to see, just like any one might do. Then Miss Hagney come back from the drug store, got the sandwich, and went in. The next thing I knew there was some kind of a murder. Pretty funny, I thought."

"You didn't see anybody else come in? Any woman?"

Clay Brooke darted an anxious glance at Barney as the answer came.

"No, sir. None except them which I've mentioned."

"Have you noticed any peculiar-looking man hanging around lately?" Brooke asked.

"No, sir," said Barney. "No more peculiar than usual."

"What do you mean by that?" the District Attorney demanded.

"Well, there's always peculiar folks goin' and comin'. It's that way around all the studios—I mean 'extra' people, and so on."

"Are you sure you can't remember who it was that came in at about quarter to seven?" Brooke asked.

"No, sir. I've been tryin' to remember, but I can't seem to. Guess I just naturally didn't notice him very well."

"All right, you can go now," finished the District Attorney. "We'll probably have to call on you again, so if you remember who this visitor was, for God's sake, don't forget it. Better write it down."

"Yes, sir."

"Carling, take him out and bring in the maid."

"Yes, sir," replied the captain of detectives following the night watchman out of the room.

"Do you think he told all he knows, Brooke?" Rawson asked.

"Could you doubt a face like that?" Brooke smiled. "His trouble is that he just doesn't remember very well. Not a very observing party, to be sure. It's curious about that 'phone ringing. Our visitor might have arranged that call and timed it to get Barney out of the way."

"We've got to discover the identity of this mysterious visitor."

"I'll wager that the Hagney woman will clear that matter up. It is apparent that he came in before she went after the aspirin."

The door opened again and Carling appeared with Margaret Hagney, one of the last persons to see Berylyn Bovary alive, a woman about thirty, and neatly dressed in a cheap sort of way. She doubtless had been pretty once, and it was evident that she was attempting to carry on the illusion.

"You are Margaret Hagney?" the District Attorney asked.

"Yes, sir."

"How long have you been employed by Miss Bovary?"

"Just a couple of weeks, sir. But I've held other good positions before this one and I can show you the best of references."

"Very good. Now I want you to tell me everything that happened this evening—everything, if you please."

"Well, sir, I arrived at the studio about five-thirty with Miss Bovary. We brought some of her gowns with us as she was to film some tests in them. We didn't expect to be here very long, but the tests took longer than usual."

"Why was that?"

"Beg pardon, sir? Oh—why did they take longer? Well, I guess Miss Bovary had a little tiff with the director. She wanted more light than he gave her during the filming and they spent a lot of time arguing about it. I think Miss Bovary got a little angry."

"H'm," said Rawson. "What is the director's name?"

Brooke stole a glance in my direction, and I knew he remembered Claire's uninvited guest.

"Wagner, sir—Frank Wagner."

"Carling, we have Wagner outside, haven't we?"

"Yes, sir," the detective-captain nodded.

"Tell me what happened next," Rawson said, turning to the woman.

"Well, I had been on the set arranging her gown and I came back to the dressing-room to get the next one ready. And there sat Mr. Dazian."

"Dazian—who's he!" said Brooke starting. "Oh, I beg your pardon," he added, turning to Rawson. Then: "Does he wear glasses?"

"No, sir."

Brooke sank back on the couch with a sigh, although he didn't appear as disappointed as I expected. The woman looked from one man to the other in a confused manner until the District Attorney indicated that she was to proceed.

"You were about to tell us of a Mr. Dazian," he prompted.

"Yes, sir. He's Carleton Dazian, a friend of Miss Bovary. He was always bobbing up at the wrong time. Whenever Miss Bovary was ready to go out with some one, Carleton Dazian was sure to appear on the scene — and then they'd have a fight."

"Who would usually appear on the scene?"

"Whoever it happened to be. For instance, tonight she was going out to dinner with Mr. Gilbert. Sure enough, Carleton Dazian appeared."

"Please tell me all you know about Dazian," the District Attorney said, "and then I'd like to hear about Mr. Gilbert."

"I never knew much about Dazian," the woman said, "except that I never liked him. I think he was on the stage or something with Miss Bovary in New York. I think he liked her pretty well, but she had gotten kind of sick of him. He was trying to sell her stocks or bonds, and I think he did manage to sell her some."

"Then you don't think that Miss Bovary and Dazian have been intimate lately—at least, not as friendly as they were in the past?"

"Oh, no! She's been trying to give him the gate for some time."

"Do you—do you think he had anything to do with what happened?"

The witness bit her lip and gazed at the floor for a moment. "I—I—don't like to say anything like that, sir. I know that Mr. Dazian has a bad temper, and I've heard him threaten her. But I guess I ought not to say things like that."

"What do you mean by 'threaten'?"

"Oh, I've heard him say things like, 'I'll fix you', and 'You'll be sorry some day', and things like that. Maybe he didn't mean it, though."

"Where does Mr. Dazian live?" Clay Brooke put in.

"At the Hotel Lowell."

"Carling!" Rawson suddenly snapped. "Call up the Lowell and see if this party is in. Find out without his knowing it—then go and get him and bring him here."

"Yes, sir," said Carling, hurrying from the room.

"Now, tell me what happened when Miss Bovary returned to the dressing-room and found Dazian there?"

"Well," Margaret Hagney continued, "first she got sarcastic with him; kidding him about hanging around too much and all that sort of stuff. She gave me the wink to try to get rid of him, but I'd like to know how I could have done that. Then she wanted some aspirin and when I left for it they were both sitting there smoking cigarets as peaceful as you please. When I came back he was gone!"

"And so was the jewelry?" Brooke put in.

"Oh—yes! All of Miss Bovary's beautiful jewels!"

"Did you see any one outside when you left the dressing-room?"

"Just the studio crew. The cameraman and two electricians walked out with Frank Wagner and me. They went over to the corner lunch-room to get something to cat."

"Where did Wagner go?"

"He stood there for a minute with me. Oh—then he looked at the sky and said it looked like it might rain and he'd better get his coat as he was going to the fights. He started back into the studio for it as I was crossing the street."

"Does Wagner happen to wear glasses?" Brooke asked leaning forward.

"No—yes, I believe he does. Those tortoise-shell kind."

The District Attorney straightened in his chair and stared at Brooke. Then he glanced swiftly around the room. "Carling!" he snapped. "Where the hell is that man, Carling!"

"You sent him to try and locate Dazian," Brooke said quietly.

"Then—Taylor, you get Carling for me—and shake it up!"

"Yes, sir," said the studio detective' hastening from the room.

The District Attorney fidgeted in his chair, glancing first at Clay Brooke, then at Margaret Hagney. The woman stared at the floor. The criminologists composure was rather astonishing, I thought, although I knew that he felt the tensity of the situation. Approaching footsteps caused John Rawson to jerk in his chair and glare in the direction of the door. Carling hurried into the room followed by Taylor.

"Dazian hasn't returned to his hotel yet," he announced, "but I've sent Leahy to root him out. He'll surely nab him."

"Good—! But how about Wagner, the director? You're holding him outside with the other witnesses, aren't you?"

"Ye—yes, sir."

"Go and get him and keep him outside the door till I call you!"

Carling gazed at his chief in puzzled amazement and hurried-from the room.

"Now then—now then," said the District Attorney rubbing his hands together nervously. "Where were we?"

"I believe you were about to ask this young woman what happened when she returned from her aspirin quest," Clay Brooke volunteered.

"Yes, sir," Margaret Hagney nodded. "I had sent the night watchman for a sandwich for Miss Bovary, and when I returned he was waiting with it. He told me that Mr. Gilbert had just gone into the studio."

"H'm," Brooke murmured. "Now, we have three men who appeared to be on the inside of the studio about the time the crime occurred."

John Rawson darted a glance of annoyance in the direction of the criminologist and was about to reply when the door burst open and Carling rushed in.

"I—I was wrong, sir!" he stammered. "I supposed Wagner was out there with the witnesses—but it's only the cameraman and the two electricians!"

"Then—then where in the devil is Wagner!"

"The cameraman said that he was going to the fights with his girl. The last they saw of him he was returning to the studio for his coat."

"All right—all right! That'll do!," snapped the District Attorney. "Now, hustle out of here and put two of your best men on his trail! We've got to find him before morning! Get that, Carling?"

"Yes, sir; I'll see to it at once! How about the other witnesses?"

"I'll see them as soon as I finish with this woman. You get your men on their way and then hustle right back here."

"Yes, sir," Carling mumbled, as he hurried from the room.

"I can imagine," Brooke smiled, "that Carling is probably the most bewildered man in the world at this moment."

"Now, then," said Rawson, ignoring Brooke and turning to the witness, "you said that Mr. Gilbert had just gone into the studio when you arrived. Tell me what happened next?"

"Well, sir, I took the sandwich from Barney and walked into the studio. I found Mr. Gilbert walking back and forth in front of the dressing-room door. He asked me if Miss Bovary was ready to leave, and I said I'd see. I came in here and didn't see her. Then I happened to look into that wardrobe and—well, I guess I must have screamed, because Mr. Gilbert rushed in. He was as shocked as I was—in fact, he carried on pretty bad. Then there was that big movie star, Claire Demoset—she arrived, too, but I don't know just where she came from. Well, we immediately put in the alarm for the police and they arrived, then Mr. Taylor and you gentlemen."

Rawson was about to put a question when Clay Brooke-quickly cut in.

"What—what do you know about Mr. Gilbert?" he asked the woman.

"Oh, Mr. Gilbert is a lovely man. He has always been most sweet to Miss Bovary, poor thing. Kind of fatherly, you know—and always sort of looking out for her welfare. He is a man in a million, sir."

"And with several?" smiled Brooke. "He gave her things, I presume?"

"Oh, yes. Lovely things—simply lovely things. All the jewels that are missing, he gave them to her. He couldn't seem to do enough for poor Miss Bovary. Mr. Gilbert never did things half-way, as the saying goes."

"And they got on well together?"

"Oh, yes, indeed! She was quite crazy for him, sir."

"She realized, of course, that he is a married man?"

"Well, I can't tell you anything about that, sir. What's my business is my business, and what ain't my business just ain't my business."

"A splendid policy, Miss Hagney," Brooke complimented. "He—er, he didn't happen to wear glasses?"

"Yes, sir. Sort of tortoise-shell ones—the kind that dangle on a black string."

"Oh!" Brooke grunted, leaning back again. "Oh, well, it doesn't matter a great deal."

"Tell me," said the District Attorney, "tell me this — Taylor has informed us that you have both noticed a mysterious stranger around the studio recently. What does he look like?"

"Oh, yes—I nearly forgot about him! He was a rather tall man, I'd say. Tall and thin, with dark hair and complexion. I noticed especially that his hair was dark. And I think—I think he wore cheaters—the kind you mention, sir," she finished with a glance at Brooke.

"Taylor," said the criminologist, "did the man you saw wear horn-rimmed glasses?"

"Well, he might have—yes, I guess maybe he did."

"How long has this man been around?" Rawson asked.

"Oh," replied the woman, "I'd say for the last few days."

"Well, I guess that'll be all for tonight, Miss Hagney," the District Attorney finished, "unless, Brooke, there's something you want to ask?" The criminologist shook his head in the negative. "Very well, you may go. But I will want to question you again, so please hold yourself in readiness until I call you. Carling has your name and address, I believe?"

"Yes, sir."

"I know where to reach her, too, sir," Taylor volunteered.

"Very good—you can go now."

Margaret Hagney departed with quiet dignity and Clay Brooke looked at the District Attorney with an expression of amusement.

"This mess is getting frightfully complicated, eh?" he said. "Now, I wonder—"

"I'm doing a lot of that myself," Rawson replied grimly. Then: "Carling!" he shouted. "I wonder where in hell that man is!"

"Here, sir!" said the detective-captain, peering in through the door. "I've been waiting outside, sir. Shall I bring in one of the other witnesses?"

"Yes; let's have the cameraman first."

In the testimony that followed, very little was of any assistance. The cameraman and the two electricians verified the facts that the director had left the studio with them, and then had returned alone for his coat. He had said that he was taking a young woman friend to the prize-fights. They had crossed the street to the lunch-room and had not seen him come out of the studio. They had not noticed any harsh words between the director and the deceased. They all had agreed at the time, however, that Berylyn Bovary was a temperamental young woman, difficult to handle. Brooke put his pet question regarding Wagner's tortoise-shell glasses. The cameraman and one electrician had not noticed them, and the other electrician wasn't sure. The witnesses were dismissed.

"Well, Clay," said the District Attorney, "it's getting late. Shall we call it a night?"

"Uh-huh," yawned Brooke. "Shall I drop around to your office in the morning? I don't think there'll be much to learn at the inquest."

"Better drop around to the office," said John Rawson reaching for his hat.

As we rose to depart a sudden knock came at the door.

"This is getting irksome," Clay Brooke remarked.

"Come in," called the District Attorney.

The door opened and a plain-clothes man entered—Inspector Edwards—followed by a seedy-looking individual who carried his cap in his hand and twisted it nervously.

"I didn't want to interrupt you, sir," apologized Edwards, "but this bozo's been raising such a hullabaloo outside that I thought it might be a good idea for you to know about it."

"Yes, chief," said the man with the cap. "Someone's stole me cab."

"Your cab?" repeated Rawson. "What do you mean?"

"Me cab! I'm a taxi driver, sir, and me cab's been standin' around the corner fer some time. When I went fer it, it was gone."

"How long was it out there?" asked Brooke with sudden interest.

"Since a little before seven o'clock, sir. When I went to look fer it a few minutes ago, the bulls outside stopped me and brung me in here."

"Do you mean to say," put in Rawson, "that you left your cab standing out there since seven o'clock? Where have you been all that time?"

"Well, sir, I ain't wantin' to get in dutch, but I might as well tell you I been shootin' craps. You see, I pulled up around the corner and went in the lunch-room fer dinner. I met some pals and we went and shot craps in a joint nearby. I didn't know the time was goin' so fast, and when I come out a few minutes ago, me cab was gone."

"H'm—I see," said the District Attorney. Then turning to the inspector he added, "Take this man's name and have him report to me in the morning. Then send a call to police headquarters and give orders to search for that cab. You can go now."

After Inspector Edwards and his charge had departed, John Rawson turned to Brooke with a look of triumph.

"Things are looking up!" he said cheerfully.

"That so?" smiled Brooke.

"Don't you think so?" demanded the District Attorney. "The murderer stole that cab and made a getaway in it! We certainly ought to get some evidence out of that!"

"Oh!" said the criminologist. "Oh! That's right, old man—and our murderous joy-rider threw his gloves away before he got in it, didn't he? Well, shall we be getting along? It's about my bedtime."

At that moment Carling came in excitedly.

"We've got Carleton Dazian outside!" he exclaimed triumphantly.

V. THE PROP ROOM

"Bless my soul!" Brooke exclaimed. "Will wonders never cease! First somebody loses a taxicab, then somebody finds Carleton Dazian! By Jove! It's very nearly a paradox!"

"Just the same, Brooke," Rawson smiled genially, "I'll wager your prediction that things would begin to happen is coming true quicker than you supposed." Then, turning to Carling, he added, "Bring in your prisoner."

Our eyes remained fixed on the door, expectantly, through which the captain of detectives must enter with Carleton Dazian. Presently, when they came, Brooke and I gasped and exchanged glances. He was no other than the sheik-like person who had danced with the murdered girl at Claire Demoset's! He was well-dressed in a showy sort of way. I imagine that a specialist in something or other would have called him an "emotional" type.

"You are Carleton Dazian?" asked the District Attorney briskly.

"Yes, sir!" came the quick reply. "And for God's sake, will somebody tell me what happened!"

"Then you don't know?"

"No—I don't! I was grabbed at my hotel by one of your strong, silent men for no reason at all. He wouldn't explain what I was wanted for. Now I want to know what it's all about!"

"You are the chap who danced this afternoon at Miss Demoset's, are you not?" Brooke cut in. "The chap who danced the tango with Miss Bovary?"

"Yes, that's me. But you can't arrest a man for that!"

"There has been a murder," Brooke went on quietly, his eyes focused on the features of Dazian. "The victim is Berylyn Bovary!"

The man stared at Brooke with unbelieving eyes. Then he broke out:

"Murdered! You're lying to me!"

He glanced rapidly from one of us to the other. The tense expressions on our faces seemed to convince him of the horrible tragedy. He turned deathly pale, swayed perceptibly, and would have fallen had not Carling stepped forward suddenly and grasped him by the arm.

"Oh, my God—my God!" he groaned. "Berylyn murdered! Why—it isn't—it can't be—!"

The District Attorney eyed him sternly.

"You were the last person in her company—in this room!" he flung at him.

"Who killed her!" Dazian demanded hysterically. "Tell me the dirty rat's name! Tell me his name, I say!"

Blood suffused his cheeks, there was a twitching of the muscles about his mouth and throat, and he swayed as if about to fall. Carling grasped the man to steady him.

"Suppose you pull yourself together," Rawson put in, "and tell us all you know about this case—and how you've been occupying yourself this evening?"

Carleton Dazian stared at the District Attorney in inarticulate amazement. Then, with something of menace in his tone he shouted:

"You don't suspect me, for God's sake!"

"I'll suspect something if you continue to carry on in this manner."

"Yes, sir," Dazian replied apologetically. He drew a colored handkerchief from his breast-pocket and nervously ran it across his brow. "I'll—I'll tell you all I can, sir. But for God's sake, don't think that I had anything to do with it! I'll see this thing through with you if it's the last thing I do on earth!"

"Suppose," put in Brooke, with a glance seeking approval from Rawson, "suppose you tell us something about yourself first?"

"Yes, sir," Dazian nodded nervously. "Then I'll tell you first that I've loved Berylyn Bovary for some time. I've loved her with all my heart and soul! I met her in New York about two years ago when she was in the *Follies* and I was a dancer. We got up an act—'ballroom dancing', they call it. We were pretty successful at the Hotel Empress. Then something happened—I don't know what it was—and Berylyn told me she wanted to go back to the *Follies*. Well, she did, in spite of my arguing, so I got another girl and kept the act going. Of course, I still loved Berylyn, but something had come between us. Then she got her chance to get in the movies and left for Hollywood. I followed her as soon as I could, figuring I might not be so bad in pictures, myself."

Dazian paused and gave a mirthless laugh. Then:

"Well, I made a mistake right at the beginning. You see, the vogue for Spanish and Mexican sheiks was on, so I put on a Spanish accent and looked for work. Then the talking pictures came and I simply could not convince casting directors that I could speak English. They wouldn't even listen to me! Sounds like bologny, doesn't it? Well, it's God's truth! Naturally, I got sore at the whole damn picture tribe. I'd saved enough jack so I wouldn't have to worry for a while, but as a side-line, I tried selling stocks and bonds. That hasn't gone so good, although I've managed to pick up a little change here and there."

"You sold some to Miss Bovary, didn't you?" Brooke put in quietly.

"Yes, I did," Dazian replied after a moment, startled at the question. "But that didn't amount to much. Well, I tried my best to make Berylyn see our affair my way, but without any luck. The girl had a one track mind and it wasn't headed in my direction any longer. I've loved her and I've been miserable, and I've tried to make her love me as she once did."

"What happened when you called here this evening?" said the District Attorney.

"She told me this afternoon that she was coming here after Miss Demoset's party to make tests, so I thought I'd run over. I wouldn't have come at all, only she was rather nice to me this afternoon—that is, we'd had a little tiff when I first arrived at the party, but when that was over everything was fine. Well, I guess I got here a little before seven and I came right to this dressing-room."

"Did you see the watchman when you entered?" Brooke cut in.

"Who—old Barney? No, he wasn't outside when I came in. Berylyn—Miss Bovary, was working on the set, so I came in here and waited for her. Just like I've always done. Pretty soon—"

"You said you didn't see Barney when you entered the studio," Brooke Interrupted. "Do you think he could have been in one of the telephone booths?"

"Well—he might. I didn't notice."

"You may continue," the criminologist said.

Dazian paused and passed his hand vaguely across his brow in the endeavor to compose his thoughts. It was evident that the strain was telling on him.

"Well—pretty soon Miss Bovary finished and came in."

"Where was her maid all this time?" Brooke asked.

"Margaret was here, too—no, she came in just ahead of Miss Bovary. Then Berylyn asked her to get her some aspirin as she said she had a headache, so Margaret went for it. Well, everything seemed fine, so I began my old line as usual and asked her to go to dinner with me. She said she had an engagement and I couldn't get her to break it."

"With whom was this engagement?" asked the District Attorney.

"With old man Gilbert—Charles Gilbert. He's got a bank-roll big enough to choke the Trojan horse, if you know what I mean."

"Was he financially interested in the picture?"

"I wouldn't be a bit surprised!" Dazian replied drily. "Oh, what the hell—I'll shoot square and say I know damn well he was! He's one of those kind of old men who's simply lousy with money and just has to spend it on a dame and tie her up in a bundle of celluloid."

"Do you think he could have had anything to do with what happened?"

"Him!" Carleton Dazian smiled faintly for the first time. "Say, old man Gilbert wouldn't have the guts to do anything! He's—well, you ought to know the type, if you get what I mean."

John Rawson darted a half-triumphant glance at Brooke.

"What happened when Miss Bovary refused to go with you?" he asked, turning back to the prisoner.

"Well, I argued with her for awhile—but it didn't do a damn bit of good. I should have known better. Then I thought I might as well blow and console myself elsewhere because Berylyn announced that she wanted to dress. Being a gentleman, I—"

"Have you any idea what time that was?" Brooke asked.

Dazian paused before replying and eyed the ceiling thoughtfully.

"Yes—I remember perfectly, because I glanced at my wrist-watch just as I left. I was wondering if I'd have time to call another dame and kill the evening with her. It was about three minutes after seven. Well, I came out and—"

"Did you see any one outside—any one at all?" Rawson asked.

Dazian shook his head.

"No, sir. The studio stage was empty and only a couple of lights were lit—big arc-lights. I stopped for a moment at one of the 'phone booths in the waiting room and put in a call."

"Whom did you call?"

"Oh, just a dame. I wanted some one to go to the movies with me."

"Do you think," Brooke ventured, "that any one could have come into the studio without you seeing them—while you were 'phoning?"

Carleton Dazian was thoughtful for a moment. Then: "Yes—they might," he replied. "I had the door closed and I talked for several minutes I guess. I really couldn't say whether any one came in or not."

"You are sure you saw no one?" Rawson cut in. "Neither a man nor a woman?"

Dazian shook his head. "Yes, sir; I'm sure."

"Was any one outside when you went out?" Brooke asked quickly.

"No—nobody was outside—not even Barney."

"Where did you go, then?"

"Why—I met the girl I had telephoned and we went to the picture at the Pyramid Theater. We only stayed through the first show, as she's doing 'extra' work out at Burbank and she had to get up early in the morning to go out on location. She's dancing in some sort of a fiesta scene. Well, then I went to my hotel—and here I am!"

As Dazian finished it was apparent that he had regained his self-control. The color had come back to his cheeks and his nervousness had almost vanished. He looked from the District Attorney to Clay Brooke awaiting the next question. For a few moments there was silence, then Brooke slowly took a cigaret from his case and tapped it on the edge of his chair.

"Mr. Dazian," he began, looking earnestly at the man before us, "I can't help but be interested in the stock you sold Miss Bovary. Won't you tell me, about it? I might want to make a good investment myself."

"I'll be square with you," Dazian replied with an odd smile, "because I hope you're going to be square with me. The stock I sold Miss Bovary was no damned good."

"No good! What do you mean?" demanded the District Attorney.

"Just what I say, sir. It was no good and it never will be any good. I wouldn't tell you this under any other conditions—I just want a square deal from you, and that's why I'm being honest. Berylyn knew this stock was no good when she bought it. We both did. You see, in spite of all his dough, old man Gilbert doesn't unfasten his bank-roll as snappily as a person might desire. But he might be persuaded to come through if a lady he was interested in wanted to make an investment. I supplied the investment and got a percentage from Berylyn. Bum stock certificates are easier to sell and manipulate under those circumstances than good ones, and Mr. Gilbert never questioned them."

"I take back my offer," Brooke remarked grimly. "I'm afraid I'm not interested in your stock."

"Oh, I know this kind of a deal isn't on the level exactly," Dazian replied, "but it—well, it served its purpose and helped out."

"I suppose you know that Miss Bovary had priceless jewels?" said the District Attorney.

"I'll say so!" Dazian nodded. "That's the way with these old guys. They'll doll a girl up, give her diamonds and pearls, and hold back on the cold cash. They want her to look classy when they step out with her."

"What do you think Mr. Gilbert's family thought of this arrangement?"

"I can't answer that one for you, but I don't doubt that there's other families out here and plenty in New York thinking the same thing. Or else they're happy in their ignorance.. Others make the best of it, because they've got theirs. It's something that might happen in the best of families if there's an abundance of big dough. I know."

"I don't suppose you are aware of the fact that Miss Bovary's jewels are missing," stated the District Attorney. "The ones she had in this room."

"Oh, then it was a case of robbery!" Dazian exclaimed, and suddenly paling, he added, "Oh, for God's sake, don't think that I had anything to do with it! I'm not that hard up!"

"The jewels are gone!" Rawson repeated. "Which proves that this crime must have been committed by someone who knew she had them and who knew something about her activities at this studio. Have you—

have you any reason to think that there could be any other motive than robbery? In other words, do you know of any one who had reason to put Miss Bovary out of the way?"

Carleton Dazian shook his head slowly. "No, sir; I can't think of any one. I guess it looks pretty bad for me, doesn't it, sir?"

"We'll decide that later," said the District Attorney. "I suppose, this girl you mentioned would verify the fact that she met you at the theater?"

Dazian nodded.

"Then I want you to give her name and address to Carling. Carling, I'll leave that matter in your hands. Now, tell me, Dazian, did you pass any one on the way to the theater that knew you—or anyone around these studios who might have seen you?"

"No, sir. None that I can remember."

"By the way, Dazian," Brooke broke in, "do you happen to know if Miss Bovary had any letters in her possession which might be incriminating to any one— that is, any letters that some man would like to get back from her? Say, for instance, Mr. Charles Gilbert?"

"No—I couldn't say."

"Another thing," said the criminologist. "One of our witnesses tells us of overhearing you threaten Miss Bovary."

"Me—I threatened her?" Dazian repeated. "Well, I might have, but, of course, I didn't mean it seriously. You can see that I ought to know by this time that it wouldn't do any good. I guess when any one's crazy about a dame and she gets him nuts because she doesn't like him any more, he's apt to say things he doesn't mean. You know how that is."

The District Attorney tapped his fingers nervously on the edge of the chair.

"Brooke," he finally said, "are there any more questions you'd like to ask?"

"No, I don't believe so. Oh—one more thing! Dazian, you drive a car, don't you?"

"Certainly! Nearly everybody does in Hollywood."

"H'm—well, Rawson, that's all I've got to say."

The District Attorney looked from one to the other of us in a rather helpless manner.

"Carling!" he snapped, turning suddenly to the captain of detectives. "Hold this man outside until I call you!"

After they had left the room he turned to the criminologist.

"Brooke, do you see any reason why I shouldn't lock up Dazian on suspicion?"

"Why not?" Brooke replied, without hesitation. "I suppose it's your theory that he killed the girl?"

"Well, if he didn't, I'd like to know who in hell did!"

"Yes, he fits comfortably into the niche you have reserved for him. Of course, he may have killed her to pinch the jewels, but I would prefer to look on the more romantic aspect and call it a crime of passion. Much more interesting—much more interesting! Oh, well, as long as you've got an empty cell, you might as well lock him up over night. I never believe in overcrowding, though."

Rawson darted a look of annoyance at the criminologist.

"H'm!" he snorted. "Well, I'll give Carling orders to hold him until morning."

After the District Attorney stepped from the dressing-room, Clay Brooke turned to Taylor and me with an amused expression. "Poor old Rawson!" he sighed. "He's simply got to lock up some one or he wouldn't sleep a wink tonight. That's the hellish part of being a District Attorney."

A moment later Rawson returned. "Well," he said jovially, "that's one we've got!" And, glancing at his watch, he added, "it's about a quarter to eleven. Shall we call it a night?"

"I wonder," Brooke ventured, "if you'd gratify a whim of mine and let me take a peep into the property room. I'm really awfully sorry, Rawson, that I happen to be such an inquisitive soul."

"This sudden energy of yours surprises me, Brooke," Rawson grunted. "I saw you yawn only a moment ago. All right, let's take a look—it'll only take a moment. You'd better lead the way, Taylor."

Following the studio-detective, we left the dressing-room. Rawson snapped off the lights and gave the officer on duty his orders for the night. We walked across the studio stage, through the Chinese street, which Brooke again gazed at curiously, and finally came to the door of the property room. Taylor attempted to open it.

"I guess it's locked," he announced.

"Wonder who's got a key?" Rawson said. "Probably Barney has one. Do you mind fetching him, Taylor?"

The studio-detective scurried away and returned in a moment with the watchman. The latter detached a huge bunch of keys from his belt, selected one, and opened the door for us.

"I don't know how this happened," he grunted. "They usually never trouble to lock this door."

"H'm! I see it's a snap lock!" Brooke remarked. "If anybody slammed it, it would lock."

"That's right—guess it would," Barney grinned. "Want me any more?"

"No; you can go," Rawson said. "When Carling returns, please tell him we are here."

"Yes, sir," said Barney, as he turned and shuffled away.

"You said that there are antiques in here, Taylor?" Brooke asked, when we had entered. "Where do they keep them?"

"I don't know exactly, sir. They usually keep things pretty topsy-turvy in this place. It's mostly a lot of junk, as you can see."

"So it is," Brooke smiled, "but fascinating junk for a newcomer like me to the film business. Now I suppose that lion's paw that's hung up there on the wall is what the comedian gets slapped in the pants with in a close-up just after they show us a real lion on the screen."

"That's the way they make the business safe," Taylor grinned.

"Hullo!" Brooke exclaimed suddenly. "Here are a lot of pretty trinkets! H'm! Not so dusty as the rest of this junk! By Jove, Rawson, these are the real thing! Come here and take a look!"

The District Attorney hastened to the criminologist's side and looked at the sparkling articles that Brooke held in his hand.

"I tell you, Rawson, that necklace is the real thing, or I'm a pickaninny!"

"Then you think—"

"Think! Hell—I know! This crime is no jewel robbery—unless, the assassin left these jewels here and intended to return for them, which is most unlikely—most unlikely! If he'd taken the trouble to steal them, he wouldn't have gone off without them. Yes, sir! These are Berylyn Bovary's jewels, or I'm an African!"

"How in the world did you know they were in here, Brooke?" Rawson asked with admiration.

"I didn't—I just made a wild guess!"

Carling came in just then, to tell us that he'd speeded Dazian on his way to the jail.

VI. A BLOOD-STAINED COAT

Carling stepped forward and gazed in amazement at the collection of jewelry.

"Holy catfish! What's this?" And he let out a prolonged whistle of increasing astonishment when they told him.

"Carling, you take that jewelry along with our other exhibits and lock it in the safe at headquarters," the District Attorney said. Then, turning to Brooke, he asked, smiling, "Well, getting sleepy?"

"Me? Bless you, no!" replied the criminologist serenely. "Never felt so wide-awake in my life!" As if to prove it, he hastily drew a fresh cigaret from his case and lighted it. "Rawson, I've a suggestion to make. My friend Gregory, being a highly-paid constructor of scenarios, is the possessor of most excellent Scotch. Mind you, I speak of this confidentially, as one man to another, not as a criminal investigator to a District Attorney. As he has kindly taken me in as a temporary lodger, I'm sure he'll permit me to act the role of co-host and invite you to his bungalow to run over the different items of the case. What do you say, old man?"

John Rawson consulted his watch. Then he shrugged his shoulders and said, "Oh, well, it's only eleven o'clock. Suppose we might as well make a night of it. Carling, you'd better run along with your exhibits. I'll see you at the office in the morning. Be sure and see that these officers on duty get a relief, as I want this studio carefully guarded until we complete investigations."

"Yes, sir. But suppose something of importance turns up? Shall I 'phone you at Mr. Black's?"

"My name is in the 'phone book," I volunteered, "if you should want Mr. Rawson—it's Gregory Black."

Carling nodded and left us, taking Berylyn Bovary's priceless gewgaws along with the rest of the evidence.

"How about me, sir?" Taylor asked, looking at the District Attorney.

"You? Oh, to be sure! H'm! Carling has your name and address in case we should want you. You'll be called for the inquest in the morning. That's all."

The three of us piled into my coupe and were soon speeding along Sunset Boulevard in the direction of Griffith Park. It was a long time before any one spoke. Brooke and Rawson silently stared out into the darkness. Finally, the criminologist broke the silence.

"The discovery of those jewels is rather upsetting, eh, Rawson?" he remarked. "It gives the case a different aspect."

"Yes, Brooke, indeed it does," replied the District Attorney, letting his head sink forward on his chest.

"In fact, it baffles one," Brooke went on. "I'm always frightfully annoyed when I'm baffled, Rawson."

The District Attorney glanced at Clay Brooke in an annoyed manner, and there was another long silence until we pulled up at my bungalow.

"Nice little place you have here, Black," Rawson commented when we were seated in the living-room with cold drinks before us.

"Isn't it, though!" Brooke exclaimed enthusiastically. "Look at the things the fellow's got! Not Navajo rugs woven in Jersey City, but antiques—very fine antiques! And where do you think he got them, Rawson? From the different studios—the prop rooms. I rather think he stole them, although he assures me he didn't. I like that old clock up there particularly. I've spent many weary hours motoring through dusty roads in New England hunting for a clock like that. Now, if you see me talking seriously to a studio hand, you'll know I'm trying to win my way into his heart so that I can beg a prop from him."

The District Attorney shifted impatiently in his chair. "I only wish you'd win the friendship of a studio man who could give you a hint about this murder," he sighed.

"How awfully sordid you can be at times, Rawson," Brooke smiled. "Of course, I can mix business with pleasure, but it isn't my policy."

"Well, let's get down to facts," the District Attorney said, suddenly becoming serious. "We have a number of things to show for our night's work. We have a pair of tortoise-shell glasses, a pair of cotton gloves with a blood-stain on one of them, and we have found the victim's jewels."

As Rawson spoke, Brooke instinctively slipped his hand into his pocket—to assure himself that he still had the glove, I surmised. Then he put in:

"We also have—or rather, we know about a purloined taxicab. You know, that stolen cab rather tickles me. I've always had the greatest desire to steal a taxicab and drive it around. Probably because of suppressions in my youth."

"Brooke, for God's sake, please be serious!" Rawson exploded.

"I am, my dear fellow! I am perfectly serious. To prove it, here's another exhibit you probably don't know about."

To my surprise he drew the white kid glove from his pocket and tossed it to John Rawson.

"What's this?" asked the District Attorney.

"It looks very much like a lady's glove," Brooke smiled. "It belongs to Miss Claire Demoset, I believe—at least she uses the same kind of rare perfume that's on the glove. I found it when I first arrived at the studio."

Rawson sniffed of the glove and then regarded the criminologist with an odd look.

"Brooke, what do you suppose she was doing there?" he asked.

"How do I know!" Brooke ejaculated innocently. "You saw fit to send her home before I arrived. Well, there may be a perfectly good explanation. Miss Demoset gave a garden party this afternoon, and the murdered girl was one of her guests—in fact, she was good enough to entertain. Danced exquisitely for us—with Carleton

Dazian. It's entirely plausible that Miss Demoset should drop in later to see her—perhaps, to thank her. Anyway, I can't see that she figures in the case. She appeared on the scene after Charles Gilbert and the Hagney woman, according to their own testimony."

"Yes, that's right," Rawson nodded.

There was something in his tone which made me think that he was not so easily convinced. At the same time, I fancied that Brooke was simulating an air of nonchalance when he spoke of Claire—that he was a great deal more worried about her part in the affair than he dared admit. Knowing Brooke as I did, I could not help but believe that he tossed the glove to Rawson in the spirit of bravado. It was no secret that Claire Demoset had been to the studio. At the same time, if the picture star should become seriously involved, I knew that Brooke would be quite capable of building a high wall of defense around her.

"Well, then," Rawson went on, dismissing the subject, "among the suspects we have Carleton Dazian in custody. We know something of the movements of Charles Gilbert—although in my opinion he is above suspicion. We have theories concerning Wagner, the director. And we have heard testimony from Barney, the watchman, from Hagney, the maid; and from the cameraman, electricians, and Taylor. Our theory that the murder was committed for financial gain—the jewels—has been upset, so we must change our course and look for another motive."

"We mustn't overlook the mysterious stranger," Brooke put in. "No, we mustn't overlook him, because he supplies the romance. He's Mr. X until we can get a better name for him. But let's begin with the various people you have mentioned. Wagner is a fellow who interests me because I know nothing whatever about him. Still, we cannot arrive at any motive for him suddenly to kill the star he is going to direct—it would bring an end to his means of livelihood. We have been told that Miss

Bovary was temperamental and that harsh words were exchanged at the studio. But to say a lady in the movies is temperamental is about the same as to say she uses a lipstick. Am I right, Greg? Thank you—your Scotch is excellent! Wagner would have a clear case if he hadn't returned for his coat. Let's shelve Wagner until we know more about him."

"What do you think of Dazian?" Rawson asked.

"I don't know—he dances charmingly!" Brooke smiled, putting his glass down and lighting a cigaret. Then suddenly he turned to me. "What do you think of him, Greg?"

"Why—why, I don't know!" I stammered, both flattered and embarrassed that my opinion should mean anything to the criminologist. "He seemed a rather frank cuss—telling us about his fake stock and—and everything else."

"Yes, that's true," Brooke agreed. "At the same time, he might be a very clever chap—working a pet psychology of his own to hoodwink us."

"You know, Brooke," the District Attorney ventured, "there's a point of interest in the fact that Dazian dislikes the maid, Margaret Hagney, and that she dislikes him. When we questioned her, it was obvious that she wouldn't mind seeing Dazian get in a fix."

"Right-o!" Brooke agreed. "Now, let's get to that charming old rogue, Charles Gilbert. He fascinates me, because I have known the type—that is, certain versions of it. I'll wager that he insists upon mixing the salad-dressing himself at the dinner table. He is the fastidious, benevolent old party with a wife and family, and he's doing his utmost to play the gay boy and get a kick out of life, scattering *louis d'or* as he trips along."

The District Attorney threw back his head and laughed heartily at Clay Brooke's imaginary sketch of the millionaire.

"Your picture of him sounds more like a role in a musical comedy," he chuckled.

"Doesn't it, though!" Brooke nodded. "Can't you just see him singing, 'Girls, girls, girls—dear little charming girls', behind the footlights with a score of chorus beauties matching his dancing gyrations? That's Charles Gilbert as his family doesn't know him—nor many of his business associates. Now, then, in a case like this, the outstanding motive for Charles Gilbert would be fear."

"Fear?" repeated John Rawson.

"Yes. Fear of discovery, fear of a wrecked home, fear of unwelcome notoriety. But let's put the old fellow under a microscope. According to Dazian, he is an old play-boy. Spends his money but likes to have it show when he spends it. Buys beautiful stones for his inamorata so that he can see them glitter. Finances a motion picture production because there's a fascination to it, and there's also a chance he'll get his money back. Anyway, Charles Gilbert picked out Berylyn Bovary. And how do we know but what the lady might have gotten ambitious, high-falutin' ideas when she opened her eyes and realized how prettily she was situated? She knew that Gilbert was crazy about her, and she was clever enough to know that she could get him crazier. In other words, she began to have visions that she could get him to marry her."

"Marry her!" the District Attorney exploded. "Brooke, do you really believe all you are saying?"

It was the criminologist's turn to laugh heartily.

"Bless my soul, Rawson! What do you think I'm doing—making these speculations to entertain you? Well, possibly I am. But why shouldn't she induce him to marry her—it's been done before! Let us suppose she had letters in her possession which could easily make old Gilbert writhe. I don't doubt that he could almost see the newspaper headlines. What about his wife—his child, or rather, his grown-up child? What about them! I'll wager he's been doing plenty of old-fashioned writhing—'reeling and writhing and fainting in coils', as Lewis Carrol puts it. But Gilbert puzzles me. He has the mind of an angry child rather than that of a criminal. And the mind of an angry child is difficult to fathom."

John Rawson regarded Brooke thoughtfully as the latter tossed his cigaret away and lighted a fresh one.

"Brooke, you're putting suspicious thoughts in my mind," the District Attorney said, "and I resent it. I'm beginning to see Gilbert, arriving at the studio and entering the dressing-room. Then, when Bovary started on the unwelcome subject, as you suggest, the old fellow might have let loose in a mad frenzy, struck her over the head, and saw her drop. Then when he came to his senses he probably took her jewels, and hid them to make it look like a robbery. But before he could get out of the studio he most likely heard her maid approaching, so he pulled himself together and paced back and forth as if nothing had happened. Sounds fairly logical."

"It does until you think it over," Brooke smiled. "Of course, I have not had the pleasure of meeting Mr. Charles Gilbert, but I cannot reconcile myself to imagining him running from the dressing-room to the property room with his lady friend's jewels. Nor can I picture him carrying the dead form of his lady love from one room to another. You see, Rawson, it simply doesn't fit!"

"Then, why in the devil do you start me on these false scents!" Rawson exclaimed in an annoyed manner. "Here you had me thinking Gilbert was the guilty man when it's the last thing in the world I want to believe. Well, then, this finishes us as far as our suspects are concerned."

"Tut! Tut!" Clay Brooke protested. "We must not overlook the most fascinating individual of the lot, our one breath of romance, our unknown quantity—the algebraic Mr. X. Why did he want to kill the Bovary girl? After all—why do people kill other people? It's a strange phenomenon. Authorities—including myself—say that the two great causes for crime are lust and laziness. Now, Greg, don't prick up your ears, because I don't necessarily mean carnal lust, but lust in its dictionary sense—the eagerness to possess or enjoy—a crime for gain. Fear comes, under this classification, as does a crime for revenge, because both of these motives are a gain of some sort. The criminal commits his offense because he is too lazy to gain by the slow method of honesty. He is too incapable, perhaps, mentally, or otherwise. Let me give you a few illustrations."

In his exposition that followed, Brooke began with Ronald True, whom he described as a "vainglorious megalomaniac", a man who flew into ingovernable tempers when balked. Brooke compared him with Carleton Dazian. Next he discussed Armstrong, the smug type of murderer who lived complacently and unsuspected, an example of the repression of a complex, or a lust which surpassed all other considerations.

"Armstrong was a young edition of Charles Gilbert," Brooke said, "but more ruthless, I fancy. A similar case is that of Patrick Mahon, the born philanderer who intrigued with women and disdained to cut himself adrift from his home life. He was the coward who had not the moral courage to face his wife and have the matter out. Mahon's victim was the sort of woman who would not be satisfied with a temporary liaison, so the man was cornered and found himself in an affair which he could not dismiss. He methodically arranged a plan to do away with the lady rather than cut himself adrift from the other woman in his life. Are you still awake, Rawson?"

"Oh, yes, indeed. Please continue."

"Well, then, our Mr X could have had these motives and possibly others for wanting to do away with Berylyn Bovary. It might have been for revenge— probably not, as melodrama has gone out of fashion. It might have been because of unrequited love—ha! that's interesting!—take Dazian as an example. And Mr. X might have killed her out of fear of disclosure, as I have pointed out, using Gilbert as an example."

"For Heaven's sake, Brooke!" Rawson protested. "Please don't agitate me over Charles Gilbert again—

besides, I think it's quite impossible. I'd much rather think that Dazian is the guilty man."

The criminologist chuckled at Rawson1 s discomfiture. "Well, let's dismiss our motives and see how Mr. X might have performed his foul deed."

As Clay Brooke spoke he rose from his chair and walked to the table where he crushed out his cigaret, then selected a cigar from the humidor. After lighting it, he returned to his chair.

"To begin, Barney was out of the way for approximately eight minutes. And part of the time Dazian was in the dressing-room. We'll put X in front of the studio and see how he can enter without being seen. Dazian has come from the dressing-room and is in the 'phone booth. That makes the coast clear, so Mr. X sneaks in. Dazian finishes his call and leaves. Mr. X is outside the door of the dressing-room of his victim. He looks about for a hide-out in case of emergency and finds the door of the office unlocked. He does one of two things —he either enters the office and attracts Bovary's attention, then finishes her when she steps in; or he walks into the dressing-room, confronts her, and starts things, and—"

"But how about what happened in the office?" Rawson interrupted.

"I was coming to that. He confronts the girl and some kind of a struggle followed in which either the victim or assassin backed into the office where the murder took place."

"Yes, that sounds fairly logical," the District Attorney commented.

"It does—and it doesn't," Brooke said thoughtfully. "I cannot understand why the murderer bothered to carry the body back into the dressing-room. And why did he deposit it in the wardrobe? I can see no reason for that. Now, then, Mr. X realizes he must get out of his predicament. He takes the jewels and leaves them in the property room—another act of madness—then tiptoes to the landing at the top of the stairs. Then—I assume—he sees old Gilbert talking to Barney. He opens the window, slips out and closes it after him. But why did he trouble to close it when he didn't bother to carry away his cotton gloves? And when he left his glasses in the wardrobe? His movements aren't consistent. Rawson, do you suppose there were two of them mixed up in this affair? Do you suppose that"

"Please Brooke!" the District Attorney groaned. "Please don't make this case any more complicated than it is."

"Bless you—I'm not trying to!" laughed the criminologist. "What is your theory, then?"

"My theory," said Rawson, stifling a yawn, "is that it is damned late and I am going to break away from this delightful company. I refuse to think any more about the tragedy until tomorrow. I've enjoyed this mental relaxation immensely, and I appreciate your help and interest, Brooke."

"Well—you know how I am, Rawson—the sport of the thing gets me. To tell the truth, I'd like to continue on the case." A pleased smile of acquiescence was his answer. "Well, now that's settled," laughed Brooke. "I wonder if you can give me an assistant—someone who knows the geography of the studios."

"Delighted! How about Carling, or Leahy? Take your choice—any one of them!"

"Rawson, I'll make a confession to you," Brooke said with mock seriousness. "I abhor officialdom. I'd like nothing better than to have that fellow, Taylor. He knows the ground, and has the entree to studiodom."

Rawson frowned. "Taylor hardly comes under my jurisdiction," he replied, "but if you want him, I'll press him into service."

"That's very good of you. By the way, may I suggest you wire to New York for all available information concerning the Bovary girl?"

"I have already attended to that," Rawson returned .tolerantly. "I—"

At that moment the telephone bell rang and I hastened to answer it. The call was for the District Attorney. I was able to detect the excited voice of Carling on the other end of the wire. Brooke and I waited expectantly until John Rawson returned to the living-room.

"Have they found Wagner?" Brooke asked eagerly, gazing up at the District Attorney.

"No, not yet—but they've located the missing taxicab. Found it up in Beverly Hills, and in the rear seat was an overcoat with blood-stains. I gave Carling orders not to handle it until morning and to hold the cab for our examination."

VII. A Startling Message

When I awoke the next morning I beheld Clay Brooke standing at the foot of my bed fully dressed.

"What—what time is it?" I asked.

"Just about eight-thirty. I wouldn't have disturbed you, but I wanted to ask if you'd mind covering the inquest. See how observant you can be, then give me a full report of the proceedings. The inquest is set for ten o'clock, so you've got plenty of time."

"All right—but where are you going so early?"

"I'm going to look over the ground at the studio. Have a feeling that I may stumble onto an interesting bit of evidence that Rawson's pack may have overlooked. Well, I'll see you at the District Attorney's office after the inquest—then we'll go to lunch."

"Okay!" I answered. "Oh, wait a minute, Brooke! Remember that Claire wanted us to come to some sort of a Whoopee Party tonight?"

Brooke paused before replying. "By Jove—yes! And I want to see her—very much! But I wonder if she'll call off the party because of the tragedy?"

"It's rather unlikely," I said, eyeing Brooke steadily. "You see, she is—unfortunately—mixed up in the affair, and I have an idea she'd give the party just the same to show she hasn't any worries. Claire is like that."

"I fancy so—I fancy so," Brooke murmured. "Well, it would be wise to give her a ring and make sure. I wish you'd call her."

There was a hint of appeal in his eyes.

"All right, old.-timer, I'll take care of it. See you later at the Hall of Justice."

I arose and dressed; then, after snatching some breakfast, I telephoned Claire Demoset. The star's secretary answered the 'phone and said that Claire was out—she had been summoned to the inquest. Yes, the party was still on.

After giving my servant instructions for the day I started for the mortuary. So, Claire Demoset would be there! I was curious to hear her on the stand and learn what part she had played in the tragedy—how much she would admit. Then I remembered young Gilbert. I had said nothing to Brooke about the conversation I had overheard. It might be wiser for me to do so—not yet, I decided—perhaps later when a more opportune time would come.

When I arrived at the mortuary I realized that Hollywood was aghast at the mysterious tragedy. Noted film stars drew up in front of the building in their motor cars and the huge crowd that had gathered peered eagerly forward to catch glimpses of them. Policemen were stationed around the building and at the doors with instructions to clear the sidewalks at the first sign of a demonstration. I was fortunate enough to encounter the autopsy surgeon, Dr. Jeffreys, at the entrance, or I might have had difficulty entering. A throng of men and women had crowded the small inquest room.

The coroner's jury had been selected and were ready and waiting for the testimony. Among the witnesses I recognized Samuel McLevy, producer and supervisor of the picture Berylyn Bovary was to have starred in; Paul. Brimmer, manager of the studio in which the crime took place; Carleton Dazian, who was in Detective Captain Carling's custody; Barney, Taylor, Margaret Hagney, the cameraman and electricians, and a gray-haired man whom I suspected to be Mr. Charles Gilbert. Behind Charles Gilbert, Claire Demoset sat, exceedingly pale, but lovelier than ever.

"Hello, Greg! What do you think of this mess?" a voice beside me murmured, and turning, I saw Hale Douglas, one of the highest-priced "villains" in pictures.

"I don't know," I replied. "Pretty terrible, isn't it?"

"I hear that a committee from the studios is raising a fund of money as a reward for evidence that will bring a conviction."

"That so?"

"Yeh!" he laughed nervously. "Say, there was some excitement a minute ago that you missed. Claire Demoset collapsed when she saw the body and they had to revive her. Bovary's maid almost flopped, too. Caused quite a stir."

"You don't say!" I murmured, trying to conceal my excitement. "Well, it looks like the real fireworks are about to commence."

Coroner Loeb was about to begin the inquest when two huge bunches of American Beauty roses were brought in. My curiosity was aroused as to the identity of the senders, and I determined to make the discovery before quitting the place. The idea of serious amateur observations on my part suddenly amused me when I noted that the entire staff of detectives and police inspectors working on the case were on hand in the hope that the testimony would uncover some clue. The coroner again prepared to begin the questioning and a hush came over the room. The first witness was Dr. Jeffreys.

"Please tell us what you know of this unfortunate situation?" Coroner Loeb asked.

The doctor related briefly what he knew: that his conclusion, after examining the body, was that the murder had been committed some time around seven o'clock. Yes, he had performed an autopsy on the deceased. There were very evident signs of a struggle and of near-strangulation, but that it was the blow on Berylyn Bovary's head that had caused her death.

The next witness was Samuel McLevy, the producer. His testimony, given in a business-like manner, had little or no bearing on the case; it only covered production items. He was unacquainted with the victim outside of the studio. After his dismissal, Paul Brimmer was called to the stand. He, too, knew very little about the victim, or of the circumstances surrounding the murder. His testimony was concerned with the general geography of the studio, entrances and exits. He also told about the contents of the safe and said that nothing was missing.

Charles Gilbert was next on the stand. As he took his place the occupants of the room leaned forward expectantly. I could see that the millionaire was extremely ill at ease and cared little for the publicity that the sensational murder suddenly had brought down on him. When Coroner Loeb asked him to tell what he knew of the case he took up a recital of the incidents beginning with his entrance to the studio, up to the time when the body of the victim was discovered. I noticed that Clair Demoset was listening intently as he talked.

"What was your first act after you saw the body?"

"I called the night watchman and ordered him to notify the police. I waited until the District Attorney arrived with his men, and then I was permitted to depart"

"When did you see the victim last?"

"I think it was the day before—no, two days before."

"Did she seem to fear anything—show any signs of impending disaster?"

"No—on the contrary, she was very gay and animated. She was particularly enthusiastic over the picture she was to star in."

As he spoke a nervous titter ran through the inquest room.

"Mr. Gilbert, when did Miss Claire Demoset enter the studio?"

I glanced in the direction of the film star and saw her face go deathly pale. Charles Gilbert hesitated before replying.

"She appeared directly after we discovered the body — in fact, just as we were about to notify the watchman to send for the police."

A slight murmur passed-through the room as Charles Gilbert was dismissed. The next witness was Margaret

Hagney, the victim's maid. She verified all of Mr. Gilbert's statements and testified as to the movements of Carleton Dazian, Wagner, and the studio crew. She also made mention of the stranger she had seen around the studio.

The cameraman and two electricians were called next, in succession, and gave their slight testimony. James Taylor, the studio detective, followed and told what he knew up to the arrival of the District Attorney, including the discovery of the implement of the crime, which was found in the office.

Carling took the stand next. He declared that he had been called to the scene of the murder about ten minutes after seven, and that he had arrived a few moments before the District Attorney. He stated that he immediately began the preliminary investigation, which he reported in detail.

"I found the body lying in the wardrobe," he said, "just as Mr. Gilbert and the other witnesses have testified."

Q. Did you discover any evidence of violence?

A. Not in the dressing-room. We found signs of violence and a struggle in the room which is used as an office. The victim also showed clearly the signs of a struggle, as Dr. Jeffreys stated in his autopsy.

Q. Did you find the weapon the murderer used?

A. In the office—yes. It was a heavy notary seal.

Carleton Dazian was then called to the witness stand. A hush fell on the room as he gave his testimony in an unhesitating voice. He stated his part in the affair clearly and concisely. Then, when he had concluded, he quietly took his place beside Carling.

"Miss Claire Demoset!" Coroner Loeb called. As the beautiful star took the stand, necks craned forward and a loud murmur filled the room. The coroner hammered for silence, then asked the girl to tell what she knew of the tragedy.

"I hardly know how—how to begin—" She was making an overwhelming effort at self-control, but her voice shook with' the nervousness which she plainly felt. "I—I went to the studio to see Miss Bovary—she had been kind enough to dance at my party in the afternoon. I thought it would be a gracious thing to stop in to tell her how pleased my guests were. But just as I got there—just as I entered—I learned that— that she—had been murdered."

"Was she a friend of yours?"

"Yes—no—that is, I didn't know her intimately. She was new to Hollywood, you see. She—she offered to dance for my guests. I—"

She swayed perceptibly and I thought she was going to fall, but in a moment she steadied herself.

"What were you about to say, Miss Demoset?"

"I don't know—oh, why am I drawn into this!" She looked at the coroner appealingly. "I—I don't know anything about it!"

"You might have telephoned your message to Miss Bovary, mightn't you, Miss Demoset?" the coroner suggested in a tone of innuendo.

Her face turned pale as she caught the unpleasant implication, and she clutched the railing for support. I sincerely pitied her. Then she seemed to regain her self-control.

"Yes—I might have, I suppose—but—" She broke off with a little hysterical laugh, as if she were sparring for time in which to collect herself, in which to marshal her thoughts.

"As a matter of fact," she began again, and now her tone and manner were more composed, "when I started out I really didn't intend to go to the studio. I was motoring along Sunset Boulevard on my way to see about a gown for my next picture when I noticed that I was passing the Eclaire Studio. And as—as I've already told you—I thought it would be nice to step in and thank Miss Bovary for dancing at my garden party."

"Is that all you can tell me?"

"Yes—that's all."

The coroner signified that she was dismissed and Claire Demoset sank back into her chair, relieved. It was plain that the ordeal had sapped her strength.

"That is all," came from Coroner Loeb, and the inquest ended abruptly.

Many of the spectators, anticipating the questioning of others in motion picture circles, appeared dazed by the abrupt termination of the questioning. The coroner's jury then made a formal statement declaring: "Berylyn Bovary was killed by a blunt instrument; namely, a notary seal, by person or persons unknown to this jury, with intent to kill."

As the spectators filed out of the room, I got the impression that they believed Charles Gilbert had not told all he knew. Others suspected Carleton Dazian. Claire Demoset had won their sympathy. I looked about for her, but she had gone. I made my way unobtrusively forward to the two bunches of roses and observed that neither one of them bore a card. Then, as there was nothing further of interest, I quickly left the unsavory atmosphere of the place and hastened to the Hall of Justice.

When I arrived I found Clay Brooke in the District Attorney's office, John Rawson facing him expectantly. Both greeted me cordially.

"Pull up a chair, Greg," Brooke said. "I just beat you by a minute or so. Anything interesting turn up at the inquest?"

I had decided to say nothing of Claire Demoset's agitation during the questioning, and merely remarked that she was among those present and that nothing had been brought to light which we did not already know. When I told of my attempt to find a clue from the American Beauties, Brooke chuckled softly. Then I remembered Hale Douglas's remark concerning Margaret Hagney's collapse as she viewed the body and I recounted it to them—but I omitted Claire Demoset's name from this episode.

"Very good, Greg!" smiled the criminologist. "Now, let me tell you of my own investigation, as Rawson has nothing on his chest and he's agog with impatience to hear of my secret expedition."

"For Heaven's sake, Brooke, get going—get going!" Rawson snorted.

"Well, gentlemen, before going to the studio I felt it my duty to check up on Brimmer's alibi. I found it sound. I wanted to be sure about the man, you see. Then, going to the studio, I combed the ground thoroughly. I re-enacted the crime—a rather difficult feat for one person to accomplish successfully, as I endeavored to assume the roles of all of our suspects at once. I may want to do this again, Rawson, with your assistance. Now then—where was I? Oh, yes—I combed the ground thoroughly and I found the astonishing array of foot-prints as described to us last night by Leahy. Then I looked around a little bit more— became frightfully inquisitive, in fact—and I found this crumpled piece of paper. Observe it carefully, gentlemen."

Brooke drew out his exhibit and handed it to the District Attorney. I noticed that there were pencil marks on one side of it, and a peculiar reddish tinge on the other side.

"What do you make of this, Brooke?" Rawson asked curiously.

"That? Why, bless your soul, Rawson!" laughed the criminologist. "That is a prize exhibit! Note the pencil scrawl, 'Paid to, F. B. fifty bucks.' Buck, as you know, is a synonym for dollar, iron sailor, cartwheel, *ad infinitum*. Of course, it would be jolly to know who F. B. is, because then we could ask him who paid him the fifty dollars which makes him so singularly prosperous. Then, there's that star-like design in pencil in one corner. What do you make of that? At first I thought it was the mark of some secret society. But I dismissed the idea, as it threatened to let my imagination run away with me.

"Now, note the other side of the paper. See that red smear? That, gentlemen, is blood. It is my theory that a certain party—call him X again—hopped out of the studio window, tossed away his gloves as we know he did, and then noticed that some of the blood on the glove had seeped through to his hand. He was smart enough not to wipe it off on his clothes, but reached in his pocket for a piece of paper and found this. Then he wiped off the stain on his hand and threw the paper away without the slightest idea that Mrs. Brooke's little son would pounce on it. Simple, is it not?"

"Very," said the District Attorney drily. "This all you found?"

"Why, Rawson!" Brooke protested. "I'm ashamed of you! I'll find the man you want by means of that scrap of paper. That's right—you'd better put it safely into your desk drawer!"

At that moment the door opened and Carling entered. He nodded at Brooke and myself and then turned to the District Attorney.

"I don't know what to think of this guy, Dazian," he said. "He came through the inquest without batting an eye. He can't be phazed."

"Have you questioned him thoroughly?" Rawson asked.

"Have I! I've given him the works! I've bullied him and wrangled with him. I've even shed tears and talked about his dear old mother. The third degree means nothing to him. He's as cool as a cucumber and he still says he's innocent."

"And you think he is—don't you, Carling?" Brooke put in blandly.

"No, damn it—well, I don't know," the detective-captain replied, scratching his head. "He's a peculiar cuss. One of these kind that you can't tell anything about. Why, would you believe it, he wants me to turn him loose so he can help us find the murderer!"

"Not a bad idea!" grinned Brooke.

"Well, keep him locked up until further orders," Rawson said. "We've got to check up on his alibi next. How about Wagner—any news of him yet?" Carling shook his head in the negative. "Oh, by the way, Carling, bring in that coat you found in the cab and let Brooke have a look at it."

Carling left the room and returned in a few minutes with the coat. Brooke took it from him and stepped to the window to examine it. On the right side, just below the shoulder, was a large blood-stain, a trifle streaked. The criminologist examined the coat inside and out with the utmost care, and studied the label inside the collar. While he was making his investigation, the District Attorney showed Carling the evidence that Brooke had discovered.

"A snappy garment," Brooke finally commented, "although a bit collegiate. Too collegiate for a Hollywood director, if it happens to be Wagner's—or am I wrong, Gregory? I imagine the owner is about your height and fairly well-built. Can't make much out of the label, as the manufacturer boasts of headquarters in New York, Philadelphia, and Chicago, as well as Los Angeles. I suppose you've questioned the clothing stores without success, Carling?" The captain of detectives nodded. "Tell me about the taxicab," the criminologist continued. "Did you find any clues, any blood-stains, finger-prints, or what-nots?"

"Nothing," Carling grunted. "It was clean as a whistle as far as evidence is concerned. And it was found in Beverly Hills near the wealthy section, if you can make anything out of that."

"I can't, my dear fellow, I can't!" Brooke said shaking his head. "I had hoped for blood on the steering wheel, but how could there be any when the party used my modest little piece of paper to wipe the blood from his hand?"

At that moment the District Attorney's secretary entered.

"Mr. Charles Gilbert is here to see you, sir," he said.

"Oh—oh, yes. Tell him to—have him wait until I call you." After the secretary left the room, Rawson turned to Brooke. "Now then," he said, "I am giving you the opportunity to plan your campaign against our visitor."

"I haven't any campaign," Brooke smiled. "Your own questioning is good enough for me, provided I may be permitted to interrupt now and then in a gentlemanly fashion."

"All right, I'll have him come in, then. Carling, get that coat out of the way and then open the door and ask Mr. Gilbert to step in. I want you to remain with us."

"Yes, sir," said the detective-captain. He quickly placed the coat out of sight and was about to step to the door when it suddenly opened and Rawson's secretary appeared again.

"A wire just came for you, sir," he said to the District Attorney. "I brought it in without delay. Shall I keep Mr. Gilbert outside?"

John Rawson nodded curtly and hastily tore open the telegram. As his eyes darted over the yellow sheet of paper, the lines in his forehead deepened, and when he came to the conclusion, an exclamation of surprise escaped his lips.

"Listen to this!" he said excitedly. "It's a wire from police headquarters in New York giving me the data on the Bovary girl. I'll read it all to you, but I want you to get the last line. 'All information available regarding Berylyn Bovary follows. Appeared in musical comedy choruses. Featured beauty in Follies. Danced at Plantation Club and Hotel Empress, then returned to Follies. Was in police court once for violating traffic regulation. Married in 1925 to Frank Wagner, a stage manager.'"

Rawson gazed triumphantly at Clay Brooke.

"Do you get that, Brooke! Berylyn Bovary was the wife of Frank Wagner, the missing director! Carling, that man has got to be found!"

VIII. A Surprising Elopement

It was apparent that Detective-Captain Carling was rapidly becoming accustomed to the District Attorney's sudden and explosive orders. He swallowed hard and returned John Rawson's gaze without flinching.

"Then you think it was Wagner done the trick, sir?" he asked.

"Nothing could be plainer!" Rawson snapped. "Don't you think so, Brooke?"

"Why, my dear fellow!" Clay Brooke replied. "How should I know! I'll admit that it isn't difficult to establish a motive. Wagner may have murdered the girl out of jealousy, or revenge, because she refused to do her wifely duty and come back to him. Then there is the flash of madness which possibly occurred during one of their little tiffs when he realized that her career was budding and his own standing still. Or he might have some less obvious reason."

"But don't you see how it all dovetails, Brooke? Wagner knows his studio. He knows the location of the prop room, which is naturally his inspiration as a place to hide the jewels and put us on a false scent. Again, there are the cotton gloves—common around a studio—and the tortoise-shell glasses. Don't you see how it all fits, Brooke?"

"Yes, you make it very clear, Rawson," replied the criminologist, "That being the case, I imagine you are going to give Carling orders to free Dazian, and also send word out to Charles Gilbert that an interview with him is no longer necessary."

The District Attorney scowled deeply and reached for his humidor.

"No, Brooke," he replied lighting a cigar, "I'm not going to let either of those gentlemen out of my sight for a while."

"But what I want to know," Carling began, "is what in hell—"

The detective captain was interrupted by the sudden entrance of the District Attorney's secretary.

"Beg pardon, sir," he said addressing Rawson, "but Mr. Gilbert requested me to inform you that it is the lunch hour, and he would be pleased to have you as his luncheon guest at the Union Club."

John Rawson glanced at his watch and then looked at Brooke. "What do you say, Clay?" he asked.

"Why not?" replied the criminologist. "And I'm sure that Greg will be delighted, also," he added with a glance in my direction.

"Tell Mr. Gilbert that I will be very pleased to accept his invitation if it includes two of my friends," Rawson told his secretary. "We'll be with him in a few minutes. And now," he added, turning to Brooke, "now you will be able to see your old roue, face to face."

"And at his own expense," Brooke finished.

I found it difficult to refrain from smiling when the District Attorney presented us to Mr. Charles Gilbert. Under a closer observation than I had been able to obtain at the inquest, he fitted Clay Brooke's musical comedy description perfectly. He was above the average height, very well-groomed, and immaculately tailored. His hair was white and his complexion ruddy. He wore tortoise-shell nose-glasses attached to a black cord. Following the introductions, Gilbert led us to his motor car and we were soon whizzing to the Union Club.

"I am greatly interested in meeting you, Mr. Brooke," Gilbert began. "I've followed a number of your personal exploits with great interest. I was particularly fascinated by your investigation which cleared the mystery that surrounded the New Haven hammer murder."

"Is that so?" Brooke replied with evident pleasure. "I'm surprised that you know of my connection with that case. I have never gone in for publicity, you know."

"And probably for good reasons," Gilbert nodded. "You see, I am a sort of amateur criminologist myself. I find it a most fascinating study. I have been particularly interested in the writings of Havelock Ellis and Lombroso on the subject. Lombroso has a most interesting theory on the subject of tattooings which criminals used to undergo. You can see that I've delved into the subject, Mr. Brooke."

"Yes, indeed," the criminologist smiled. "Then, I imagine, you must have certain theories on this unfortunate case which is bringing gray hairs to my good friend, John Rawson."

"Yes, I have a number of ideas which might be worth discussing," Gilbert replied. "One of them—but, here we are gentlemen!"

We entered the grill of the Union Club and our host selected a table in a far corner of the room. After we had given our order, Charles Gilbert turned with a smile to Clay Brooke and said, "I trust that the quiet of this place isn't too deadly for you after lunching at some of the Hollywood show places which you must have visited?"

Clay Brooke looked in my direction with amused eyes. "I'll admit that it isn't so distracting as some of the restaurants Gregory has taken me to," he remarked. "Now yesterday noon we dined at the Montmartre, and there were so many pretty women surrounding us—movie stars, you know—that I can't for the life of me remember what we had to eat."

Gilbert chuckled. "Ah, yes! An amazing place is this celluloid offspring of Los Angeles, with its pretty women, mountebanks, polyglots, irreproachable climate, unsurpassed birth-rate, chamber of commerce exhibits, lion, ostrich and alligator farms, tourist-bearing automobiles, and astounding alfalfa production. Now, would you believe that there is a weekly payroll of over one million dollars in the motion picture industry alone?

And I won't permit you to overlook our Los Angeles Harbor, which handled $804,014,311 worth of commerce in 1926—mind you—and leads the world in oil exporting, having produced 160,254,415 barrels of oil in 1926."

"To say nothing of a chamber of commerce," Rawson added, "with a membership of 12,443 in 1926, which is now the largest organization of its kind in the world."

"But think how it must have increased since 1926!" Brooke smiled in an amused manner. "I had hardly arrived when I was assured by members of your organization that you have an average of three hundred and fifty-four days a year of sunshine; and that earthquakes are mythical bugaboos, only giving an impatient little shrug perhaps once every few years, and from which there has never been a death or serious accident."

"Yes, indeed—yes, indeed!" Gilbert beamed, nodding his head. "You really should settle here, Mr. Brooke. But let's get to this very unpleasant case, gentlemen, as I know you are more interested in that at the moment than the beauties of our native state."

"A few moments ago, Mr. Gilbert," Rawson began, "you declared that you have certain theories concerning this puzzling tragedy. I am sure that we would be more than interested to hear them."

"To be sure! To be sure!" Gilbert agreed enthusiastically. "I'll begin by telling you of my own connection with this very unfortunate happening. I was, as you know, interested in Miss Bovary in a business way. That is, I was financially interested in her film debut, and I have not a doubt in the world that she would have been a great success on the screen, both artistically and financially."

The millionaire's story was interrupted by the appearance of the waiter. As soon as he left us, Gilbert continued.

"To get on with my story, I received a telephone, call yesterday morning at my office from Miss Bovary asking if I could conveniently call at the studio around seven o'clock when she expected to be finished with her camera tests. She said she wanted to discuss certain production items concerning her role, and she also wanted my advice about certain stock which she thought might be a good investment. I will return to the stock later. Well, I went to the studio, as you know, and a few moments later discovered the horrible tragedy that had taken place."

"Mr. Gilbert," Brooke cut in, "before you continue, I wish you would tell us all you know concerning the victim. Who have been her friends in Hollywood—and how long have you known her?"

The millionaire hesitated before replying. Then: "Miss Bovary seemed to have made no intimate friends. She usually remained aloof except when she was invited to the usual parties which included everyone of note. You see, she had not yet made a name for herself."

"I see—and your own friendship with her?"

Charles Gilbert darted a quick glance at each one of us. An expression bordering on fear came over his face, then suddenly he began to speak and made a frank disclosure which amazed us all.

"Gentlemen, I am going to tell you more than I had intended, but I am doing it in confidence and I trust that it will go no further. You will think it strange, I am sure, when I say that I—a man of my age, married, and with a grown son—have been very much in love with Miss Bovary. I am being frank with you—very frank. I met Miss Bovary in New York about a year ago when she was dancing at the Hotel Empress. I admired her greatly and we became very good friends. Now, a financial investment in a motion picture production was not a new experience for me, and I saw no reason why a girl of Miss Bovary's beauty and talent could not be built into a star of real drawing power. We discussed this and she was just mildly interested, so I dismissed the thought. About four months later I made another business trip to New York and found that she had joined the Follies. I saw quite a bit of her then, and when I was about to leave she brought up the subject of my motion picture proposition. And that is how she happened to come to Hollywood, a most unfortunate circumstance, gentlemen, which I regret more than I can tell you."

There was silence around the table as Charles Gilbert finished.

John Rawson was the first to speak. "Did—did anything Miss Bovary ever say to you lead you to believe that she had been married at some time or other?"

"My word—no!" Gilbert exclaimed. "The idea is absurd!"

"Possible, though," Brooke smiled. "A lot of people have done it. May I ask you, Mr. Gilbert, if you ever chanced to meet Miss Bovary's dancing partner during your trips to New York?"

"You mean Carleton Dazian, I presume," Gilbert said with a frown. "Yes, indeed. It was through Dazian that I met Miss Bovary. He, by the way, is the man I was going to refer to relative to Miss Bovary's investments. But to go back to the time of this meeting, I really believe that the fellow cared for her—if a sponge can care for anything! I'll admit that Dazian did things for her— helped her make a name, brought her to prominence, and all that. And I understand he was pretty badly cut up when she left the Empress ballroom and returned to the *Follies.* Anyway, he followed her to Hollywood and took a fling at the movies himself without success. Then he became interested in the stock market and began to urge Miss Bovary to buy certain certificates, which she did. Now the mysterious part of this, gentlemen, is the fact that every bit of stock Miss Bovary purchased was worthless."

"Worthless!" echoed Brooke, with an amused glance at Rawson.

"Absolutely worthless!" Gilbert repeated with emphasis. "I tried to convince her of this, but she wouldn't listen to me. I'd point out that the money she was investing was being thrown away, but she'd laugh at me. She declared that she had inside information concerning the certificates and it would only be a matter of time before she would make a great deal of money. I knew different, but it was a waste of time to tell her so, so I stopped."

"And do you know where these certificates are?" Rawson asked.

"Of course not! I suppose she put them aside somewhere. But what I'm getting at, gentlemen, is the fact that I think Carleton Dazian knows more about this horrible business than he says."

"Dazian has sworn that he loved Miss Bovary," Rawson remarked.

"And is not thwarted love a most likely motive!" Gilbert exclaimed, bringing his fist down on the table. "And didn't he have the fact staring him in the face that some time he would be found out regarding his fraudulent dealings! I'll wager, gentlemen, that this crooked stock dealing on the part of Dazian is news to you all."

"On the contrary," Rawson smiled, "Dazian told us of it himself."

"Oh, indeed?" Gilbert replied, visibly perturbed. "Well, now—that is strange, is it not?" He was silent for a moment, then turning to the District Attorney, he continued, "A moment ago you asked me if I had ever supposed Miss Bovary to be married. Did you mean to infer that she may have been secretly married to Carleton Dazian?"

The District Attorney shot a glance at Clay Brooke. "Why, no," he replied after a moment, "I didn't intend to infer that. Naturally, I have been trying to fathom every possible twist in this case."

"Then you think," Brooke said, turning to Gilbert, "that we have every reason to suspect Dazian?"

"I don't like to say so," Gilbert replied grimly, "but it appears to me that all circumstances point to the man.

According to the testimony, I understand that he was the last one seen in her company, overlooking the fact that the director returned to the studio. To suspect Wagner is rather absurd."

"Then I must tell you in confidence," said Rawson drily, "that Berylyn Bovary was the wife of Frank Wagner."

"Wh-what!" gasped Charles Gilbert. "Why—I don't believe it! It's impossible!"

"It isn't impossible. I received that information this morning from New York."

Gilbert was silent for a moment; then, "Gentlemen, this is a most puzzling case. A moment ago I would have sworn that Dazian is the guilty man. Now my suspicions swerve to Wagner. H'm—now it comes back to me. Miss Bovary, I plainly recall, did not relish the idea of working with Wagner. That was one of her complaints to me over the telephone and I dismissed it as temperament. Why, I see it all now! Where is the fellow? Have you got him?"

"Not yet. He hasn't been seen since he returned to the studio for his coat. But we'll have him before the day is over."

"By the way, Mr. Gilbert," Brooke put in, "do you recall that Miss Bovary ever spoke about a party named Bronson—well, maybe it wasn't Bronson, but the initials were F.B.?"

"No, I'm afraid not. No, I've never heard of any one with those initials whom I can recall at the moment. You have a clue, I take it!"

"We have a number of them," Rawson replied, "quite a chain, in fact. Unfortunately, there are a number of missing links."

"Another question, if you please," Brooke said. "Rawson has kindly assigned an assistant to me, and I wonder if you can tell me anything about his capabilities. It's just possible that you can, you know. I am referring to the studio detective."

"Oh, you mean Taylor?" Gilbert said. "Not much of a detective, I suppose, is your criticism? Well, Taylor is a trustworthy fellow, so far as I know. He worked for a time in the Sunset City Bank on Santa Monica Boulevard. I happen to know that, as I make some investments through that bank. I understand that he wanted outside work, and that is how he happened to leave and take a job at the studios. Perhaps he was bitten by the movie bug and has a desire to get in pictures. What's the trouble—is he too much of a nuisance to you?"

"Oh, no, indeed!" Brooke smiled. "He was very helpful to us during our investigations last night. I asked about him because I like to know everything about a man I'm going to work with."

"Well, I can't guarantee his ability as a disciple of Vidocq," Gilbert smiled, "but he's thoroughly trustworthy. He was well-liked at the bank and I am sure he left a good enough record."

"To return to our subject," the District Attorney cut in. "There is one thing I'm curious about—Miss Claire Demoset's part in the affair."

As Rawson spoke I noticed Clay Brooke's fingers tighten on the arm of his chair.

"I don't quite understand you," Charles Gilbert replied slowly. "Miss Demoset was innocently involved—like myself. She had come merely to see Miss Bovary, as I had. In fact, she must have followed me into the studio, for she appeared just as I was about to notify the police."

Rawson nodded slowly. "Then you don't think she could have been in the studio before you entered?"

"No, of course not! At least, I didn't see her."

"By the way, Mr. Gilbert," Brooke ventured, "I am among those fortunate enough to be invited to Miss Demoset's party tonight—Greg has told me that she is giving it in spite of the tragedy. I suppose I will have the pleasure of seeing you there?"

"No—I think not. I am hardly in the mood for parties."

"Well, gentlemen," cut in Rawson, consulting his watch, "I've already exceeded my lunch hour and there's plenty of work ahead of me."

"Dear me—yes, it's getting late," said Gilbert, reaching for the check. "Well, I hope to see a great deal of you, Mr. Brooke. I've enjoyed this friendly conference notwithstanding the circumstances, and. I know that it is only a matter of time before you'll apprehend the guilty man."

"Yes, only a matter of time," repeated the District Attorney.

As we left the table, Gilbert asked, "May I instruct my chauffeur to drive you back to your office?"

John Rawson readily accepted, so we left Charles Gilbert at his club and drove back to the Hall of Justice.

"Well, Brooke, what do you think of Brother Gilbert?" Rawson asked when we were seated once more in his office.

"A most agreeable old gentleman," Clay Brooke replied. "He's very quick to jump at conclusions—did you notice that, Rawson? He was convinced that Dazian was the murderer until he. learned to his astonishment that Wagner was Bovary's husband. And now he thinks Wagner is the assassin."

The District Attorney appeared not to be listening. He sat staring silently at his desk. Then:

"Brooke, do you see this pile of letters before me? Well, I haven't opened them yet, but I'll wager they're from 'Pro Bono Publico', 'John Smith', 'American Legion', 'A Voter', and so on, demanding that I find the culprit— demanding justice!"

"My dear fellow, don't let them excite you!" Brooke smiled. "Turn them over to Carling. They should add to his comprehension of human nature. You know, Rawson, there have been times when items of actual value have been contained in just such—"

A sudden knock came on the door of the office and Carling burst into the room.

"We've got Wagner!" he exclaimed breathlessly. "Just got a wire from Donovan! He's—he's bringing him back from Tia Juana. The guy must be crazy—he didn't make any trouble about extradition! And guess what—Wagner eloped there with an 'extra' girl and got married! What the hell do you think of that, sir!"

IX. A Secret Mission

For a long moment the District Attorney stared in silent amazement at Carling. Then he brought his fist down with a bang upon his desk, and turned to Clay Brooke.

"What about this development, Clay! Looks bad for Wagner! Looks as if he put his wife out of the way so he could turn about and marry this girl with whom he eloped!"

"It's one way to look at it," Brooke nodded. Then turning to Carling, he asked, "Do you happen to know the name of the girl he married?"

"Yeh—the dame's name is Joy Egan."

"Pretty name," Brooke commented. "Exceedingly celluloidian, isn't it? I was hoping it might be Fannie Buckle, or something to fit the initials F.B. We've got to find some one to fit those initials, Rawson. You don't happen to have any F.B.'s listed in your memory, do you, Carling?"

"No, sir. None I can recollect."

"Hang your confounded F.B.!" Rawson snorted. "Let's talk about Wagner and see how he fits into our case. In the first place, it looks to me as though this elopement is a pretty sudden affair."

"Elopements usually are," Brooke smiled. "At least, all of mine were."

"Can't you see Wagner's position?" Rawson continued ignoring Brooke's interruption. "He's a man in love, and the only thing standing in his way is his marriage to Berylyn Bovary. We have learned from various sources that he quarreled with Bovary. Gilbert also stated that Bovary was annoyed because Wagner was directing her. The fellow has doubtless been demanding his freedom so that he could marry this Egan girl, and Bovary refused to give him a divorce because it would ruin her with old Gilbert. To go even further, the publicity she would get from a divorce would be most unwelcome at the time of embarking upon a motion picture career. Yes, it looks to me as though Wagner got desperate and put Bovary out of the way so he could marry this Egan girl."

"Splendid! Splendid!" Brooke applauded. "But, Rawson, if I may pick a flaw—and I assure you I feel pretty low about doing so—don't you think that Wagner might have married again in perfect safety without fear of a protest from Bovary? Don't you think that she was just as anxious to forgive and forget as Wagner?"

"I'll grant that there might be truth in that," Rawson nodded. "But, on the other hand, I can't bring myself to look at it in that light. If that were the case, why should Wagner have quarreled with Bovary, as we know he did? And why would she look with distaste upon having Wagner as a director? And what of the tortoise-shell glasses which we are pretty sure he wore?"

"Ah, you are winning me!" Clay Brooke smiled. "Then you believe that Wagner evidently had a pretty big chip on his shoulder following the arguments he had with Bovary during the making of the tests? All fight—good enough! Possibly he broached the subject of a divorce and Bovary refused for the very good reasons which you have mentioned. He walked out of the studio with his cheek still smarting, and with thoughts of the Egan girl. Then he got outside and decided to go back for his coat—either with the idea of murder, or actually to get his coat. Once in the studio he decided to have it out with Bovary again, and the tragedy is the result. He hid the jewels as a blind, made a getaway by the window, then—and here's where my paper with the initials F.B. comes in! Who in the devil is F.B.! Then, I presume, he stole the taxicab, ditched it a good distance away, got his girl and eloped with her. Does the girl live in Beverly Hills, Carling?"

"Hell—no!" the detective-captain grunted. "'Extras' don't make enough jack to live in that section!"

"Oh—then there's the blood-stained coat, Rawson! And it's quite probable that this coat is the one that brought Wagner back into the studio. H'm, Rawson, I'll wager that I'll be able to tell you in the morning whether Wagner is the guilty man or not."

The District Attorney looked at the criminologist with sudden interest, and even Carling pricked up his ears.

"What are you driving at, Brooke?" Rawson demanded.

"Just what I say. I'll wager that in the morning I'll be able to tell you whether Wagner is the guilty man or not. I'll go even further than that—I'll be able to give you the name of the owner of that blood-stained coat."

"Is this a theory you've got to work out—something you've got to be sure of before making a disclosure?"

Brooke chuckled. "Naturally, I want to be sure of it! But it isn't just a theory—it's a clue, and a pretty sure one."

"I refuse to play guessing games with you," the District Attorney retorted impatiently. "I suppose you're giving me my cue to be patient—although I'm sure I don't know what you're talking about."

"Good!" Brooke blandly replied. "Now to change the subject, why not get acquainted again with Dazian? We know a great deal more now than we did when we first interviewed him. Let's see if our sheik can help us unravel a few tangled strings."

"A good idea," Rawson agreed grudgingly, "although I must confess that your mysterious wager disturbs me. Carling, have Dazian brought in."

After the door closed on the captain of detectives, John Rawson consulted his memorandum pad, then reached for the telephone and disposed of a number of important matters which had accumulated during the noon hour. Then he summoned his secretary and handed over some correspondence which had come in on the late mail, giving orders and instructions as to their contents and disposal.

Before long, Carling appeared with his prisoner. Carleton Dazian smiled agreeably and sat down in a chair which the District Attorney indicated. He was a trifle paler than when we last saw him, and had lost some of his accustomed jauntiness.

"Dazian," Rawson began, after glancing at a sheet of paper Carling had placed on his desk, "we have investigated your alibi and find that you have told us the truth as to your movements following the crime. The lady you took to the theater has corroborated your statements of last night. That, however, does not clear you and we must continue to hold you under suspicion until we are further convinced of your innocence. During the time which intervened between your call on your victim and your engagement at the theater, you might easily have committed the crime for which we are holding you."

"I understand, sir," Dazian nodded.

"Since our questioning of last night," Rawson continued, "we have learned a number of interesting facts. Perhaps you can clear matters for us. If you can, so much the better for you, as all the assistance you can possibly give will react when the time comes to try to establish your innocence."

"Yes, sir."

"Your own part in the affair, such of it as you have admitted to us, is very clear, and at the inquest you told the same story. Now I am wondering if there are any small details you might have omitted. Think hard and see if there are any facts concerned with the case, which you can recall."

Carleton Dazian returned the gaze of the District Attorney and shifted uncomfortably in his chair.

"I have told you all that I know," he replied. "I have also told you that I loved Miss Bovary, and that I'm anxious to help bring her murderer to justice. When I'm freed I will prove that to you by trying to assist your investigation in every way that I can."

"Then you can give us no new facts?"

"No, sir."

"Carling," Rawson said, swinging around, "get me that exhibit you found in the taxicab." The detective produced the coat and Rawson held it up before Dazian, concealing the blood-stains. "Is this yours?"

"No, sir."

"H'm—will you do me the favor of trying it on?"

Dazian did as the District Attorney requested, paling suddenly as he saw the dull blood-stains below the shoulder. Had the coat been half a size smaller it would have fitted him perfectly.

"This isn't mine!" Dazian said defiantly. "Margaret, Berylyn's maid, could have told you that I came to the studio without any coat."

Rawson pondered the fact for several minutes.

"You've never seen this coat before, then—on any one?"

"No, sir, I haven't."

"All right. Put it away, Carling," Rawson snapped impatiently.

"Excuse me, may I have a word?" Brooke put in suddenly. Rawson nodded and the criminologist turned to Carleton Dazian. "Tell me," he said, "have you ever run into a chap around the studios named Fred Bronson? I believe that is his name—at least, the initials are F. B."

Dazian hesitated before making a reply.

"No, sir; I guess not—nobody by the name of Bronson."

"Can you recall any acquaintance of yours who has those initials?"

"No; I guess I can't, sir."

"H'm! That's too bad," Brooke sighed, lapsing into silence again.

"Dazian," the District Attorney began, "do you know anything about this fellow, Wagner, who was directing Miss Bovary?"

"No—not much. I always thought he was a nice fellow, though."

"What do you know about him?"

"Not very much, sir. I just know him slightly because he's been running with a girl that I used to play around with."

"What is her name?"

"Miss Egan—Joy Egan. She's an 'extra' girl and a good kid. I guess he's been filling her full of the usual apple-sauce that he can get her a great job and make her a star. They all pull that kind of bull, and the dames fall for it, too."

"Wagner and Miss Bovary were always pretty friendly, weren't they?"

"Well—no. I wouldn't say they were friendly. I mean, they got on all right as far as I know—if any director can get along with a girl who's been a musical comedy queen and is new to the movies. Berylyn never saw him outside of the studio."

"I see," said Rawson, pausing for a moment. Then: "You told us last night of your career as a dancer with Miss Bovary. How did your partnership come to a termination?"

"That's something I could never find out, sir. I think I told you that last night. Miss Bovary said she wanted to go back to the *Follies,* that's all there was to it. Maybe she got sick of ballroom routine and wanted the smell of scenery again. Dope it out any way you want to."

"You knew Charles Gilbert in New York, did you not?"

"Yes—slightly. He picked up a sort of a friendship with me in the hotel—guess he thought I'd run him up against a lot of celebrities."

"And you introduced him to Miss Bovary?"

"Why—yes, I did."

"Tell me, did Miss Bovary leave for Hollywood right after the introduction?"

"Let's see—no, she didn't. Old man Gilbert went back west, and right after that, Berylyn went into the *Follies*. Then I think the old man paid another visit to New York, and it was after that that Berylyn came out here."

"Why do you say 'I think' that Mr. Gilbert paid another visit?"

"Did I say that? I mean I know he made another .trip."

"I see," Rawson nodded. "I presume you knew Miss Bovary pretty well—her friends in New York, and all that?"

"Yes, I guess I did."

"I don't suppose Miss Bovary was ever married?"

"Berylyn? I should say not! I tried to get her to marry me, but she couldn't see it. She always said that marriage was the bunk."

"Then your only theory that she was never married comes from the fact that she refused to marry you?"

"Well, I'd hardly say that," Dazian smiled faintly. "Sounds sort of conceited, doesn't it?"

"Then," Rawson said, eyeing Dazian carefully, "you couldn't have known that Berylyn Bovary was married to a New York stage manager?"

"What's that!" Carleton Dazian exclaimed, straightening in his chair. Then he recovered himself and smiled. "Oh, you're trying to kid me!"

"I mean it," the District Attorney replied sternly. "The murdered girl was married in 1925 to Frank Wagner, a stage manager. I have positive proof of it."

"Is this on the level?" Dazian demanded, glancing from one to the other of us. "Well, I'll be damned! I wonder if he could have been working at the Amsterdam Theater? And in 1925—let's see! Then, she must have been married a year or so before I ran into her. And she was married to him—Frank Wagner! My God! That's the

same name as the guy who directed her—the same guy! Where is he! For God's
   sake, tell me that you've got him!"
   "Pipe down! Pipe down!" Carling broke in. "Cut out the shouting, Dazian, and leave that part of the case to us!"
   The prisoner sank back in his chair and nervously pushed his hair back from his forehead. It was plain that the fellow was hard hit by the sudden disclosure.
   "Can you tell us anything about Wagner now?" the District Attorney asked quietly.
   Dazian recovered himself and returned Rawson's gaze calmly.
   "No, I can't," he said. "I only wish to God I could. If you've got him, though, I should think you'd have enough reason to turn me loose."
   "Unfortunately, we haven't got quite enough reason," Rawson replied drily.
   "May I interrupt again?" Brooke cut in. "It—er—it very nearly slipped my mind, Rawson, that I did more investigating this morning than I told you about. Devilish absent-minded of me, I'm sure. After I finished looking over the studio, I sent for Taylor, and we whisked ourselves over to Miss Bovary's bungalow. Fortunately, the officer on duty was one who had seen me with you— he knew Taylor, too—so he permitted us to enter. I examined the house thoroughly, and outside of encountering a number of lively red ants, I found these."
   Brooke reached into his inside pocket and drew out a large manila envelope which contained an assortment of stock certificates. "Now, these," he went on, turning to Dazian, "I imagine are the certificates you sold to Miss Bovary."
   He tossed the envelope to Carleton Dazian, who examined each one.
   "I sold her all of these except three," he said, after a moment. "I'll admit to all except those of the Monte Cristo Mining Company. I've never seen them before."

"You're sure of that?"

"Yes—are they any good?"

"I made some inquiries and they seem to be worthless. Oh, well, let's drop the matter for the present. No more questions from me, Rawson."

The District Attorney looked at Brooke oddly, and it was evident he was annoyed that the criminologist had not mentioned the certificates before. Then, after a few more brief interrogations, he dismissed Dazian.

"And now," he said, turning to Brooke, "will you kindly tell me what all the mystery on your part means?"

"About the certificates?" Brooke asked, smiling. "Why, my dear fellow, you want my assistance on this case, and I'm doing my utmost to give it to you." He paused and lighted a cigaret, then regarded the ceiling. "What a strange creature Berylyn Bovary must have been! I have known any number of stamp collectors, but never any one who collected worthless stock certificates! Just a fetish, I suppose—a fetish, so to speak, to fleece old Gilbert. Better place these certificates with the other exhibits, Rawson."

The District Attorney deposited the envelope in his desk drawer, then turned to the criminologist.

"You have an uncanny habit of finding things, Brooke," he said. "I only hope they'll soon lead us to something concrete. But Jell me, now that you've had another look at Dazian, what do you think of him?"

"Well, in my opinion, that chap is either innocent, or else he's a damn fine actor." Then, turning to me suddenly, he asked, "What do you think, Greg?"

"It appears that Dazian isn't a very good actor," I replied, "because I have not seen his classic features adorning the billboards along the highways. Using that argument as a sort of logic, he might be innocent."

"Very well said," Brooke chuckled.

"Just the same, I'm going to keep him locked up," Rawson snorted. "We'll have Wagner back tonight and question him in the morning."

"Heigh-ho!" Brooke ejaculated, rising from his chair. "We'll have an interesting day before us tomorrow. Well, I must be off. I have business to attend to at the post office before it closes for the day, and I'd better be toddling along."

"The post office," Rawson repeated, "what in the world are you going to attend to at the post office?"

"I have one simple question to ask," Brooke smiled, walking toward the door. "You know, I can never for the life of me remember how many stamps a fellow must put on a letter that's going to Afghanistan."

"Afghanistan!" Rawson regarded Brooke wonderingly. "I can find that out for you, if you really mean it."

"Of course you can!" Brooke chuckled. "But if I find out for myself I'll never forget—just like the elephant! And a walk will do me good. Besides, I've got to dress for an orgy we're taking in tonight. Come on, Greg! See you in the morning, Rawson."

The District Attorney shook his head bewilderedly as Clay Brooke and I quitted his office.

"Frankly, I take the greatest delight in worrying poor old Rawson," Brooke remarked when we reached the street. "Now, I've put him in a frightful pet! But I wouldn't for the world disturb him by telling him all I know. Well, Greg, I'm going to hop into this taxi and whisk along to the post office. Don't try to shadow me, or I'll pull Lecoq's sly trick and get in one door and out the other. This case is getting interesting—damnably mysterious, too. Well, see you later at the house!"

X. ENIGMAS

It was about six o'clock when Brooke joined me at my bungalow. I was more than anxious to see him to learn the outcome of his mysterious afternoon mission; so much so that when he entered I completely forgot about the outlandish costume I was wearing. When he saw me he gasped with astonishment and broke into loud laughter.

"Little Lord Fauntleroy, as I live!" he exclaimed. "Will you kindly tell me, Gregory, what you're doing in those clothes?"

"Don't tell me you've forgotten!" I managed to grin. "This party tonight is a kiddie party. All the guests must come dressed as kids."

"A kiddie party!" Brooke threw his hands up in mock horror and sank into the nearest chair. "A kiddie party! Great Grief! This Hollywood of yours will be the death of me! But, Greg, where in the world did you get that outfit—do I have to wear one?"

"That's what the invitation says."

"Well, I won't do it—I'll be damned if I'll do it! My legs are funny! Now I can see why our friend, Gilbert, isn't going. Not in the mood for parties, said he. Not in the mood—can't you just see him in rompers!"

Brooke burst into laughter. I waited until he had finished, and then asked:

"Now you've got to tell me where you went this afternoon."

"Oh, hang this afternoon! Well, to tell the truth, my time was very well spent and I am one of the most astonished mortals in Hollywood—in fact, I am still astonished. But don't ask me any more about it now—it will keep till later. Greg, what am I going to wear tonight?"

"Oh, wear a pair of pajamas and carry a mouth organ," I suggested.

"Is that kiddie-like? I can't afford to upset my dignity, you know. I've got it—I'll run out and buy a collar and tie!"

"A collar and tie!" I repeated.

"Yes—one of those wide, overturned collars, and a loose, black bow tie. Then I can wear my dinner suit in quiet dignity and appear as an Eton school boy. I'll borrow your car and dash down to the haberdasher's now—be back in a minute."

Later, after Clay had dressed for the occasion, we jumped into my coupe and drove to Claire Demoset's house in Beverly Hills. On the way I tried to pry my friend's secret from him, but he refused to talk on that subject. He seemed deep in thought and I wondered if it was Claire Demoset's part in the tragedy which was causing him to frown. He really had not been greatly interested in the case until he. learned that the lovely film star was involved, and I fancied that this was the cause of his occasional moody silences.

Finally I turned up the drive, and after parking the car we approached the house. A huge, colored butler, dressed as a southern pickaninny, took our things; and suddenly Claire appeared before us looking very boyish and charming as Gainsborough's *Blue Boy*. After greeting me, she turned to Clay Brooke and held out her hand, an expression of apprehension mingled with gladness in her eyes, as if she were looking to him for some sort of protection.

"Oh, I'm so glad you've come!" she murmured. "I—I— was afraid you—you mightn't."

"You've stepped right out of the canvas," he smiled with admiration, "only you're lovelier than any work in oils. Now, you're probably wondering about me. I'm an Eton school boy despite my age. I know you've read about me in *Tom Brown's School Days*."

"I haven't read many college books," she replied, "but I like school boys."

Claire took Brooke's arm and we passed through the large foyer from which all the rooms on the ground floor radiated. The criminologist appeared amused at the sight before us, alternating his gaze from the juvenile costumes of the guests to the Spanish decorations and furnishings in the huge living-room.

"Just make yourselves at home," Claire said to us. "I've so many things to attend to that I can't act as a studio supervisor to everyone. You'll find a gang downstairs in the den having lots of fun—there's an orchestra down there if you care for dancing."

"Oh, but I want to talk to you!" Brooke said in a tone almost of caress.

A wistful look came in her eyes as she returned his gaze. And there was just a suggestion of indecision in her manner.

"I'm too busy right now," she murmured, and with that she darted away. Clay Brooke gazed after her; then he drew a cigaret from his case and leisurely lighted it.

"Well, ain't everybody got fun!" I remarked, lapsing into the vernacular of the studio. "Look, there's Hale Douglas dressed as Peck's Bad Boy. He's the highest-priced villain in pictures and he's even shaved his mustache for the party."

"Art means nothing, does it!" Brooke replied drily. "By the way, didn't you say you saw him at the inquest? H'm—I thought so. Yes, you're right, Greg, every- body sure has got fun."

As the screen fan magazines would put it, here, indeed, was Hollywood at play. In one corner, Billy Francis, the comedian, dressed as Simple Simon, was displaying his cleverness as a magician to a group of admiring ingenues in rompers and large gay hair ribbons. Roland Mendez, the Spanish star, and Carol Grant, a pretty comedienne, as a Bowery boy and girl, were trying to perform an Apache dance in the small space allotted to them. Paul Gallet, a handsome juvenile, dressed as Buster Brown, had even brought his dog, Tige.

"Who's that girl over there in the corner," Brooke suddenly asked, "the one in the Elsie Dinsmore get-up?"

"I don't know," I replied, looking in the direction he had indicated. "I don't remember ever seeing her before. I don't think she's one of the regular movie crowd."

"I don't think so either. I suppose it's perfectly good form to scrape an acquaintance?"

"Sure—you heard what Claire said. Obey your hostess."

"I will. You run along, Greg, and have your fun. I'll get along all right."

Clay Brooke started toward the strange girl, so I pushed my way to the den on the floor below. Here I found the highest-priced orchestra in the world, grinding out jazz; for a group of stars, musically inclined, had taken the places of the regular musicians. Buddy Rodgeton was at the drums and traps, Doug Arden was playing the saxophone, Arthur Pond was successfully making the noise of two banjos on one, and George O'Neil, Rod LaTour, and Harry Cooper completed the orchestra. Nick Cluett and Sue Merril were giving a lively exhibition of the latest version of the "Breakaway" in front of the band, while an admiring throng of celebrities clapped their hands to the syncopation of the jazz.

"Here's Johnny Dines and Lotus Yong!" Nick cried when their dance finished. "How about a little Chinese dance? Any Chinese music, Professor?"

After a few false starts the band swung into *Chinatown,* and the pretty oriental ingenue and Johnny Dines, the comedian, began their dance. Johnny lighted a cigaret which he puffed furiously while pretending to lean against a lamp-post, and Lotus tiptoed lightly around him, holding her forefingers upward in regulation Chinese fashion. When the band reached the chorus, the dancers put broad comedy into their steps, and shouts of approval greeted their whirlwind finish.

I suddenly wondered how Clay Brooke was getting along, so I started up the stairs to look for him. I went first where the strange girl had been sitting, but a young man was with her and Brooke was nowhere around, nor did he seem to be anywhere in the big living-room. Then I thought of the conservatory. It was just possible that my friend would seek refuge there to enjoy a smoke in peace and quiet. As I was about to enter, Brooke's voice came to me, and I halted.

"But, Claire," he was saying in a pleading manner, "you've got to tell me! It would be better—better in every way."

"Oh, I can't—I can't!" came the girl's voice. "It's all so—so horrible—so bewildering! I—I can't think of anything else! It's making me ill—" Her voice broke in a sound like a sob.

"Can't you see that I want to help you?" pleaded Brooke.

"You—you want to help me?" she echoed incredulously. "You—you really mean that?"

"More than you know," said Brooke in a voice of suppressed emotion. "I can't bear to think that you're apt to be dragged into this ghastly business—dragged through it, I mean."

"But you're helping the District Attorney, aren't you?" she asked in mingled suspicion and bewilderment.

"I am. But above all, I want to help you—and how can I when you refuse to tell me everything?"

"If—if I thought you cared—" She broke off and looked searchingly at him.

Brooke was silent for a moment. Then: "But—but I do, Claire—I do!"

"Oh! And I care for you, Clay—so—so awfully much!"

There was silence. Then it dawned on me that I was hardly a gentleman to play the role of eavesdropper. I started to go, but something made me remain.

"Now, will you tell me everything?" I heard Brooke ask softly. "You must, dear—"

"Oh, I wish I could, but—"

"But you must, Claire—everything depends on it."

"Will it make any difference—will you still care for me no matter what—"

"No matter what!"

"Very well, then," she began again, with a new resolution. "On the night—"

"Miss Demoset! Miss Demoset!"

I turned quickly and saw Claire's butler approaching, so I hurried from the spot. Suddenly Clay Brooke appeared from the conservatory. He paused for a moment and looked about, then slowly and deliberately he lighted a cigaret and took several deep inhalations. A group surrounding the piano lustily singing old bal- lads of the gay '90's held his attention for a moment in an absent sort of way; then he saw me and walked slowly in my direction.

"Enjoying yourself, Greg?" he asked, eyeing me strangely.

"Pretty much," I managed to reply. "Oh, by the way, your little girl friend seems to have a suitor." I indicated the strange young couple seated by themselves in the corner of the room.

"H'm! So she has! Who is he, do you know?"

"No; I don't. If he's in the movies I've never seen him before."

"The girl's name is Evelyn Halloway, and she's really very charming. She's a sort of a protegee of Miss Demoset, but she isn't in pictures."

"Oh, so you've met her!" I laughed.

"Yes, and I managed it rather well. I fancy the chap she's with now is some sort of a fiance, but just the same I'm going to try to edge into supper with her."

I wondered what Brooke's interest could be, especially after what I had overheard. I glanced at the girl again and as I did so I fancied she was telling her escort Clay Brooke's identity. Then she looked toward us and smiled, nodding pleasantly to the criminologist. The young chap with her gazed at us coolly and lighted a cigaret.

"Jealousy!" Brooke murmured under his breath, in an amused manner. "But he can't frighten me away! Greg, why don't you go over to the piano and sing? Your elegant baritone has just the kind of a sob in it to go well with that rendition of *She is More to Be Pitied Than Censored*."

I wondered why Brooke wanted to get rid of me, but my reply was cut short by the sudden booming of a Chinese gong. The guests who had been performing in the den below came clattering up the stairs, headed by Johnny Dines. Then there was another booming of the gong and Claire Demoset appeared.

"Ladies and gentlemen, and stars of the cinema!" she cried gaily. "You will find the groceries waiting for you in the dining-room! Help yourselves and sit wherever you can find a place!"

Clay Brooke, without a word, left my side and darted toward the dining-room. I quickly followed, but by the time I reached the long table he had secured two plates of food and was scurrying back to the living room. From where I stood I could see him seek a place beside Evelyn Halloway and offer her one of the plates, which she accepted. She was an exceedingly pretty girl, and when she smiled her soft features took on a glowing charm that was irresistible. She was dark, with strange blue eyes and a lovely complexion.

As I watched, the girl's escort appeared with two plates piled high with chicken patties and sandwiches. He seemed greatly embarrassed as he acknowledged the introduction to Clay Brooke, awkwardly holding a plate in each hand. Then Brooke saw me watching and came to the young man's rescue by motioning for me to join their little group. I hastened to comply with his suggestion.

"Gregory Black will gladly relieve you of one of those," Brooke said as I came up. "Greg, I want to present you to Miss Halloway and Mr. Gilbert—Mr. Mitchell Gilbert. I fancy you must know-his father— he dabbles in the movies."

"Oh, yes, indeed!" I said, endeavoring to conceal my surprise. "How do you do?"

It was not until then that I remembered him as the young man at Claire's garden party who had stated his intention of having it out with Berylyn Bovary. And a rather handsome young man he was, too. I judged him to be pretty close to six feet in height; he was slender, but with good shoulders. His hair was blond and he had light blue eyes that looked timidly through a pair of spectacles. I fancied that he was a little annoyed with Clay Brooke and me for breaking in on his tete-a-tete.

Brooke evidently sensed his thoughts, for he said, "Mr. Gilbert, we really owe you an apology for bursting in on you this way, but Greg has been declaring all evening that he is fed up with movie people and that he would like to meet someone who has absolutely nothing to do with pictures."

"That's us, then," Mitchell Gilbert smiled awkwardly.

"What do you do in the movies, Mr. Black?" the girl asked.

"Scenarios. I'm one of these fellows who takes a famous author's perfectly good novel and changes it so that he will never recognize it when it appears on the screen."

"Oh!" the girl laughed. "I should think your famous author would sell it over again!"

"Well," I replied, "I know of one chap who writes original stories for the screen, and he tells me he's sold the same story seven times."

"I suppose," Brooke ventured, "that all he does is change the setting from Palm Beach to a wild west locale, and instead of a chase in motor boats he puts his characters on horses."

"Or on dog sleds in Alaska," I added.

"Your work must be awfully interesting," the girl said to me. "I wish I could write—it must be wonderful!"

"Have you ever thought of going into pictures?" Brooke asked.

The girl laughed. "Oh, of course I've thought of it. But I doubt if I could ever be a very good actress."

"Evelyn would photograph swell," the young man put in enthusiastically. "But then, it's a pretty hard struggle if you want to get anywhere—and go it straight."

"Does anybody want some ice cream and cake?" the girl asked, changing the subject.

"Not for me, thank you," Brooke said rising. "I'm a hard-working man and it's about my bed time. Gregory is my slave-driver, you know. He's got me here to help him write stories of the underworld, and it's time we were sneaking out of this revel if I'm to do any work tomorrow."

Mitchell Gilbert rose and bade us good night, and the girl smiled prettily as she extended her hand.

"Nice kids, aren't they?" Brooke said, as we walked away. "Now, if you'll pardon me a moment, Greg, I'd like to see Miss Demoset alone before we leave."

"Certainly, that's all right with me. I'll see you out by the car."

"Oh! You aren't going this early!"

We both turned and saw Claire smiling charmingly at us.

"I'm afraid we must," Brooke replied, taking her hand and holding it lingeringly. "I've enjoyed your party ever so much, but I've got a lot to do tomorrow. Greg, don't you want to go and get the car?"

As he spoke he darted a significant glance in my direction. Perhaps Claire sensed the fact that he wanted to see her alone, for she clasped her free hand on my arm and walked with us both to the door.

"Oh, let me come with you!" she said. "Goodness knows, I need some fresh air."

"But—"

"Oh, but I want to! It's so stuffy inside."

As we walked along the gravel drive, I wondered what was going on in the minds of my two companions. The conversation I had overheard between Claire and Brooke perplexed me, but what was even more startling was the sudden avowal of love between them. We had reached the spot where my car was parked and I said good night to the picture star and climbed into the front seat. The girl and Brooke were standing in the shadows, but I saw her raise herself and kiss him full on the mouth. Then she turned and darted toward the house. When Brooke approached I was discreetly lighting a cigaret.

The criminologist was silent and thoughtful as we drove toward my bungalow in Griffith Park. He sat hunched in the seat beside me, staring at the road ahead and puffing furiously on his cigaret. Finally I decided to break the silence.

"Quite a revel!" I ventured. "Did you enjoy yourself?"

"You ought to know, Greg," he answered, a strange tone in his voice.

"I ought to know! I don't get you?"

"Then, perhaps I should explain that while I was in the conservatory with Miss Demoset I saw the reflection of your startled face in one of the wall mirrors."

He had caught me completely by surprise, and I was about to stammer an apology when he suddenly changed the subject.

"A very nice girl, Miss Halloway," he said, "very nice, and very pretty. What do you think of her escort, young Gilbert?"

"He seems to be a likeable enough chap."

"Yes; doesn't he!" Brooke replied. He paused for a moment. Then: "Tomorrow morning I'm going to tell you something that will surprise you. As for old John Rawson, he'll simply be dumbfounded!"

XI. The Uninvited Guest

When I stepped into the dining-room the next morning I found Clay Brooke already eating his breakfast. He darted an impatient glance in my direction and murmured something to the effect that if I wanted to accompany him to the District Attorney's office I'd better hurry. It was apparent that, something of importance was on his mind, and I wondered what could have happened at Claire Demoset's party. Remembering the enigmatic remark he had made on the way home, I was on the verge of asking for an explanation, but there was something strangely forbidding in his manner.

About fifteen minutes later we arrived at the Hall of Justice. Brooke brushed past Rawson's surprised secretary and stepped into the District Attorney's office. Rawson raised his eyebrows and simulated astonishment at Brooke's precipitous entrance.

"Well, well!" he greeted. "You're around bright and early!"

"Rawson, I want you to give one of your men orders to bring Charles Gilbert's son to this office immediately — Mitchell Gilbert is his name!"

The District Attorney stared at Brooke as though he thought the man suddenly had gone out of his mind.

"You—you want me to send for Charles Gilbert's son!" he replied. "What for—what does this mean?"

An expression of annoyance appeared on the criminologist's face.

"You've got to let me have my own way if you want me to find the murderer of the Bovary girl!" he said with emphatic precision. "You get Mitchell Gilbert here and I'll prove just how important it is."

"But—"

"If there are to be any 'buts' in the matter, I'll drop the case!"

Rawson continued to stare at Clay Brooke, then he grunted irritably and pressed the button which summoned his secretary.

"Is Carling around, Shapiro?" he asked.

"Yes, sir."

"Get him for me!"

The secretary disappeared and before long the door opened and the captain of detectives entered. Carling smiled triumphantly, in the manner of the proverbial cat that ate the canary.

"Shall I bring Wagner in, sir?" he asked.

"Not yet, Carling. I want you to send one of your men to bring Mitchell Gilbert here—he's Charles Gilbert's son. Immediately, Carling, do you understand?"

"Ye—yes, sir!" Carling stammered, in disappointment. "But I thought you wanted to see Wagner the first thing this morning, sir?"

"I'll see him in a few moments. Get Mitchell Gilbert to this office as quickly as possible. We've got to have him!"

Carling whistled softly. "Is he mixed up in this mess, sir?"

"That remains to be seen. Hurry along and get your man on his way. I'll send for you when I'm ready to see Wagner."

"Pardon me, Rawson," Brooke cut in, "but I see no reason why we should not see Wagner now. Heaven knows, it's something we've been looking forward to. Let's have a look at the director and hear his story while we're waiting for young Gilbert."

The District Attorney glared at Brooke and then turned to Carling.

"All right, Carling, bring Wagner in as soon as you've got your man on his way."

Carling smiled happily. "Yes, sir." Then he turned and hurried from the room.

Rawson drummed his fingers nervously on his desk for a moment, then swinging around to Clay Brooke he demanded, "Just what have you got on Mitchell Gilbert?"

Brooke slowly drew a cigaret from his case and tapped it on the arm of his chair. After lighting it thoughtfully, he turned to the District Attorney.

"Rawson, must I remind you again that I insist on having my way in this matter? I can assure you, old fellow, that there is a reason for this stubbornness. You'll find out soon enough, and I can promise you a delightful surprise."

The District Attorney grunted, then turned back to his desk and occupied himself signing a number of documents. Clay Brooke rose nervously from his chair and paced the room in silence, stopping now and then to stare out of the window. Finally a sharp knock came at the door. Brooke wheeled around and returned to his chair.

"Come in!" Rawson snapped.

The door opened and Carling appeared with the missing film director. Wagner was a tall, rangy man whom I judged to be about thirty-four. His face had a somewhat dissipated appearance, and what good looks he possessed were marred by a heavy-hanging jaw. There was something disquietingly familiar about him, and I wondered where I had seen him before. He walked forward defiantly and seated himself in the chair that Rawson indicated.

"You are Frank Wagner?" the District Attorney began.

"Yes, sir."

"You have been told about the murder of Berylyn Bovary?"

Wagner nodded indifferently. "Yes, sir."

"You know that you are suspected of this crime?"

"I—er—I assume so, sir."

Rawson was silent for a moment. Then:

"Wagner, I want you to tell me all you can concerning what occurred at the studio on the night of the crime."

Frank Wagner darted an apprehensive glance at each one of us; then he cleared his throat nervously and began.

"Well, sir, as you already know, I went there late in the afternoon to direct Miss Bovary in some film tests. She brought some gowns and the tests were to decide which ones would show up best in the picture. We must have photographed six or eight. Well, we finished about seven o'clock—or maybe it was closer to quarter of seven. Then we knocked off and left the studio. I walked out with the cameramen and electricians—Miss Bovary's maid was with us, too. She sent Barney for sandwiches, and then she went to the drug store for some aspirin. The boys wanted me to go over to the lunch-room for some chow, but I told them I was going to the fights. They crossed the street and then I happened to think that I'd forgotten my coat, so I went back to the studio for it. Then I came out and went my way."

"What kind of a coat was it?" Rawson asked eagerly.

Wagner hesitated. It was clear that he was on his guard.

"A tan coat, sir—sort of a gabardine."

"Carling, get that coat out of the locker—you know the one I mean."

The captain of detectives stepped quickly to the locker in a far corner of the room and returned with the blood-stained coat.

"Try that on, Wagner!" Rawson ordered.

The director's face blanched. But quickly recovering himself he did as the District Attorney instructed. While the coat was a rather snug fit, it could not have been called too small for the man.

"Too tight for me," Wagner said in a tone' of triumph. "Well, does this let me out, sir?"

"I'll tell you when we're through with you!" Rawson retorted. "Now answer this—have you seen any one around the studio wearing a coat like that one?"

"No, sir—it's a little too classy, if you get what I mean. It might have belonged to some ham actor, though."

"Now, tell me this, Wagner. Why was it necessary for you to quarrel with Miss Bovary during the tests?"

A frown clouded the director's face. "I didn't quarrel with her—she quarreled-with me! I mean she tried to tell me my business. You know how it is with these scrappy dames that think they know it all! I really wasn't sore, but a dame like that always gets my goat. But who told you I'd battled with her?"

"Never mind that! Now, answer this question. Have you worked in many pictures with Miss Bovary?"

"No, sir. You see, she's new to the studios. That's what was the matter with her. All of the new ones tell you what you ought to do, and how you ought to photograph 'em."

"Then you didn't know her very well?"

Wagner shook his head. "No, not very."

"Well enough to argue with her, though?"

"Well—you can't help but argue back when someone argues with you, can you?"

"I am doing the questioning!" Rawson reminded him sternly.

"Yes, sir. Excuse me."

"Tell me this, Wagner. How long were you in the studio when you returned for your coat?"

"Just long enough to get it, sir. I came right out."

"You saw no one loitering about?"

"No, sir—oh, yes!" he exclaimed excitedly. "There was a guy in Miss Bovary's dressing-room! By God! He's the one! The man you want is Dazian—Carleton Dazian!"

"We've got him," Rawson replied drily. "What do you know about the fellow?"

Wagner glanced at each one of us, his hands twitching nervously. "He's a little sneak! Dazian's the man that did it if anybody did, I tell you! He was stuck on the girl—stuck on her and sore because she couldn't see him for dust!"

"How do you happen to know all this?" Rawson asked coolly.

The director caught himself quickly. "Why—why, any guy could see that with half an eye! That's the way I doped it out."

"I see. Now, tell me why you said you were going to the fights when you were going to Tia Juana?"

"Because it was nobody's business where I was going, if you'll pardon me for saying it this way. Well, you know what happened. I didn't want to broadcast it to the world that I was eloping and getting married to a classy little girl—yes, sir, a classy girl and a great picture bet!"

"Her name is Joy Egan, is it not?" Rawson asked.

Wagner nodded. "Where did you meet her after you left the studio?"

"At her house—a boarding house on Bronson Avenue."

"Carling," the District Attorney said, turning in his chair, "make a note of that and give me a report on it. Verify everything that this man tells us."

"Yes, sir."

"How long have you known this girl?" Rawson continued, turning to the director.

"About two months, sir—maybe a little more."

"I don't suppose," the District Attorney went on, eyeing Wagner closely, "it ever occurred to you that you might be arrested for committing bigamy?"

"Bigamy! I don't get you!"

"You will!" Rawson replied coolly. "And it's about time you came clean and told us the truth! When I say that you were committing bigamy I mean that you married this Egan girl when you already had a wife—Berylyn Bovary!"

The director's eyes widened and his lips hung open. His normally pale face turned a sickly yellow, and his fingers tightened over the arms of his chair.

Rawson coughed nervously. "Wagner," he said after a moment, "I think you can see that you're in a tight place—a mighty tight place! Take my advice and tell us what you can of this tragedy and the circumstances which link you with the case."

Wagner made an effort to steady himself.

"Yes, sir," he nodded, then, after a short pause, "Well, sir, what I've told you is the truth—I mean about me returning to the studio for my coat. I got the coat, came right out, then met my girl and we jumped in my bus and drove to Tia Juana and got married. She'll tell you this, too."

Again he lapsed into a silence. Then he began again: "And it's true that I was married to Berylyn Bovary, as you say; but about me committing bigamy—well, I guess I didn't look at it that way. You see, sir, I've forgotten that Berylyn and me were ever married. I guess she did, too—or she would have liked to." He paused and scowled angrily. "Berylyn and me didn't stay married long—only for a short time. In the beginning I fell for her hard, but I couldn't keep up with her. She wanted the earth and I couldn't give it to her. Well, we busted up and drifted apart, and then I heard she took up with this sneak, Dazian!"

Wagner stopped and looked at the District Attorney as if to see the effect of his words.

"They put on a dance act together," he went on. "Then I pulled out of New York and came out here to get work in the movies. I haven't done so bad if I do say it myself. I've always worked pretty steady and I haven't had many lay-offs between pictures. And if I do say it myself, I haven't ever made a flop. Well, you can imagine I got the shock of my life when Berylyn arrived to go into pictures—and to star in 'em, at that! Then this sneak, Dazian, he follows her out! Well, I wasn't holding any grudges any more because I'd walked out of her life a long time ago. I'd had enough—plenty! Of course, it gave me a pain in the neck when I directed her and when she'd try to lord it over me and tell me my business. Seemed most like we was married again!"

"Did you ever suggest that she get a divorce?" Rawson cut in.

Wagner smiled ruefully. "After a fashion, sir. You see, Berylyn told me to keep my mouth shut about being married to her. Well, I hadn't meant to do any bragging—I'd got mine, and I was through! I doped it out that she meant to forget, the same as I did. Nobody knew about us, so what was the difference?"

"Now, tell me what you know about Carleton Dazian?"

An expression akin to hatred appeared on Wagner's face as the man's name was mentioned, and his eyes flashed dangerously.

"Dazian's what I said—a little snake in the grass!" His tone was of contempt mingled with disgust. Then he raised his eyes and looked at the District Attorney. "In my way of thinking, sir, if you're looking for the guy that did the killing, Dazian's the bird! I never liked the guy—well, I never knew him very well. I mean, I was never chummy with him. He bobbed up just as I checked out of Berylyn's life. He took her out of the *Follies*, taught her to hoof, and put her on the floor at the Hotel Empress."

"Did he know you were married to Miss Bovary?" Brooke cut in.

Wagner looked at the new questioner with surprise. "He must have! Well—maybe he didn't. Berylyn wasn't the bragging kind when it came to talking about her matrimonial plunge with me. Maybe he knew about it and maybe he didn't."

"Are you acquainted with Mr. Charles Gilbert?" Rawson asked.

"The sucker, you mean? Sure, I know him! He was back of Berylyn's picture. She hooked him, too! Oh, Gilbert's the type she craved! He's put money in pictures before and I've been on his payroll. That's about all I know about him—we don't move in the same circle."

"I see," Rawson nodded, then turning to the criminologist, he asked, "Brooke, is there anything you want 1 to ask this man?"

Brooke was thoughtful for a moment. "H'm—yes, there might be a question or two. Tell me this, Wagner.

Do you happen to know any one around the studio by the name of Fred, or Frank, Bronson? It might not be Bronson—it might even be Bloom. Anyway, the initials are F. B."

Wagner shook his head. "No, sir. I don't know any Bronson or Bloom."

"Any one with those initials?"

"No—nobody that I can think of."

"I see. H'm—do you happen to know anything about Miss Bovary's investments since she's been out here? Any stock she might have bought?"

"No; of course not! I wouldn't know that. I've hardly seen her except at the studio. I didn't know she knew anything about playing the market."

"Thank you," Brooke finished abruptly. "That's all for me, Rawson."

The District Attorney stared thoughtfully at his desk, then turning to the director he said, "Wagner, I'm going to hold you until I have favorable enough evidence to release you. Meanwhile, try to recall anything concerning this case which might he to your advantage. Take him out, Carling, and let me know if our other visitor has arrived."

Wagner returned the District Attorney's gaze with expressionless eyes and walked from the room with Carling.

"Well, Brooke, what do you think of the fellow?" Rawson asked.

"Rather an obvious exhibit of injured innocence," Brooke commented. "The sort that lies as long as you'll let him, and tells the truth when he's pinned down. His hysterics were rather genuine, although hardened criminals and innocent folk are equally capable of hysterics when they have their backs to the wall. I imagine it's the dramatic instinct in us all. Wagner's had his hard knocks where the Bovary woman was concerned and that—but have patience—have patience. I fancy—"

"Brooke," I interrupted, "do you recall—"

"Yes, I think I do, Greg," the criminologist cut in. "I believe you were about to refer to a gentleman who sat behind us at Miss Demoset's garden party and made a few remarks which were in exceedingly bad taste for such a happy occasion. It was a little drama which we might title, 'The Blonde Dancer and the Uninvited Guest.'"

Rawson gazed at Brooke bewilderedly and Was about to speak when the door opened and Carling popped his head in.

"Leahy nabbed young Gilbert!" he announced, his face wreathed in smiles. "Shall I bring him in?"

"By all means!" snapped the District Attorney.

"May I have one of your atrocious cigars, Rawson?" Clay Brooke asked.

XII. The Blue Slip

When Detective Captain Carling ushered in Mitchell Gilbert, the young man's eyes fell questioningly on the stern features of the District Attorney, and then shifted to Clay Brooke. A pleasant smile of recognition appeared on his face as the criminologist bowed a friendly greeting. Then he nodded in my direction and seated himself. Carling dropped into a chair in the corner and looked expectantly at the District Attorney.

"You are Mitchell Gilbert?" Rawson began,

"Yes, sir."

"The son of Mr. Charles Gilbert, the banker?"

"Yes, sir."

Rawson paused and looked helplessly at Clay Brooke, perplexed as to what his next question should be. The criminologist was studying the young man closely.

"Rather an enjoyable evening last night?" Brooke finally ventured.

"Yes, indeed; it was," young Gilbert replied, shifting nervously in his chair. It was plain that he was wondering why he had been sent for, and was wishing that the District Attorney would come to the point.

Suddenly Brooke swung around and flung these words mercilessly at him.

"Gilbert, I want to know how you got those bloodstains from the murdered woman on your overcoat!"

The young man's face turned a dead white. His lips went dry and parched. He could not speak and there was a moment of deathly silence.

"I—I don't know what you mean," he finally stammered.

"You know what I mean! And I want you to tell me why you stole that taxicab and abandoned it in the Beverly Hills section!"

"Just—just a minute, Brooke!" cut in the bewildered District Attorney. "I think—"

"I'm handling this!" Brooke snapped. "You can ask any questions you want when I've finished. Well, Gilbert, what have you got to say?"

The young man looked up at the criminologist and passed his hand vaguely across his forehead.

"I don't know what you're talking about," he murmured.

"Oh, you don't!" Brooke swung about and faced Carling. "Get this young fellow's coat out of the locker!" he ordered. "I mean the one with the blood-stains!"

The detective-captain sprang to his feet with amazing alacrity and scurried to the locker in the corner of the office. He returned holding the blood-stained coat before him.

"Try that on!" Brooke commanded, turning to Mitchell Gilbert.

The young man rose sullenly, and evading each one of us with his eyes, slipped into the coat. It was a perfect fit.

"I might as well inform you, Gilbert," Brooke went on, "that it was unnecessary for you to try on that garment— let us say that it was my love of drama that made me so insistent. I knew last night that you were the owner of that coat." Brooke then turned to Rawson, "You might as well give this young man his glasses the ones we found in the wardrobe with the murdered girl."

The District Attorney opened a drawer of his desk and drew out the tortoise-shell glasses which he handed to young Gilbert. At the same time, Carling took the coat and placed it in the locker. The young man sank back in his chair, completely crushed.

"Well, what have you got to say now?" Brooke asked quietly.

"What do you want to know?" Gilbert returned, half defiantly.

"About this Bovary girl—you didn't care much for her, did you?"

"No—I hated her!" Mitchell Gilbert suddenly sprang to his feet. "I hated her—I tell you! You don't know what sort of a woman she was! She had my father in her clutches—it was killing my mother!—Oh, you ought to know how it is! She got just what was coming to her! Death was too good for her!"

As he finished speaking he sank back into his chair. The suppressed nervous excitement that had fired him died out and he was now almost listless and indifferent.

"Suppose you tell us all you can of the tragedy," Brooke ventured.

Mitchell Gilbert glanced at each one of us before replying. Then:

"All right. But I didn't kill her, I tell you! I didn't do it!"

"It will be interesting to hear your explanation of the blood-stains," Brooke cut in.

The young man looked unflinchingly at the criminologist. After a moment's effort he steadied himself.

"I'll—I'll tell you the whole thing. In the first place, you know of my father's infatuation for the murdered girl—unfortunately," he added bitterly, "that is now common property. Well, I decided to put an end to it because the affair was becoming serious to my mother's state of mind and her health. She was on the verge of a nervous, break-down. It—it was killing her! Well, for a long time I wondered what to do. Then I decided it was up to me to put an end to it."

As he paused, Clay Brooke darted a glance at the District Attorney, but Rawson was staring at the son of Charles Gilbert as though he could not believe his ears.

"Night before last," Gilbert went on slowly, "I was going to a fraternity dance. I was taking a young lady—the girl you met at Miss Demoset's," he added, turning to

Brooke. "I knew that Miss Bovary was working at the studio and I decided to call on her and have a talk. I intended to insist that she break the hold she had on father—to bring an end to everything. I saw no reason why she should not continue with the picture, but I was going to insist that she keep her relations with father on a strictly business basis. I determined to make my argument brief and to the point, then call for Miss Halloway and continue to the dance. I—"

"Did you go to the dance?" Rawson interrupted, regarding the young man intently.

"Yes, sir; but the circumstances which intervened were so horrible that I don't see how I ever managed it. But to get on with my story, I left the house around quarter to seven. I took a cab and dismissed it at the studio door. Then I entered the studio and went directly to the—to Miss Bovary's dressing-room."

"Just a minute," Rawson cut in. "Did any one see you enter the studio?"

"No; I don't believe so. No one was outside. In fact, there didn't seem to be any one around at all."

"All right. Please continue."

"Then I knocked on Miss Bovary's dressing-room door."

"How did you know which door was hers?" Brooke asked.

"I really didn't. The door I came to was slightly ajar and there was a light inside, so I supposed it was hers. Well, I knocked and there was no answer, so I knocked again. There was still no reply, so I opened the door and entered. The room was empty."

"Empty!" echoed the District Attorney. "What did you do then?"

"I don't know—I guess I stood there for a moment and waited. Then—all of a sudden—a horrible sound like a low, distant groan came to my ears. I was frightened stiff—it was so sudden and unexpected! I stood there as though I was glued to the spot. Then, there was a pause—

then a sound of uneven footsteps, as though someone was staggering. I—I don't know what impelled me to do it—but I got the sudden impulse to hide. I looked about wildly—then hurried to the wardrobe closet and hid behind the garments that were hanging inside. Then—then something happened which I shall never forget as long as I live! Some one entered carrying the body of Miss Bovary and—and thrust it into the closet almost on top of me! Oh, my God! It was too horrible—too horrible!"

As he finished he sank back weakly in his chair, and there was a twitching of the muscles about his neck and throat.

"This man!" exclaimed the District Attorney. "Who was he!"

"I—I don't know! I was paralyzed with fear! All I saw was a pair of legs and shoes; I've been dreaming about those legs and shoes! I can't seem to get them out of my mind! And I can still hear that dismal groan, and the steady tread of footsteps coming nearer and nearer!"

"Would you know the legs and shoes if you saw them again?" Brooke asked casually.

"I might—I don't know. It was a dark suit—a sort of a dark gray suit, and the shoes were black shoes—not very new."

"You're sure you didn't see his face?" Rawson asked eagerly.

"I couldn't see it. He held the body of the girl in front of him, and as he pushed it toward me even the slight view I had was shut off. Then he scurried from the room. I tried to follow and shout for help, but I was petrified with fear. It was—it was horrible!"

"H'm!" murmured the District Attorney, lighting his cigar which had gone out. "Do you think he saw you—knew you were concealed there?"

"No, sir; I don't believe he did. He might have, but I hardly think so."

"Very interesting," Brooke remarked drily. "What did you do next—and please don't overlook the part played by your father?"

Young Gilbert eyed Brooke wearily. "I am coming to that, sir. Now, you must realize that I felt pretty wobbly. Then my senses began to return, and my first thought was that I wanted to get away as quickly as I could. I—I don't think I even wondered if the girl was dead or alive—I just wanted to get away, do you understand? Well, I managed to get out of the wardrobe, then I noticed the blood on my overcoat. I quickly took it off, folded it inside out, then tiptoed to the dressing-room door. I guess I was still trembling, because I couldn't seem to move fast enough. Somehow or other, I managed to get out of the horrible place and pick my way to the stairs and the door leading to the street. I—"

"Just a minute!" Rawson interrupted. "Did you see any one around—a man, or a woman? Did you see anything at all of a woman?"

Brooke stared at Rawson and darted an uneasy glance at Gilbert.

"No, sir; I did not."

"Thank you, Mr. Gilbert," the criminologist smiled amiably.

"Well, I was about to hurry down the stairs to the door when I saw my father standing there."

"He was outside?" Rawson asked eagerly, eyeing Brooke with triumph.

"Yes, sir. He was standing outside the door talking to a man who looked like he might be a studio hand."

"You're sure it was your father you saw?"

"Yes, sir; I'm positive. Well, the door was opened inward, and I succeeded in reaching it without them hearing me, so I hid behind it. After a time father entered the studio and I slipped out without being seen. When I got around the corner I saw an empty taxicab standing there, and as the driver was nowhere to be seen I decided to borrow it. I threw my coat in the rear seat, jumped in the front, and in a second I was getting away from the studio as fast as I could travel. I guess the night air must have brought me back to my senses, because I wondered whether I should notify the police or keep quiet. Then I decided to keep quiet as I knew it would be impossible for me to identify the murderer—and, at the same time, the circumstantial evidence might point pretty close to me. Well— that's all there is—that's my story."

As he finished, Mitchell Gilbert looked first at Clay Brooke, then his eyes rested on the District Attorney.

"Then, I suppose, you called for the young lady and went on to the dance?" Rawson ventured pleasantly.

"Yes, sir. I left the cab on a corner in Beverly Hills, then I called for Miss Halloway."

"A most amazing experience!" Rawson exclaimed. "Most amazing! What do you say to it, Brooke?"

"I repeat—most amazing!" said the criminologist blandly. Then, turning to Gilbert, he asked, "Did you notice if any one was in the telephone booth in the waiting room when you entered the studio?"

"I didn't notice. I didn't hear any one talking."

For a moment Brooke regarded Mitchell Gilbert with such an expression of disarming friendliness, that the young man's composure returned. Then a slight frown clouded the criminologist's face.

"A moment ago," he said, turning again to Gilbert, "when you spoke of seeing your father, you inferred that he had just arrived at the studio. Now, why are you so sure that he had not already been in the studio?"

"Why—why—because I am sure that he had just arrived," Gilbert replied hesitatingly. "If you're trying to make me say that he was the man I saw from the wardrobe, you won't succeed, because it could not have been. There was all the difference in the world in the appearance of that man and my father—father is always well-groomed and—"

"But you said you were not so sure that you could recognize the man who carried the body—then how can you be positive that this was not your father?"

The unhappy young man was obviously perplexed. "Well," he began slowly, "I might have been able to, and I might not. But if you're trying to make me implicate my father, you won't succeed."

John Rawson was clearly annoyed with the criminologist. "Brooke," he said, "I'm rather inclined to believe this young man's story."

"It's colorful, to say the least," Brooke smiled grimly. "Answer this question, Mr. Gilbert. When you entered the dressing-room, did you notice any jewelry?"

"Yes, sir; on the dressing-table I saw a number of jewels—a string of pearls, and other things on a jewel tray."

'When you came out of the wardrobe did you notice if that tray was still there?"

"No, I didn't. When I came out, all I wanted was to get out of the place. I didn't notice anything."

"Now, tell me this. After this—er, strange man had thrust the body into the wardrobe, did you notice if he went over to the dressing table and took the jewels?"

"No—I was so paralyzed with fright that I didn't know anything until he had gone."

"Did you notice anything different in the studio when you left—any doors or windows open that were not open before?"

"No, sir."

"Have you confided your part in the tragedy to any member of your family, or to any one else?"

"I have kept it entirely to myself."

There was a short pause. Then Rawson spoke. "I don't suppose you know anything of the private life of the victim—her friends outside of your father, or any details.which might assist our investigation?"

"No, sir—of course not."

"Do you know anything of her financial investments?"

Mitchell Gilbert shook his head. At this point, Clay Brooke could not suppress a grin in the direction of the District Attorney.

"Your father," Brooke said, with a twinkle in his eye, "has never had any dealings with the Monte Cristo Mining Company, has he?"

"I can't answer that, Mr. Brooke. I am unfamiliar with his business, as I am not interested in it. I am studying to be an architect."

"Oh, indeed?" the criminologist replied with interest. "H'm! Tell me this, Gilbert, have you among your acquaintances any one with the initials 'F. B.'? Or any one with a name like Fred Bowen, Frank Bronson, or any name similar?"

"I can't recall any," the young man replied, shaking his head.

Clay Brooke lighted a cigaret and during the interval of silence, John Rawson regarded him rather uncomfortably. Then he turned to Mitchell Gilbert.

"I suppose, young man," he said slowly, "you must realize that I have enough circumstantial evidence to put you under arrest?"

Gilbert paled perceptibly. "Ye-yes, sir; I suppose you have."

"On the contrary," Brooke smiled, "we are going to permit you to have your liberty. Mr. Rawson will probably make the request that you will remain within reach so that he can get in touch with you at a moment's notice."

The District Attorney stared at Brooke unbelievingly, then affirmed Brooke's statement with a sudden nod.

"Thank you—-that's very good of you," Gilbert replied gratefully.

Clay Brooke looked at the District Attorney between half-closed lids, an expression of amusement on his face.

"You may go now, Gilbert," Rawson said.

"Oh, just a moment!" Brooke cut in. "On second thought, I think it will be advisable for you to report to this office at two-thirty this afternoon. That's all."

"Yes, sir. I'll be here at two-thirty."

Mitchell Gilbert rose from his chair awkwardly and left the room.

"Brooke, do you think I'm doing right turning him loose?" Rawson demanded suddenly.

"I was just about to suggest you have Carling put two of his best men on his trail," Brooke replied.

"Carling, carry out those orders!"

The captain of detectives hurried from the room and Rawson turned again to the criminologist.

"I didn't like to let him go, and I didn't want to, lock him up," Rawson murmured, half to himself. "The boy has such a fine family, such fine connections, Brooke."

"Rawson, have you got the fine-family complex?" Brooke laughed. "You should live in Virginia where they have F.F.V.'s. I tell you, old fellow, it is often a very good move to let a fellow run loose—some one you aren't sure of. It is so easy for him to implicate himself deeper than he has already—especially when he is being shadowed." Brooke smiled brightly.

The District Attorney was silent for a moment. Then suddenly he turned to Brooke and demanded, "How in the devil did you know that young Gilbert was implicated in this, murder?"

In answer the criminologist drew his wallet from his pocket and extracted a blue slip of paper which he handed to the District Attorney.

"What in the devil is this?" Rawson, asked.

"It's a money order receipt—the stub they tear off for the purchaser to retain."

"A money order receipt—well, what of it?"

"It was in the small pocket inside of the large pocket on the right-hand side of the blood-stained overcoat. When you permitted me to examine the coat, I found it. Evidently your men overlooked it. I thought it was quite a curiosity—so much so that I took the liberty of confiscating it when you were busy with Carling. Then I hied myself to the General Post Office and hunted up the chief of the Money Order Division. To my great delight I discovered that the purchaser of the money order was Mitchell Gilbert. You see, Rawson, like most of us, he crumpled up the receipt and put it into his pocket and forgot it, which jolly well proved that he was the owner of the coat."

"Why in the devil didn't you tell me this before?"

"My dear fellow," Brooke smiled blandly, "if I told you everything I know, your mind would be a maze of confusion—just as mine is at the present moment. But to change this subject which is embarrassing to both of us, I have a very interesting idea which I am turning over in my mind. I may put it into execution this afternoon. It's— it has a touch of the gruesome, but I have great hopes for it, Rawson, great hopes."

XIII. Clay Brooke's Plan

The District Attorney eyed Brooke reproachfully. But he remained silent, for he had learned that the criminologist was insistent upon keeping his ideas and theories to himself, and that it was useless to demand an explanation of the man's veiled remark. When I first knew Brooke, I wondered if he affected this pose to arouse my curiosity, but I soon learned that there was usually something significant connected with his artful insinuations. Rawson finally shrugged his shoulders and consulted his watch.

"Well, it's about lunch-time," he announced. "Shall we dine at my club?"

"Heaven forbid!" Brooke exclaimed, raising his hands in polite protestation. "We've been eating at your club altogether too often. It can't be possible you've no other place to go, old fellow! If you don't mind my saying so, I'd like a change of diet."

"Would some spaghetti appeal to you?"

"Would it! Now that you've brought up the subject, I'll tell you that it's spaghetti I've been craving ever since I arrived here. That's one dish that has me home-sick for the side streets of New York."

"All right," Rawson smiled, rising from his chair. "We'll go to Barbatti's!"

In a few minutes we were in John Rawson's car on the way to the best spaghetti house in Hollywood. I had been to Barbatti's a number of times, and I wondered if the District Attorney knew that the place on Vermont Avenue masked a speak-easy where one could get a drink if they knew one. There was a dining-room on the first floor with the kitchen in the rear. On the second floor were two large dining-rooms where gay parties often' took place—

parties given by societies of studio people, camera-men, electricians, studio hands, carpenters, and that type. I assumed that Barbatti used the top floor for his living quarters.

Finally we drew up to the restaurant and Rawson instructed his chauffeur to wait. On entering, we were greeted genially by a short, stocky man rather powerfully built, whom I knew to be Barbatti. His smiling features were sharp, and his low forehead was crowned with a shock of coarse black hair. Leaning on the counter, picking his teeth, was a vaguely familiar figure whose eyes lighted when he saw the criminologist.

"Why, hello, Mr. Brooke!" he said, stepping forward.

"Hello, Taylor," Brooke smiled. "By Jove—this is luck! You're the very person I wanted to see!" Then turning to Rawson and me, he said, "If you'll get a table, I'll join you in a moment."

Rawson and I seated ourselves and after a moment Brooke joined us. It was evident that Brooke was highly pleased about something. Rawson stared intently at his menu and said nothing. When I next looked toward the counter, Taylor was gone.

"What do they have here, Rawson," Brooke asked cheerfully, "Italian table d'hote? Good! Waiter put me down for the antipasto, minestrone, spaghetti, and the whole business—don't stop until you reach the spumoni!"

When the waiter left us, John Rawson plunged into the recent developments of the murder case. I could see that Clay Brooke was somewhat bored, but he managed to be most attentive to all of the District Attorney's remarks as he summed up the various perplexing incidents surrounding the Bovary murder. He began by discussing each one of the suspects and endeavoring to eliminate names as he came to them. It was plain that he regarded Frank Wagner as a suspect to be reckoned with. Brooke had very little to say, and I fancied that he was holding something back; for expressions of impatience crossed his face as Rawson carefully weighed each of his arguments.

When the waiter brought our orders, the subject turned to golf for a moment, a subject which Brooke seemed to want to linger on, but the District Attorney soon returned to the tragedy. The name of Paul Brimmer, the studio manager, came up and there was a flash of interest in Brooke's eye, but it quickly died away when Rawson returned to his discussion of Wagner.

"You'll have to agree, Brooke," the District Attorney went on, "that Wagner is the most cantankerous party connected with the crime. Of course, we have Dazian to reckon with, but I'm placing my odds on Wagner. Our pair of Gilberts are innocent to my way of thinking:—I simply can't bring myself to believe either of them had anything to do with it. Yes, Wagner looks like the man we want."

"Don't tell me, old fellow," Brooke smiled, "that you have wiped the name of Miss Claire Demoset from the slate!" Rawson dropped his eyes and became interested in the plate in front of him. "We must remember," Brooke went on, "that we must not grasp too quickly for the obvious. There are a number of most important items to be cleared up and considered before we can be sure of our theories. Don't overlook my particular pet, Mr. X—now don't smile at me so peculiarly. I'm going to prove to you that there is a Mr. X—an unknown quantity—in the wood pile before you're many days older."

"Why not now?" Rawson asked inquisitively.

"Oh, you mustn't press me, Rawson," Brooke protested, "especially after the excellent lunch I've eaten. I never make any statements or disclosures before turning them over carefully in my mind. I look for loopholes, and if I have the bad fortune to find one I begin again in a different channel. The drive back in your motor will drive away the fog, I'm sure."

John Rawson shook his head impatiently. "You take devilish enjoyment in being mysterious, don't you, Brooke?" he said, paying the check.

As we drove back to the Hall of Justice, Clay Brooke was silent, a faint smile playing over his features at intervals. John Rawson watched him in a curious and half annoyed manner, but did not venture to disturb whatever thoughts he might have had. Finally we drew up to the curb and alighted.

"We'll step into the office by my private entrance," the District Attorney said, as we left the elevator, "young Gilbert might be waiting in the reception room and there are a number of things I want to attend to before seeing him."

We entered Rawson's office by a door which led directly from the corridor, and after depositing our hats on the rack, the District Attorney rang for his secretary.

"Is Mr. Mitchell Gilbert outside?" he asked.

"No, sir. He hasn't arrived. But there's a lady to see you, sir."

Brooke started slightly and stared at the speaker.

"A lady!" Rawson exclaimed. "What's her name?"

"Miss Halloway, sir."

"Ah, at last the love interest!" Brooke ejaculated with pleasure, and, I thought, with some degree of relief. "Greg, it's our charming acquaintance of the kiddie party! By all means, Rawson, let her come in."

"Who is she?" Rawson demanded. "What does she want to see me for?"

"Perhaps she doesn't," Brooke smiled. "Perhaps she wants to see me!"

Rawson snorted and turned to his secretary.

"Tell her I'm too busy to see her today," he said.

"I think you're making a mistake, old fellow," Brooke cut in. "Miss Halloway, besides being very lovely and charming, is the young lady to whom Mitchell Gilbert is engaged."

Rawson's eyes widened. "Oh, I see!" Then turning again to his secretary, he said: "Tell her I'll see her."

Shapiro stepped outside, and then ushered Evelyn Halloway in. She looked exceedingly pretty in a charming little sports outfit which clung snugly to her slender figure. She glanced shyly at each one of us, her eyes finally alighting on Clay Brooke.

"Oh! How do you do, Mr. Brooke!" she exclaimed. "I—I really didn't expect to have the pleasure of seeing you so soon again."

"No, indeed!" Brooke smiled, rising and helping her to a chair. "I presume you came to see the District Attorney, Miss Halloway? This is Mr. Rawson. And I am sure you remember Gregory Black, although you probably don't recognize him without his Lord Fauntleroy get-up. He seldom wears it in the day-time."

"Now tell me what brought you here, Miss Halloway?" Rawson asked, when amenities were concluded.

The girl glanced in the direction of Clay Brooke and myself in an embarrassed manner before making a reply.

"Please don't be disturbed at my presence, Miss Halloway," Brooke put in kindly. "I can guess why you have come to this office, and I can assure you that it will do no harm for me to hear what you have to say. You see, I am working on the case which involves Mitchell Gilbert."

A look of apprehension flashed into the girl's eyes, but quickly vanished.

"Then I have been told the truth," she said calmly, "you sent for Mitchell today. But I can assure you that he had nothing to do with that horrible murder. He has told me the entire story—how he had gone to the studio before taking me to the dance, and how he hid himself in the closet. Oh, I think it is all too dreadful for words!"

"Yes, it is," the District Attorney nodded grimly, exchanging glances with Clay Brooke. "When did he tell you this?"

Evelyn Halloway hesitated for a moment, fearing that she might have said too much. Then:

"On our way from the dance he told me. I could see that he was very nervous, not at all like himself—so I made him tell me what it was. He finally confided in me because he wanted my advice. We—we are engaged to be married, you see."

"So I understand," Rawson nodded. "Tell me, what was the advice he desired?"

"He asked me what he should do—whether he should notify the police as to his unfortunate presence in the— the affair, or whether he should say nothing about it. He explained it carefully to me, saying that his being at the studio at the time of the murder might cause him to—to be looked upon with suspicion. He thought if he said nothing it might not ever be discovered that he was there."

"We have a way of finding out those things, Miss Halloway," the District Attorney smiled. "However, I can understand your point of view, and I can't say that I blame either of you for not confiding in the police—but it was unfortunate that you did not do so immediately."

The girl became genuinely perturbed at his words. She looked helplessly from one of us to the other.

"But the reason I have come here," she faltered, "is to tell you that Mitchell had nothing to do with the horrible crime. Oh, please believe me, won't you! If you could have listened to his story as I did, you would be convinced that he is innocent. I—I think I know him better than any one, and I can assure you that there isn't a bit of cruelty or meanness in his character. I know he is innocent, Mr. Rawson—I am positive of it!"

"Just why are you so positive, Miss Halloway!" Brooke fairly flung the words at her. "Were you there—were you in that studio on the night the murder was committed?"

A look of terror came on the girl's face, and she stared at the criminologist, aghast.

"Why—why, no! Of course not!" she stammered.

"Then why are you so sure that the boy is innocent! Is it because he so carefully outlined every move to you—every movement he made from the time he entered the studio to the time he left?"

"Why—yes, of course."

"Then you know every move he made—just as though you had been there?"

The girl replied with some slight hesitation. "Ye—yes."

Brooke rose from his chair and approached her triumphantly.

"So that you could come here and tell us your most convincing story—the same story that he told us—so carefully thought out!"

"Oh, no—no!" the girl cried, almost hysterical. "I did not mean that!"

"Come, come, Brooke," Rawson cut in. "I am—"

"One minute!" Brooke snapped. "So, Miss Halloway, you both practically planned these movements together—there was no chance that either of you would tell a different story!"

The color had gone from the girl's face and she groped uncertainly for words.

"But I did not mean it that way!" she cried.

"Another thing!" Brooke flung at her. "You knew of all this the night I met you at Miss Demoset's party, didn't you?"

"Why—yes, I did."

"And you knew who I was, didn't you? You knew that I was working on this murder case!"

"Yes, I think I did. But—"

"Then why didn't you confide in me before—before the boy was found out!"

"I just said a minute ago, Mr. Brooke, that—"

"I'll tell you why you didn't!" Brooke interrupted. "Because Mitchell Gilbert wouldn't let you! Because he wanted to be sure that his story hung together—. and he wanted to be sure that you knew your role, too!"

Brooke paused and regarded the girl intently. She dropped her eyes and suddenly broke into spasmodic sobs. I wondered why the criminologist kept hammering at her so relentlessly. I supposed that he had a deep regard for the girl. Perhaps this was one of his strange methods of arriving at some sort of a conclusion.

"Another thing!" he resumed suddenly. "A woman's glove was found in that studio the night of the murder! Was that your glove, Miss Halloway, or was it Claire Demoset's!"

"It—it was not mine!" the girl sobbed, looking up through her tears. "You—you can't bring me into this case any more than you can Claire Demoset. She is one of my best friends, and—"

She was suddenly interrupted by a sharp knock on the door.

"Just a moment, Carling!" the District Attorney called, then turning to Brooke, he added, "Have you finished with Miss Halloway? I believe Carling has the young man with him—we made an appointment, you know."

"Oh, yes—Mitchell Gilbert," Brooke said, eyeing the girl casually.

Evelyn Halloway looked up, startled. "Is—is Mitchell here!" she demanded with frightened eyes.

"H'm—yes," Rawson nodded uneasily. "We have some things to talk over."

"It's really nothing to worry about, Miss Halloway," Brooke put in, in a kindly tone. "But I imagine that you would not care to have him see you here; so, if you wish, you may leave by Mr. Rawson's private entrance."

The girl regarded Clay Brooke perplexedly and appeared suspicious of his sudden change of manner. She started to speak but dropped her eyes and said nothing. It was plain that her spirit was utterly crushed, for she had come to defend the boy she loved, but under Brooke's bombardment she had made matters worse.

"Thank you," she replied, rising and looking uneasily at the door.

"I hope to see you soon again under much happier circumstances," Brooke smiled, as she stepped into the hall. Then closing the door, he turned and regarded us quizzically.

"Brooke, what in the devil did all that mean?" Rawson demanded.

"That was pretty low of me, wasn't it?" the criminologist replied. "Oh, I can be brutal to a pretty woman when I want to. God help the future Mrs. Clay Brooke! Well, Rawson, I had a reason for doing that, and perhaps it was a silly one—a very silly one."

At that moment a shrill cry, followed by voices, came from the outer office, and Brooke reached the door in two bounds and flung it open. To our astonishment, we beheld Carling struggling with Mitchell Gilbert and Evelyn Halloway.

"Keep them apart!" Brooke cried. "Don't let the girl speak to him!"

With an effort, Carling fairly hurled young Gilbert into the District Attorney's office and slammed the door. Brooke was left in the reception room, and I imagined him trying to comfort Evelyn Halloway.

"What does all this mean!" Gilbert demanded. "I want—"

"Pipe down!" Carling bellowed. "I've had enough from you already!"

"Just a moment—just a moment!" protested Rawson.

At that moment Brooke returned.

"Everything is all right," he announced pleasantly. "Ah, good afternoon, Mr. Gilbert. You've arrived promptly."

"Where is Evelyn?" the young man demanded.

"I believe at this moment she is stepping into her car and saying 'Home, James!' She said she had a dinner engagement with you, so you can verify my statement later." He paused for a moment and lighted a cigaret.

"Rawson," he said finally, "at luncheon, I told you something about a particularly bright idea I have. I suggest that Mr. Gilbert be detained outside a few more moments while I impart it to you, and then we will get down to business."

"All right, Carling, take Mr. Gilbert into the reception room."

When they had gone, Brooke drew a chair up to Rawson's desk and seated himself.

"Now then, here's the idea," he began. "There's just the barest chance that it might prove something. Briefly, it's to release your two prisoners, Dazian and Wagner, and pile them into an automobile and take them to the studio. Mr. Charles Gilbert must be summoned to the studio at the same time. And I insist that we make sure that each one of these gentlemen is wearing the same clothes that he wore on the night of the murder."

"What in the devil are you driving at!" Rawson demanded perplexedly.

"Just this. We'll put Mitchell Gilbert into that wardrobe—just the way he was when the crime took place. We'll get hold of a dummy—there ought to be one in the prop room—and we'll have each one of our suspects carry it from the office and deposit it. in the wardrobe. In other words, we'll re-enact the crime as closely as possible."

"I see!" Rawson exclaimed enthusiastically. "Then young Gilbert may be able to identify the murderer when he sees the trousers and shoes of each one of the suspects!"

"That's just about it," Brooke smiled affably.

"Brooke, I think we're on the right track at last! And while each one is re-enacting the crime, we'll be able to make our own observations."

"Exactly. It sounds like good entertainment, doesn't it?"

Rawson studied the top of his desk for a moment, then he brought his fist down with a bang.

"I'm going to put your plan into execution immediately, Brooke," he declared. "We can take young Gilbert and Carling to the studio in my car, and I'll have Leahy see that the prisoners are safely delivered. In the meantime, Shapiro can be locating Mr. Charles Gilbert. Brooke, I think your plan is a good one."

Rawson pushed the buzzer on his desk and told his secretary to send Carling in.

"Ho-hum!" sighed Clay Brooke, leaning back in his chair and studying the ceiling. "It's nice to be appreciated—even though one has been brutal with a lady."

XIV: Re-enacting the Crime

Fifteen minutes later, John Rawson, Clay Brooke, Mitchell Gilbert, Carling, and myself were in the District Attorney's limousine heading for the Eclaire Studio. Detectives Leahy and McGregory were to follow, bringing Dazian and Wagner in separate cars. Rawson had located Charles Gilbert, and, although the millionaire had pleaded a pressing business engagement, he finally agreed to join us at the studio within the next half hour.

As we sped along Sunset Boulevard, Brooke explained to young Gilbert the role he was to play in the strange performance which was to be enacted. Carling, in the front seat, listened attentively and nodded his enthusiastic approval as Brooke outlined his plan to his decidedly nervous listener.

"Now, are you sure that you understand everything?" the criminologist asked when he had finished.

"Oh, yes, Mr. Brooke," young Gilbert replied seriously.

A little later, when we pulled up at the studio, we found James Taylor waiting. He gave Brooke a knowing glance, as if they had some secret between them, and opened the door of the car for us to alight.

A police officer on duty also stepped forward and saluted the District Attorney respectfully, while Barney, the watchman, remained in the background and eyed us wonderingly.

"Drive the car around the corner and wait for us, Joseph," Rawson told his chauffeur; then he turned and led the way into the studio.

"Well, Brooke," he said,' when we reached the studio stage, "what is the first thing on the program?"

"The first thing I want to do is get a dummy and a pair of white cotton gloves—I demand realism, Rawson. Taylor, do you think you can dig those articles up for me?"

"Yes, sir!" the studio detective nodded with enthusiasm. "I think I can find what you want in the prop room."

"Good! Oh, just a minute, Taylor—before you start your search, I wish you'd ask the watchman to step in. I also want you to instruct the officer on duty to tell Leahy when he arrives that I want him to place his prisoners in separate dressing-rooms upstairs, and to hold them there until he hears from me. Is that clear to you?"

"Yes, Mr. Brooke," Taylor replied, hastily leaving us.

The criminologist then stepped into the dressing-room. The room had remained undisturbed, just as it was the night of the crime. He peered into the wardrobe and examined the garments hanging there, then turned to Mitchell Gilbert.

"I suppose this is the way the wardrobe was the night of the murder?" he asked.

"Yes—I believe so," young Gilbert replied, looking reluctantly into the closet. "I don't recall everything, but I remember that pink smock."

"Do you mind getting in and showing me what position you were in?"

Mitchell Gilbert stepped gingerly into the wardrobe and it was plain that the task was most distasteful to him. Then he shrank into the furthest corner, concealing himself as best he could behind the garments that hung there. Suddenly there was a knock on the door and a moment later, responding to Rawson's call to enter, Barney stepped in.

"Taylor said you wanted me," he announced.

"Oh, yes!" came from Brooke. "I want you to make sure that the gate on the stairway leading to the upstairs dressing-rooms is unlocked. Two of Carling's men are coming with a pair of our prisoners and I want to make sure he gets them upstairs and puts them under lock and key. And I wish you'd let me know when those people arrive."

Barney nodded and departed, and, at the same time, Taylor returned.

"I've got the stuff you wanted, Mr. Brooke," he said. "I put it all in the office in case you want to look it over."

"Good! I'll look at it immediately!" Brooke said enthusiastically, and without further ceremony he turned and led the way into the office with the rest of us following. "By Jove—this is splendid!" he went on. "Quite a realistic lady dummy you dug up for our melodrama— and she's a blonde, too! Ah, you can't carry realism too far to suit me! I suppose this fair creature of sawdust has been hurled from many burning buildings and speeding motors in place of the star of the picture. Where are the cotton gloves—oh, I see! And all of these came from the property room, Taylor?"

"Yes, sir."

"H'm! I couldn't ask for better paraphernalia. Now, if you gentlemen will excuse me for a few moments, I'd like to look around a bit—while we're waiting for our guests to arrive. Want to come along, Greg?"

John Rawson and Carling gazed perplexedly at Clay Brooke as he strolled from the office and left them. He walked slowly to the head of the stairs which led to the reception room below and the telephone booths, then paused and approached the gate at the bottom of the other flight of stairs which led above to the dressing-rooms. Swinging the gate open, he fingered the padlock which hung loosely on the gate. Then he stepped back and surveyed the premises.

"H'm!" he murmured, half to himself. "The studio crew has left . . . maid gone for aspirin . . . Barney is after the sandwiches. Dazian, if he told the truth, comes from the dressing-room, goes down the steps and enters the 'phone booth. At this point, Wagner probably returned for his coat—h'm!"

Brooke stopped abruptly in his monologue and walked quickly in the direction of the dressing-room door. Here he paused, then suddenly changing his mind, he entered the office where Berylyn Bovary had met her death. He surveyed the office carefully, then scowled deeply, and drawing a cigaret from his case, lighted it.

"You know, Greg," he said, eyeing me peculiarly, "it was here that the murderer performed the one act which I cannot comprehend. It shows the strange working of a terrified brain. He picked up the body, dragged it out of the room, carried it into the dressing-room and deposited it fairly on top of our young friend— but you know all that, don't you. Now, let's step outside again."

The "set" representing the Chinese street which had so fascinated the criminologist on the night of the murder again drew his attention. He walked through it silently and paused when he reached the spot where he had found the perfumed glove. He carefully surveyed the entire studio from where he stood, and I wondered what thoughts were racing through his mind, and just how deeply Claire Demoset was concerned in them. Suddenly he shrugged as though to shake off disagreeable theories and walked to the door of the property room. Then he turned about and faced the Chinese street.

"A most bizarre hiding place!" he remarked, indicating the "set". "Greg, it's my theory that the murderer came in this direction with the idea that this was a good place to conceal himself for a time—at least, until the storm blew over. Then he saw the door of the property room, and disposed of the jewels inside. While he was doing this, young Gilbert made his getaway. Now, right here is a bit of curious psychology. The murderer easily might have made his escape as young Gilbert did, but he lacked the courage and quick thinking to do it. That's interesting— most interesting! I wonder—oh, well, let's rejoin our friends."

As we approached the dressing-room, Brooke was silent. I fancied that he knew a great deal more about the tragedy than any of us suspected. But why was he being so abstruse about it?

"Anything happened, Rawson?" Brooke asked, as we entered.

"Not yet," the District Attorney replied, "but our prisoners ought to be here by this time."

Brooke turned suddenly to Mitchell Gilbert. "Now, there's just one thing more I want to explain to you," he said. "I'm going to have our various suspects enter—one at a time, of course—and I want you to keep tab on them according'to number so our record of your observations will be absolutely correct and in writing. For instance, the first to enter will be No. 1—" Brooke paused and tore a sheet of paper from his notebook— "and after No. 1 on this piece of paper, I want you to write your remarks as to whether you think the party is a possibility—any remarks which occur to you as having a bearing on the murder. The same goes for Numbers 2 and 3. Do you understand?"

"Yes, Mr. Brooke."

"I've got the birds here," Leahy announced cheerfully, coming in. "They're locked in their perches upstairs."

"I hope they enjoyed the ride," Brooke smiled pleasantly. "Now, Leahy, in a minute I want you to bring either one of them down and hold him in the office until I come for him. Do you understand that? All right, go up and pick your favorite and let me know when he's in the office."

"Yes, sir," said Leahy, hastily quitting the room.

Brooke then placed the piece of notebook paper and a pencil on the dressing-table, indicating his action to Mitchell Gilbert.

"Now, young man," he said, "take your place in the wardrobe—just as you were on the night of the murder. Don't try to see the face—look for the shoes and trouser legs. Now, I'm going to step into the office and see that Leahy's choice makes a good start. Rawson, I should prefer it if you and Greg would take places outside—

several paces from both doors where you can watch the movements of our candidates as they drag the dummy from the office to the dressing-room. Carling, you and Taylor will be in this room with me. Now then, Gilbert, I'll let you know when to get ready. I'm going to be here with Carling and Taylor on the couch to watch this part of the show. All right—now to prepare for act one."

Rawson and I followed Brooke from the dressing-room and took our places just as Leahy led Carleton Dazian into the office. Brooke followed them in to give his instructions, but reappeared in a moment.

"We're off!" he called in our direction before disappearing into the dressing-room.

"All right—start!" came his voice after a moment.

The door of the office opened and Carleton Dazian appeared, grimly carrying the horrible dummy in his arms and wearing the white cotton gloves. His face was deathly pale from what I could see of it, and his steps faltered. The door of the dressing-room was ajar and Dazian disappeared inside with the dummy. Rawson and I breathlessly waited for him to come out, and I found myself drawing my handkerchief from my pocket and running it across my brow, so horribly realistic was this strange performance.

After a moment, Dazian reappeared without the dummy. His jaw sagged slightly and his labored breathing was quite audible. He leaned against Carling for support and stared blindly ahead of him.

"All right, Leahy!" Carling called. "Take this bird back and fetch the other. Better give this fellow a good stiff glass of water."

Leahy grimly took the arm of the prisoner and conducted him toward the stairs, then disappeared around the corner to the dressing-rooms above. At that moment Brooke appeared, smiling dubiously.

"What's the verdict, Brooke?" Rawson demanded.

"The boy's writing it now. I'm not going to look at his report until the entire show's over. Come on, Carling, we've got to get our star ready for the next act."

Brooke and Carling returned to the dressing-room as Leahy arrived with Frank Wagner and led him into the office. Presently Brooke appeared and followed them in, only to emerge a moment later and return to the dressing-room.

"All right!" came his cry.

Wagner appeared with the dummy, a grim smile on his face. As he entered the dressing-room he stumbled, and I feared he was going to fall headlong, but he caught his balance and disappeared inside. When he reappeared his self-assuredness had vanished. He was licking his lips nervously and his eyes dilated. Leahy was waiting for him and promptly led him upstairs.

"Has Charles Gilbert arrived?" Brooke asked, stepping from the dressing-room.

"No; but he'll be here," Rawson replied, "he ought to be here any minute. For God's sake, Brooke, tell us what's happened in there?"

"Can't—don't know myself!" Brooke shook his head stubbornly. "Say, I've got an idea—it's a hunch to confuse the boy in the wardrobe." I could feel the criminologist's eyes on me and it gave me a most uncomfortable feeling. "Greg," he went on, "I'm going to ask a big favor of you, and I hope you won't disappoint me."

"What is it?" I asked dubiously.

"Would you mind going through this rigmarole you've been watching?"

"Me!" I gasped. "Why do you want me to do it?"

"Just as a—as a movie gag," Brooke grinned. "Besides, I'd like your reaction—what information you can give me as to Gilbert's position in the wardrobe. You know—visibility, and that sort of thing."

Brooke continued to plead with me and almost before I realized it I had donned the white gloves and was embracing the ghastly dummy which he shoved in my direction.

"Now, Greg," he instructed, "when you chuck that sawdust beauty into the wardrobe, take a good look and see how much of Mitchell Gilbert you can observe. But don't let him see your face. I'll shout when I'm ready."

Before I could reply, Brooke had left the office, leaving me with the objects which represented the victim and a clue of a brutal murder.

"All right!" he shouted from the next room. So, holding the dummy grimly before me, I stepped from the office into the studio, then turned and almost stumbled into the dressing-room. From the corner of my eye I could see Clay Brooke, Carling, and Taylor watching me from the couch—something which did not add to my pleasure—but I headed for the wardrobe, attempting to keep well covered and still observe a trace of Mitchell Gilbert. I could see one foot and a portion of his elbow and arm as I thrust the dummy forward. Then I turned tail and fled as Brooke had instructed. The criminologist joined me outside.

"Well, what about it, Greg?" he asked.

"I couldn't see enough to identify him," I replied, explaining what portions of the young man's anatomy had been visible. "I would say that the actual murderer would not have observed anything."

"I see," Brooke nodded. "I see, but—"

He was interrupted by Leahy who came toward us with a broad grin.

"Old man Gilbert is here," he announced. "McGregory's been holding him outside. Shall I trot him in?"

"Just a minute!" Brooke said. Then he turned to the District Attorney and asked, "Does Gilbert have any idea what we want him for, Rawson? Well, it might save the old chap some embarrassment if the situation were explained to him before Leahy trots him in."

"Maybe you're right," Rawson said. "Leahy, explain to Gilbert why we've sent for him. And be as diplomatic as possible."

Leahy nodded doubtfully and proceeded in the direction of the waiting-room. It was plain that he did not relish the idea of being the one to offer explanations. In a few moments he returned looking unusually troubled.

"He refuses to go through with it," he announced. "He said that the whole thing is a lot of foolishness, and he won't do it."

"Oh, he won't!" Carling snapped. "Ask him if he'd prefer sleeping in a cell tonight instead of helping us clear up this case! I mean it, Mr. Rawson!"

"Bravo, Carling!" Brooke applauded. "Pardon me for saying so, but I believe that you're the very man to make Mr. Gilbert see the light."

"I'll just do that!" Carling grunted. "I'll just do that! I'll have a little chat with him and see if I can't change his mind!"

"Be careful, Carling!" Rawson warned. "Remember that Mr. Gilbert is a respected citizen and a very powerful and influential man!"

"I'll be careful!" the detective-captain snorted. "So he won't do it! Huh!" He turned smartly on his heel and started for the. waiting-room.

"Great fellow, Carling!" Brooke said admiringly. "That was almost a perfect exit speech. I fancy he learned that from your talking pictures."

The detective-captain, at length, returned with Charles Gilbert. That the millionaire was exceedingly ill at ease was evident, although he greeted us pleasantly enough.

"Mr. Rawson," he began, "this masquerade is utterly absurd! But if your officials insist that I go through with it, I suppose I must."

"Really, Mr. Gilbert, it doesn't mean a great deal," Brooke put in. "It's just a matter of routine to help us freshen our minds on what happened here a few nights ago."

"Oh, don't misunderstand me," Gilbert protested. "I want to help you clear up this unfortunate tragedy— to help in every way that I can. But you can hardly blame me for hesitating to go through with something of such a ridiculous nature."

"Of course—of course!" Brooke replied impatiently. "Now, if you'll step into the office with me, we'll start the show and get it over as speedily as possible."

Charles Gilbert reluctantly followed Clay Brooke into the office while John Rawson and I remained in our positions. Carling had returned to the dressing-room. Then the thought came to me of the predicament of Mitchell Gilbert, and I wondered if he would recognize his father in the little drama which was to be enacted. And if he recognized him, would he admit as much to us?

Brooke suddenly appeared from the office, smiled broadly at Rawson, and slipped into the dressing-room.

"All right—start!" came the cry again, and Charles Gilbert appeared with the dummy in his arms, the white cotton gloves on his hands. The millionaire made such an absurd picture that I could not refrain from smiling as I watched him cover the distance between the doors and disappear into the dressing-room. In a moment he emerged white and trembling, beads of perspiration on his brow. Brooke followed him out.

"What a horrible experience!" Gilbert murmured agitatedly. "I was extremely startled to see Mr. Brooke and the others seated there! I—I hope you have finished with me and that it won't be necessary for me to repeat that ghastly performance!"

"No; there's no need for us to detain you any longer," Brooke said. "Leahy, will you show him out? Thank you for coming, Mr. Gilbert."

The millionaire mumbled an incoherent reply and left us. When he was out of sight, Carling burst into loud laughter.

"He's rather upset!" he chuckled. "Well, Mr. Brooke, let's go in and take a look at the young feller's report."

We were about to enter the dressing-room when Leahy came hurrying up.

"There's a lady outside!" he said with excited awe. "Claire Demoset, the movie star!"

"Claire Demoset!" Brooke exclaimed, coloring slightly. "What—what does she want!"

"She said she was sent for, Mr. Brooke."

The criminologist turned suddenly to the District Attorney. "What in the devil does this mean, Rawson!" he demanded.

"I don't know—I'm as surprised as you are!" He paused bewilderedly, then: "I know—I told Shapiro to have each one of the suspects come to this studio, and I—I imagine Miss Demoset's name is still on the list."

"I see—I see," Brooke replied, thinking rapidly.

"All right—show her in, Leahy."

As Claire Demoset approached, she was more beautiful than ever, except that her face was exceedingly pale. She avoided Clay Brooke's gaze and looked directly at the District Attorney.

"You sent for me," she said in a low voice. "What is it you want?"

It was John Rawson's turn to flush with embarrassment.

"Well—er—I tell you, Miss Demoset," he began hesitatingly, "we're trying to get to the bottom of the Bovary tragedy and it's quite possible that you can help us, if you will. We've been re-enacting the crime, and now, if you don't mind, I'd like to ask for your assistance on a point we're endeavoring to clear up. It will only detain you a moment."

Clay Brooke stared at the District Attorney in wide-eyed amazement.

"Rawson, it isn't possible that you're going to ask Miss Demoset to—to carry that dummy from the one place to the other!"

"Why not?" Rawson asked drily.

Suddenly Brooke's face changed and a triumphant smile appeared.

"Very well," he said with apparent resignation, "but I'm afraid the consequences will be rather hilarious. It doesn't seem to have occurred to you that Miss Demoset does not wear a gentleman's shoes or trousers."

Carling burst into hearty laughter which startled us all, and John Rawson turned a deep red and regarded Brooke irritably.

"I hardly think we need detain Miss Demoset any longer," the criminologist went on. "However, I want to have a few words with the lady." The movie star gazed at Brooke in bewilderment.

Without waiting for a reply Brooke led Claire toward the Chinese "set" and paused when he came to the spot where he had found the glove. I fancied that he was pleading with her to tell him what she knew. But the girl continued to shake her head. Then, when he continued with something of vexed persistence, she raised her handkerchief convulsively to her face, her body trembled with sobs, and she attempted to turn away from the criminologist. He appeared to be deeply shaken and presently he took her arm and led her from the studio, her face still buried in her handkerchief. Then Brooke returned to us, puffing furiously on his cigaret.

"Now, we'll go in and look at the boy's report," he said bruskly.

Mitchell Gilbert regarded us questioningly as we entered the dressing-room; and still seated on the couch, Taylor was attempting to re-light the very short stub of a cigar. Brooke apologized for the delay, took the slip of paper which Gilbert offered, and seated himself on the couch beside Taylor. Rawson had recovered his composure and was eyeing Brooke anxiously.

"H'm! 'Number 1'," he read, " 'Number 1'—that's our dancing man—of him Gilbert has to say, 'I am certain he is not the murderer because he wears light gray trousers, whereas the trousers I saw were a dark oxford gray. He wears patent leather shoes, while the murderer wore black shoes, but not patent leathers.' Well," Brooke said, looking up, "that seems to check Dazian out of the running.'"

"What about the next—the director?" Rawson asked eagerly.

"'Number 2'," Brooke read, "'is not the man because he is wearing a blue suit and tan shoes. This does not fit my description.'"

"Now, the old man!" Carling demanded.

"'Number 4'," Brooke read, "'is not the murderer because he is well-groomed and does not bear the slightest resemblance to the man I saw. I believe that Number 4 is my father who was outside of the studio when the murder took place.'"

"Well, that's all, then!" Rawson said, with a sigh of disappointment.

"No," young Gilbert cut in. "Read—"

A burst of laughter from Clay Brooke interrupted him.

"Good Lord!" the criminologist exclaimed. "I skipped Number 3. Gilbert says that Number 3 is the murderer of Berylyn Bovary. Gregory—that's you!"

XV. The Inductive Method

During our trip back to the Hall of Justice in John Rawson's car, Clay Brooke continued to chuckle over Mitchell Gilbert's written statement which appeared to involve me in the murder case. Indeed, this disquieting incident seemed to have driven from his mind all thought of the reappearance of Claire Demoset into the case. I would not have minded Brooke's hilarity so much if the District Attorney had not been present, but I could feel that Rawson was beginning to eye me with suspicion.

"Greg," Brooke went on gaily, "I'm going to insist that you get a new man to take care of your things—to see that your boots are blacked and your trousers pressed. For a high-priced scenario man, you can't afford to run around this way—being mistaken for a murderer who is far from a Beau Brummel, if young Gilbert can be relied on. This is the best joke ever!"

"But, Brooke," I protested, "you'll remember that I was with you when the telephone call came—the very moment we learned of the murder."

I glanced at the District Attorney to note his reaction, but he was staring ahead in silence. One could see that he was exceedingly downcast, following the failure of the experiment—except to incriminate me.

"Devil take it, Brooke!" he exclaimed impatiently after a time. "I'll admit that the idea was a good one, but where did it get us? It proved that we've been holding innocent men, and now we've got to release them and look elsewhere for the murderer."

As he slowly spoke the last words a little shudder went up my spine.

"Yes; and we're going to find him!" Brooke replied, in the best of spirits. "Mark my words, Rawson! Well, here we are back at your stuffy old office. Let's enter as if we hadn't a care in the world, Rawson—not a care in the word!"

"I don't see how you can be so all-fired cheerful!" the District Attorney snorted as the car stopped at the curb. "I'm as glum as a—as a—"

"A llama?" Brooke finished with a smile as he alighted from the car. "Now don't misunderstand me, Rawson, because there isn't the slightest resemblance between you and a llama."

"Thanks," Rawson grunted. We entered the Hall of Justice and proceeded in the direction of his office.

"Any calls for me, Shapiro?" he asked his secretary as he opened the door leading into his inner-sanctum.

"No, sir."

"Well, here we are again!" Brooke announced, when we were seated in the District Attorney's office. "Rawson, I do wish you'd change the interior decorations of this place. I'm getting rather fed up looking at the same pictures on the walls all the time. It reminds me of when I was a kid in school. We had to sit at our desks and gaze all day at two enormous black and white portraits—one of them was Longfellow, including his beard, and the other was John Greenleaf Whittier, also of the era of whiskers. Those two pictures are stamped indelibly on my mind, and it's a wonder I ever became a lover of poetry. I used to plan with ghoulish glee difforont things I would like to do to those pictures. You can see how easily I might have become a criminal rather than a hunter of criminals."

"H'm," the District Attorney commented drily, "is there anything I can do to encourage you in your hunting ability? I'll gladly change those pictures on my wall if it will help you solve the mystery."

"Say no more—I'll take the hint!" Clay Brooke replied with a grin. "And now to work. Please hand me that pad on your desk. I think I have a pencil."

The District Attorney handed the pad to the criminologist and watched him curiously. Brooke began to write slowly, frowning now and then as he did so. Then after studying one sheet for a moment, he tore it off and began scribbling on the next. When he finished the second, he looked it over carefully and turned to John Rawson.

"I've written two advertisements," he announced. "I suggest that you have your secretary make sufficient copies of each one of them and rush someone to all of the local papers with them. Have them inserted in the agony column—you know, the personal column— so that they will appear tomorrow morning and to-morrow evening." He glanced' at his watch. "We've got plenty of time to make it before the dead-line."

The criminologist handed each one of the slips of paper to the District Attorney.

"'F. B. take notice,' " he read, looking at the first slip, " 'if you are in need of more money do not 'phone me. Write a note to the undersigned, care of this paper. X.Y.Z.'"

John Rawson glanced at Brooke curiously, then read the other slip aloud, "'Monte Cristo Mining Stock wanted by man with money. Chance for quick sale. Cash given. Write care of this paper. Calhoun.'"

"You see, Rawson," Brooke explained, "this is just a blind idea of mine. It may work beautifully and it may not. We know that a party with the initials F. B. got money from the murderer because of the blood-stained piece of paper I stumbled onto. He might have more coming to him, and if he sees this advertisement we can get in touch with' him in the hope of prying the identity of the murderer from his lips. We also know that someone sold Bovary some stock certificates—Monte Cristo Mining Stock. There is a possibility that the fellow who did so secured it from a source which we may discover and thus prove his identity. Or else he had some worthless stock reposing in a safety deposit vault, as nearly everyone has at some time or other. I am hoping that he secured it from someone who has more to get rid of, and if we can discover the name of the party in this way we may get a clue worth following."

The District Attorney nodded. "It's a long chance, of course, but it's worth trying—everything is worth trying at this stage of the game."

He pressed the button on his desk and his secretary entered.

"Make enough copies of these advertisements for all of the local papers," he said, handing over the two slips. "Wait! Better than that—do it by telephone. It'll be quicker and you might make a late edition to-day. But do it under your own name, Shapiro, so they won't know it comes from this office. I'll leave it to you—it's most important."

"Yes, sir," the secretary replied, hurrying from the room.

Rawson tapped his fingers nervously on his desk for a moment; then he suddenly swung around in his chair and faced Clay Brooke.

"Do you see any reason why I should hold Dazian and Wagner in custody any longer?" he demanded. "I mean, after this afternoon's experiment?" And before Brooke replied, "I think they should both be released immediately. Do you agree on that point, Brooke?"

"I never like to think of any one languishing in jail," the criminologist smiled. "Of course—"

"Of course, what?" Rawson demanded. Then he turned back to his desk and summoned his secretary. "Has Carling returned?" he asked, as the man entered.

"No, sir."

"When he does, have him come in. I want to see him."

"Yes, sir," replied the secretary turning to go. "The advertisements have been placed by telephone, sir," he added, "and I think you'll make one of the late editions."

"Good!" Rawson grunted. "And now, Brooke, we've got to start all over again from the very beginning. What do you propose to do first?"

"A number of things," the criminologist replied seriously. "First and easiest, you'd better make a note to have one of your men follow up those advertisements. I'm not pinning a great deal of hope on them, although there's a chance. We're apt to be smothered with mail from all of the F. B. parties who want money, and it may take a lot of time to go through that batch of mail. The Monte Cristo advertisement is a wild chance, too. However, murders have been solved through stranger means."

"Have you any other ideas?"

"Yes, a number," Brooke replied, smiling, "but please don't ask me, Rawson. They're not in concrete form yet and I've got to think them out. In fact, I've got a number of hunches I want to follow up tomorrow."

"God knows, I hope you'll be successful," the District Attorney said shaking his head. "But what—"

He was interrupted by a knock at the door and Carling appeared before us.

"You wanted to see me, sir?" he said addressing Rawson.

"Yes, Carling. There are a number of things I want done and you can take care of them for me. First, put through the proper orders so that the Eclaire Studio can be reopened. I've been worried to death by Brimmer, and I see no reason why we should keep them from work any longer. Will you see to this?"

"Yes, sir."

"The next thing I want you to do," the District Attorney said slowly, "is to release your prisoners, Carleton Dazian and Frank Wagner."

"What!" Carling gasped, as if he couldn't believe his ears.

"Do you see any reason why we should hold them any longer?"

"Why, no, sir; I can't say that I do," the detective-captain admitted, "but—"

"But, what!" Rawson demanded.

"I have never seen a detective who didn't hate to release a prisoner," Brooke interposed, smiling.

"We have no further reason to hold either of them, Carling," the District Attorney said. "What evidence we have against them does not hold water, and according to this afternoon's work neither of them is the one who killed Bovary and carried her into the dressing-room. Consequently, I am of the opinion that we should release them. However, I want you to warn both Dazian and Wagner that they are not to leave the city, but must keep within our reach should we need them for information or anything that might come up. Tell them that any attempt to leave town will result in their arrests. I also think you should have them both trailed and get reports of their movements."

"Yes, sir," Carling replied. "You want me to see to this at once?"

The District Attorney nodded and Carling hesitated for a moment, then turned and left the room.

"Odd, isn't it," Brooke put in. "Carling, I am sure, is one of the kindest-hearted chaps in the world, and yet he simply hates to let those two men out of his grasp."

"Carling's a good man," Rawson commented.

"Well, now the happy bride, Mrs. Frank Wagner, can kill the fatted calf and welcome home her absent bridegroom," Brooke said. "Let us hope they will continue their interrupted honeymoon like two cooing doves. Ah, young love—young love!"

"Please, Clay," Rawson protested, "this office is for prosecuting crime, not for sentimentalizing. Now I'd greatly appreciate any little hint you care to throw my way as to your next move."

"Well, then," Brooke said seriously, "it is only right that I should inform you that I am going to apply to myself the chief characteristics of the Parisian detective. I shall follow the example of sly old Vidocq's school of detection and use the inductive method for finding our unknown murderer. So far, we have followed clues and theories as they have presented themselves. From now on I shall attempt to pursue my investigatlon by assuming things. I shall induce various arguments to try to prove that the murderer did this and that—that he must have done so, and that his motive was this or that. Then I shall attempt to prove that my inductions are correct. Do you follow me?"

"Yes," Rawson admitted with hesitation. "But how are you going to start?"

"That's my secret," Brooke replied blandly. "I am going to attempt to confirm certain theories which I have been pre-supposing. Don't sneer, Rawson. I've been doing a lot of thinking in secret—really I have! So now I'm going to work by intuition and with the aid, I sincerely hope, of whatever inspiration I can stumble onto. A person or persons unknown killed Berylyn Bovary—we know that much. Now—"

"But don't you think, Brooke," Rawson interrupted, "that the deductive method is safer—safer and surer?"

"Yes, indeed! I'll agree with you there!" Brooke nodded. "But where has it gotten your precious Homicide Squad! At the present time they're absolutely up against it. We've stumbled on clues, but where did they lead to? At the present time, there doesn't appear to be a really tangible clue to work on—" as he said this, there was the trace of a smile on the criminologist's face—"nothing to deduce from, unless a miracle happens and we learn something from our newspaper advertisements."

The District Attorney nodded slowly and reached for a cigar.

"Yes, my dear fellow," Brooke went on, "I am not going to waste any more time. I'm going to set up my own premises—and I have some which might surprise you— and argue inductively from them. You probably didn't realize it, Rawson, but I made a beginning this afternoon. Oh, now, don't look so startled! When I was covering the ground at the studio while you were busy with Carling I was doing it principally for my own information."

"And what conclusions did you arrive at?" Rawson asked.

Clay Brooke stared out of the window in silence. Then he turned his gaze toward the District Attorney.

"Wait and see, Rawson," he smiled. "I'll tell you this much—I've a pretty definite theory covering this wretched affair, but I've got to prove my points. And that is what I am about to do."

John Rawson regarded Brooke intently. He was about to reply when the door opened and his secretary entered.

"There's a man outside to see you, sir," he announced.

"I'm very busy—who is he?"

"It's Carleton Dazian, sir."

"Oh—ho!" Brooke ejaculated. "Let's have a look at him, Rawson!"

It was evident that the District Attorney was annoyed at the interruption.

"All right—tell him to come in!" he grunted.

The secretary opened the door and Carleton Dazian entered. His step was buoyant and he seemed to have almost recovered his former exuberance.

"Thanks for seeing me, sir," he said, addressing John Rawson. "I know that you are a busy man, but I want to thank you for seeing your way clear to have me released."

"Is that what you wanted to see me for?" Rawson snorted.

"No, sir—not all. I also want to offer you my assistance, and do all that I can to help you solve this mystery. I have told you before that I want to see the murderer of Berylyn brought to justice, and I want to help you find him."

The District Attorney darted a glance at Clay Brooke.

"Well, really," he began, "I hardly think—"

"That's very good of you, Dazian," Brooke interrupted. "Who can tell but what you won't be of valuable assistance to us! Write your name and 'phone number on this slip of paper. Here's my card—wait a moment, I'll write my 'phone number on it. I'm staying with Gregory Black, you know."

Much to the District Attorney's amazement, the criminologist and the former suspect exchanged addresses and 'phone numbers.

"That's all, Dazian," Brooke said pleasantly, "unless Mr. Rawson wants to question you further."

"No, I have nothing more to say," Rawson replied.

"Thank you very much," Dazian said, addressing Brooke. "If I should happen to get hold of any news of any kind, I'll get in touch with you immediately. And if you need me, you know where to give me a buzz—at the Hotel Lowell. And thanks again for giving me my liberty," he repeated to the District Attorney.

"Don't mention it!" Rawson grunted. "Brooke," he added, after Dazian had left us, "what in the world do you expect to do with that gigolo?"

"I don't know—haven't the slightest idea at the moment. But don't forget, Rawson, that Sherlock Holmes used to have a street gamin as an aid, and if Sherlock had his gamin, I fancy I can have my gigolo."

"Let me see that card he gave you!" the District Attorney said suddenly. The criminologist handed over the card questioningly and Rawson studied it for a moment, then opened the drawer of his desk, and carefully drew out a scrap of paper.

"This is the blood-stained piece of paper you found at the scene of the crime, Brooke," he explained. "Not a bad idea to compare Dazian's handwriting on the card with the scrawl on this piece of paper, eh?"

"It won't do you any good, Rawson," Clay Brooke replied, smiling. "I took care of that sometime ago, you know. No, the handwriting on the paper isn't Dazian's, Wagner's nor the two Gilbert's. And if you want to know, it's the hasty penmanship of Mr. X."

The District Attorney returned the criminologist's amused gaze with a baffled expression.

"I mean it!" Brooke continued. "Now may I have my card back, please? You really shouldn't allow yourself to get excited, Rawson. It's bad for your blood-pressure!"

"Blood-pressure—nonsense!" snorted the District Attorney.

"Well, let's be getting along, Greg," Brooke said turning to me with a wink. "Rawson is getting just the least bit annoyed at me. I'll give you a ring in the morning, Rawson, old dear, and we'll exchange ideas and what-nots. Something might turn up in the meantime. If you want me tonight, have me paged in the Hollywood Bowl. Gregory doesn't know it, but I'm making him go to the symphony concert with me where we'll sit surrounded by beautiful movie stars. My soul is stifling and I simply must listen to Great Music. See you later, Rawson."

XVI. An Unforeseen Event

Clay Brooke slept later than usual the following morning and it was ten o'clock when we were sitting in my secluded patio enjoying our breakfast in the streaming sunshine. Brooke spoke enthusiastically about the concert we had attended and seemed particularly charmed with the rendition of Wagner's Overture to *The Flying Dutchman*, Brahms' Allegretto from *Symphony No. 2*, and Gluck's *Dance of the Spirits* from *Orpheus Ballet*.

"But after all," he finally remarked, "for an emotional orgy, give me Wagner's *Love Death* from *Tristan and Isolde*. I am really disappointed they didn't play that, Gregory. You would have enjoyed it. I suppose, though," he smiled, "that it might be dangerous to play it here in Hollywood where emotions run riot."

"No," I laughed, "I've heard it in the Bowl a number of times, and there have been no casualties to date."

"That's disappointing, too!" Brooke smiled broadly, helping himself to a piece of toast. "But possibly I've overestimated the sensibilities of you Hollywoodians.

"You know, Greg," he continued after a pause, "you know, there's a composer or two of the new school whom I'm watching with great interest—particularly Stravinsky and Ravel. I confess to being somewhat of an old fogy, inasmuch as I resent most of this modernistic art, but as far as music is concerned, I'm actually charmed with it. Why, I'll confess to you that I've even got a record home of George Gershwin's *Rhapsody in Blue* out of which I get an enormous kick. Jazz has its place—yes, there's no doubt about it, jazz is an important factor in the music of the future."

He was interrupted by the padded entrance of my Japanese house-boy. I was wanted on the telephone, so I excused myself and left Brooke for a moment. The voice at the other end of the wire proved to be John Rawson's requesting Clay Brooke. The District Attorney was in a state of almost incoherent excitement when he told me what had happened and stammered that he wanted to talk to the criminologist at once. I lost no time hastening back to the patio.

"There's been another murder, Brooke!" I exclaimed. "It's Rawson on the wire. He wants to talk to you."

"Another murder!" Brooke repeated, calmly placing his coffee cup in the saucer. "Who is the victim this time?"

"It was difficult to understand Rawson and I didn't catch the name. He said something about a speak-easy."

"H'm!" the criminologist murmured. "I suppose poor old Rawson is at his wits' end. He would be! Well, he can worry himself into a state of collapse for a moment, if he must, because I'm going to finish this cup of excellent coffee."

Finally Brooke left the table and went to the telephone. In a moment he returned, a puzzled frown on his face.

"The victim is Barbatti—Fiore Barbatti. Say, Greg, we had lunch in his place—the spaghetti house! I wonder what's at the bottom of it."

He paced the room in silence for a few minutes, puffing nervously on his cigaret.

"Fiore Barbatti!—that's it!" he exclaimed, suddenly becoming alert. "That's F. B.—I'll swear that's who it is! Our man got him, Greg—got him before we could reach him! But not a word of this to Rawson. Rawson thinks it's a vendetta—an Italian feud. Tommyrot! Well, Greg, I'll finish dressing and then we'll get on our way. Rawson is there already. Is your car in a mood to run this morning?"

Fifteen minutes later we were in my coupe on the way to Barbatti's resort on Vermont Avenue. Clay Brooke sat beside me in deep meditation for a few minutes, then he turned and asked what I knew of Fiore Barbatti and the place he had been running.

"I know scarcely anything about Barbatti," I told him, "and very little of his place. After your visit, you know almost as much about it as I do. Oh, by the way, Taylor might be able to tell you something of Barbatti—remember, we saw him there when we had lunch?"

"What a remarkable memory you have, Greg!" Brooke smiled. "Taylor can probably help a lot. I had an idea he might be useful some time. By the way, did Barbatti live in his place?"

"I think he had quarters on the top floor."

Clay Brooke lapsed into a silence until we reached our destination. The tragedy and the arrival of the police had brought out the inevitable throng of the curious, and we found the entrance to the place surrounded by a crowd. At the door, we encountered a police officer who admitted us when Brooke gave his name and stated that the District Attorney was expecting us. We were told that Rawson and his aids could be found on the third floor.

When we reached the second landing, we encountered a little man descending who proved to be our acquaintance of the first tragedy, the county autopsy surgeon.

"Well, Dr. Jeffreys!" Brooke greeted him pleasantly. "Here I meet you on a strange staircase when I was hoping that our next meeting would be on the golf links."

"Why, it's Mr. Brooke!" the other exclaimed cheerfully. "That's right—that's right! I've been looking forward to our encounter on the green. But it doesn't look as if we ever will—if this crime wave continues. Another ugly affair, Mr. Brooke, another ugly affair. And as puzzling as the last one, according to John Rawson. I'm just leaving after completing my examination of the victim."

"What's your verdict, Doctor?"

"Death from either of two causes," the autopsy surgeon replied after a slight hesitation. "The victim met his death either from strangulation, or from the result of a severe cut on the back of his head near his ear—a bad spot. The latter came from a fall that he took in which his head bumped against the iron grate of the fireplace. There's a serious abrasion at the back of his head. I can't ascertain whether Barbatti was strangled before or after his fall. At any rate, death could easily have come from either of these causes."

"And when do you think the crime took place, Doctor?"

"About one-thirty last night. Barbatti closed up at one o'clock and the crime took place about half an hour afterwards."

"Has Rawson made any arrests, or found any possible clues?"

Dr. Jeffreys slowly shook his head. "No," he replied, "I believe he has questioned two of the waiters, but that's all. McDonald was unsuccessful in his search for incriminating finger-prints. Well, I've got to be running along. And I'm not forgetting, Brooke, that we're to have that match—I've got a new driver and a new mashie I'm anxious to try out. Well, bye-bye, gentlemen!"

The little fellow scampered down the stairs with his medical kit, and Clay Brooke and I climbed the next flight, arriving at an open door which led to the scene of the tragedy. The District Attorney, Carling, and Leahy greeted us gloomily as we entered.

Seldom have I seen a room in such disorder as the one before our eyes, with the possible exception of a movie "set" on a studio stage after a strenuous film fight has been performed before a battery of cameras. Chairs were overturned, a table in one corner was in a state of collapse, the bed was rumpled, papers were strewn about in wild abandon, and chaos was apparent at every turn. In one corner near a window was a bureau with the drawers pulled out and the contents half protruding; and on the floor before the fireplace lay the body of the victim, a blanket snatched from the bed covering it.

"Nice little place you have here, Rawson," Brooke commented. "I hope you'll ask us again."

"I hope I never have to!" the District Attorney snorted. "Looks like there's been a gang fight here! What do you think of it, Clay?"

"I'd rather not—until you tell me the details."

"Well, it looks like a vendetta to me," Rawson replied irritably. "But to begin at the beginning, two waiters— both Italians—discovered the crime about nine-thirty this morning when they arrived to prepare for the lunch hour. They wondered why Barbatti had not come down; for he was an early riser as a rule. Finally one of them came up here. He saw that the door was partly open, so he entered and found the body lying where you see it now. He immediately called the police, who got in touch with Carling at headquarters. I gave both Italians a preliminary questioning, but could learn nothing of any value. Barbatti had no enemies as far as they know—they have been working here only a short time, according to their statements, and couldn't be expected to know a great deal about his habits. Both claim alibis which are being looked into at the present moment. McDonald has been here and has covered the ground pretty thoroughly. He found no signs of incriminating finger-prints—in fact, there seems to be nothing but disorder everywhere. The victim met his death either by strangulation, or—"

"Yes," Brooke cut in hastily. "I met Dr. Jeffreys on the stairs and he told me that. Then it is your theory, Rawson, that Barbatti was mixed up in a feud or a vendetta?"

"It certainly seems that way to me," the District Attorney answered.

"Well—let's have a look at him!" the criminologist replied, approaching the form under the blanket. He drew back the covering and bent over the victim, examining the body carefully from head to foot, taking special note of the ugly gash on the back of the head.

"No," Brooke finally said, rising to his feet, "I'm afraid we'll have to dismiss the romantic idea that this is a Camorrist affair. I've had experience with the Camorra of

Naples, the Mafia of Sicily, and the Nano Nera, or Black
Hand, to which order any one may elect himself who feels
in the mood for committing a crime. Nine times out of ten,
the victim of a vendetta meets his death by a knife
wound, so I'm afraid Barbatti won't qualify. Sorry to
disappoint you, Rawson."

"Then perhaps you can give me an idea who is back of
this crime?" the District Attorney replied with sarcasm.

"To tell the truth," Brooke smiled blandly, "I am the
possessor of a most persistent theory—but it will have to
keep till later. It isn't entirely assembled, you see, so it
would hardly do for me to explode it until I am absolutely
sure of each of my points."

"Then you—"

"Just a moment, my dear fellow! Have a little patience
and be so good as to permit me to make an investigation
of this place. Then, perhaps, I'll find one or two of my
missing links. Now then, let's have a look at the bed. A
bed, you know, is one of those obstreperous witnesses
which never misguides, and no counter testimony can be
given against it. This one doesn't help much, however—
just messed up in the general upheaval. Doubtless
someone's been looking for something. No sign of blood-
stains either—except near the body."

As he spoke his gaze traveled along the floor in the
direction of the dead man.

"In fact," Brooke went on, "the only blood-stains are
around the fireplace where Barbatti fell. If the murderer
strangled his victim after he fell, he must have got blood
on his hands or clothing. Have you found any blood-stains
on anything, Rawson—anything that the murderer might
have used to wipe his hands? H'm—too bad! A pretty
powerful fellow, our murderer, because Barbatti was no
lightweight."

Clay Brooke then lapsed into silence as he paced
quietly about the room, pausing to examine the upset
furniture, and occasionally kneeling to study the
surroundings. He appeared to have almost forgotten our

presence, so engrossed was he in his occupation. The broken table in the corner caught his attention suddenly and he squatted before it, to study its simple construction. Then he became interested in the bureau and carefully investigated the contents of the drawers, examining shirts, underwear, and other articles of clothing. After peering into the utmost corners of the bureau drawers, he rose and walked to the windows. For a long moment he stood silent, gazing out.

"Any one live in that house next door?" he asked suddenly.

"No," Carling replied. "It's an empty house—has been vacant for some time. Leahy managed to get in and look around. Didn't find anything in there, did you, Leahy?"

"No," grunted the detective. "Only plenty of dust and dirt. Nobody's been there for months. Didn't even see a footprint."

"I see," Brooke nodded; then he continued his slow pacing, glancing at the papers which were littered about the floor. His eyes brightened with interest suddenly as he stooped and picked up a folded newspaper which lay near an overturned chair. He gazed quizzically in the direction of the District Attorney; then he unfolded the paper, opened its pages and searched the various columns rapidly, turning from one page to the next.

"There's an item here I'm going to tear out, if I may," Brooke said, after a moment. "It's a small link in my theoretical chain."

"I wish you'd bring this mysterious pose of yours to an end!" Rawson grunted irritably. "I'd like to know what you're driving at!"

"You will—very soon," Brooke replied calmly. "H'm—I don't suppose there'll be any answers to our advertisements at your office. No—of course, not!"

Rawson smiled sarcastically at the criminologist.

"Hardly! Even if someone answered the one in the late edition last night, or the early editions this morning, we'd hardly begin to be flooded with mail till late this afternoon. Don't worry, Brooke, I've a man detailed to look after that. Why are you so interested?"

"Just curious. Well, it may interest you to know that I believe two men did this job—two men killed Barbatti. Or, perhaps I should say that two men were in this room besides the victim when the tragedy occurred, and one of them, without a doubt, helped the other when the fracas began. One has rubber-heels on his shoes—you'll notice that the victim has leather heels and they're pretty, much run down."

"But what do you surmise was the motive?" the District Attorney asked.

"There were probably several. It is most evident, however, that this mysterious pair of mine were searching for something—something incriminating to themselves. The upset condition of the room, the disturbed state of the bureau drawers—all that, points to the fact that a frenzied search was made, and, without a doubt, after the murder occurred. Our visitors were in a hurry to get away, and I can't say that I blame them. And Barbatti put up a good fight—I can almost see it! I would say that the unfortunate affair began in a more or less friendly fashion with the visitors making their demands and Barbatti refusing them until they got persistent."

Clay Brooke paused for a moment to light a cigaret. Then:

"Finally one of them flew into a rage and sprang at Barbatti. Clutching at one another wildly they toppled over on the bed, and then the second visitor came to the first's assistance. Barbatti managed to get to his feet and hurl the second attacker to that corner with such force that the table collapsed under his weight. You'll find a pair of rubber-heeled marks there. Now, by this time, the first man, who had been grappling with Barbatti on the bed, managed to rise and hurl himself on the victim—the latter lost his balance and fell over that chair, with-his attacker at his throat, With him still clinging like a bulldog, Barbatti struggled to his feet gasping for breath and clawing wildly. Then our man who had been flung toward the table re-entered the fray with a rush and Barbatti went over backwards and hit his head on the grate. Does that sound plausible to you, Rawson?"

"Ye—yes," the District Attorney admitted. "Then you think that the men ransacked the room directly after the crime?"

"Of course!" Brooke answered. "Now I wonder if there's anything we've overlooked! What's in that closet, Rawson?"

"Only an old trunk. We didn't think it necessary to bother with it."

"Dear—dear!" Brooke shook his head in dismay. "You're very perfunctory, my dear fellow. Let's have a look at it—or better yet, let's drag it into this room where we can examine it better. Lend a hand, will you, Carling?"

The criminologist and the captain of detectives pulled the battered, old-fashioned trunk into the room, and Brooke immediately knelt in front of it and carefully examined the rusty padlock which secured it.

"This is most interesting, Rawson," he murmured. "I'm really surprised you passed this up! You can see that our visitors did their best to smash the lock. Having no instruments, they tried kicking at it. The fellow with the rubber heels didn't make much of a dent, so the other took a turn. You can see the imprint of his heel. He's only had his shoes resoled a short time, and you can make out the small imprint of a horse-shoe—you know, those little metal gadgets they put around the edge of a heel to prevent it from being run down quickly."

In spite of his deep chagrin, the District Attorney knelt beside Clay Brooke and examined the markings that the criminologist pointed out.

"You see," Brooke continued, "they did their best to get this open; then they figured that they'd wake the neighborhood with the noise they were making— if they hadn't already with their free-for-all fight. So they made a bolt for the door. Get that, Rawson—they made a bolt for the door! That's a terrible crack for me to make out of a clear sky! Think I can get a job as a movie title-writer, Gregory? Well, Carling, can you get this trunk open?"

In answer, the detective-captain produced a metal implement from his pocket and began tinkering with the rusty padlock. After he had labored a few minutes, the padlock yielded to his manipulations, and he grunted triumphantly.

"Now, then, Rawson, what do you suppose we'll find in here?" Brooke smilingly ventured. "Probably a large water-color or crayon drawing of the King of Italy shaking hands with Mussolini. What's your guess?"

The District Attorney ignored the criminologist's banter and lifted the top of the trunk open. Then he unsnapped the covering on the tray and pushed it back. The left-hand partition contained a folded corduroy jacket and trousers, and a number of other discarded garments, thrown in carelessly. It was the right-hand partition, however, which immediately attracted Clay Brooke's attention, for he rapidly began to examine the heterogeneous collection of knick-knacks, souvenirs, programs, photographs, and the like.

"Ah, here we are!" the criminologist suddenly exclaimed. "Just what I hoped we'd find!" He produced a bundle of yellow and green-backed documents which were held together by a large rubber band.

"See here, Rawson!" he beamed. "Stock certificates! Stock certificates issued by the Monte Cristo Mining Company! What have you got to say about that!"

The District Attorney whistled softly and examined the certificates which Brooke passed to him.

"Then this looks," he began, "this looks as if—"

"Just a moment, Rawson!" Brooke interrupted, a twinkle of amusement in his eyes. "Here is Exhibit Number 2! What do you think of it! Guess it was taken when she was in the *Follies*!"

The criminologist handed a portrait of Berylyn Bovary to the District Attorney, who gazed at it in amazement.

"She was quite a vampish lady," Brooke commented. "That apparently was taken before the style of undraped photographs of chorus girls came into vogue. Nice picture, though."

"Great heavens, Brooke!" Rawson gasped. "This certainly looks as though Barbatti had a hand in the murder of the Bovary girl! I have it! He's the mysterious stranger, Brooke! Barbatti fits the description of the stranger described to us by Taylor and Bovary's maid! What do you say to that?"

"Well," the criminologist smiled. "There's a connection—there's certainly a connection, Rawson!"

XVII. Disclosures at the Montmartre

The District Attorney glanced up from the portrait of Berylyn Bovary and regarded Clay Brooke curiously. He was about to reply when a police officer ushered in two interns who had arrived to take the body to the mortuary.

"Let's get out of this, Rawson," Brooke suggested. "I don't believe there's anything else in here that interests me. We can discuss the case and our discoveries in the dining-room, below."

John Rawson nodded, then turning to Carling he said, "See that a temporary padlock is put on this door until I give orders to have it removed."

"Yes, sir," Carling replied, stepping aside to permit the interns to pass with their stretcher.

On the way downstairs, Clay Brooke stopped for a moment and peered into the private dining-rooms on the second floor. The District Attorney paused impatiently and waited for him.

"I doubt if you'll find anything of interest in there, Brooke," he said. "Carling's men have covered both rooms thoroughly and nothing was found."

"I suppose not," Brooke commented, returning to the head of the stairs. "I suppose the murderers got out of the building as fast as they could. Was the front door open when the waiters arrived this morning?"

"No; it was closed. There's a snap lock on it."

"I see," the criminologist nodded. "These waiters you questioned didn't say whether they noticed any one with Barbatti in the café before closing time?"

"I asked them that. They said Barbatti spent his time in the kitchen, or near the cashier's counter, or else near the door. He hadn't joined any party; nor did they notice him conversing with any one for any length of time."

"Well, let's go down to the next floor."

We descended the next flight of stairs; then the District Attorney turned to the right and led the way into the large dining-room. Clay Brooke glanced at the walls which were decorated with crude paintings of stereotyped Italian scenes, and then casually dropped into a chair at the nearest table.

"Sit down, gentlemen," he invited with a gesture, and after Rawson and I had seated ourselves, he remarked, "I suppose gallons and gallons of red ink are consumed nightly in this little place in an atmosphere supposedly Bohemian—meaning it is stifling with cigaret smoke. I fancied these places once, but—"

"Brooke," the District Attorney interrupted impatiently, "when we were upstairs you remarked that you believed there was some kind of a connection between Barbatti and the mysterious stranger who might have killed Bovary. Just what did you mean by that?"

"Just what I said," the criminologist replied producing his case and selecting a cigaret. "If you'll remember, you declared that the stock certificates and the photograph made it appear that Barbatti might have had a hand in the murder of the Bovary girl—that he fitted the description of the mysterious party described to us by Bovary's maid and our friend, Taylor. I supplemented that by stating that there is certainly a connection. Isn't that pretty obvious?"

"Confound it, Brooke! You're evading my question!" Rawson retorted irritably. "If you really know something about this case and who's at the bottom of it, for God's sake tell me! I'm being hounded to death by the newspapers and the authorities higher up to reach the solution of the murder of Berylyn Bovary. Now if you have any sound theory, I'd be exceedingly grateful for whatever information you can give me."

"My dear fellow," Brooke laughed softly, "I have told you that I am working by the inductive method—I am supposing things, and I am trying to follow up my suppositions. You wouldn't have me tell you to arrest a man when the act might make fools of us both! If it will relieve your mind, however, I'll tell you that I'm getting warm—very warm, and it won't be long before I can give you the actual facts—concrete facts."

"Then what do you advise me to do?"

"Don't do anything—no, I'll tell you what to do, Rawson. Return to your office and send for the press. Tell them that the murder of Berylyn Bovary has been solved. Tell them that Barbatti was the murderer. You have good evidence in that photograph and the stock certificates, and he jolly well seems to fit the description of Mr. X. That will doubtless give the reporters so much satisfaction that in their haste to beat one another to their typewriters they might not ask who killed Barbatti. To tell the truth, they don't care so much about Barbatti. He isn't a romantic figure—he isn't in your blessed movies! But if they should press you concerning Barbatti, explain that your present theory is that he was killed in a feud—a vendetta."

"But do you think Barbatti murdered Bovary?"

"As I said before, Rawson," the criminologist smiled broadly, "there is a connection."

"Oh, damn your secrecy!" the District Attorney snorted, bringing his fist down on the table with a bang. "Well, I'll favor you by taking your advice. I've got. to if I'm going to have any peace of mind. Well, I'm returning to the office—are you coming with me?"

"No, I shall sit here for a time, if you don't mind. Gregory is good company, you know. But you'll hear from me soon, Rawson. Oh, by the way, I wish you'd give instructions to your man at the door that I'm to have a bit of freedom here, if you don't mind, and just a mite of authority."

"All right," John Rawson grunted as he rose and started for the door. "Let me know if you have any luck, or—or if you come to a decision to let me into your confidence."

"I will, Rawson, I will." Brooke chuckled to himself.

"Now, Greg," he said, turning to me after the District Attorney had departed, "where can I meet you for lunch? I'm going to remain here in silent solitude for a time. It's good for deep thought; and besides, I'm hoping a relative will arrive."

"A relative!" I repeated in astonishment.

"Yes; a relative of Barbatti," Brooke smiled. "All Italian restaurant-keepers have relatives—didn't you know that? He's usually the cook, or the linx-eyed waiter who passes you in at the door. Of course, he can't live with Barbatti because he's married and has too big a family of kids. That's always the way with this relative. The proprietor remains a bachelor and leaves it to the relative to contribute to the population. Even I have relatives that way, so it isn't so bad as it sounds."

"Well, then—suppose I meet you at the Montmartre?"

"That's a good choice," Brooke agreed with enthusiasm. "This is such a nice day—really unusual for California—that there ought to be a lot of cuties out— what? All right, see you there between twelve-thirty and one o'clock."

The criminologist followed me to the door, and as I started my car I looked back and saw him in earnest conversation with the police officer on duty at the entrance of the resort. Arriving at my bungalow I opened my brief case intending to run over the outline of the scenario that Clay Brooke and I had begun work on. I found, however, that it was utterly impossible for me to concentrate, for my mind was continually filled with the strange details dealing with the death of Berylyn Bovary; and then thoughts came tumbling in concerning the murder of Fiore Barbatti. I wondered what Clay Brooke had up his sleeve, for he had not confided in me any more than he had in John Rawson. With a gesture of impatience I hurled the brief case back on the table and glanced at the clock. It was nearly time for me to be on my way.

Clay Brooke was in the best of spirits when he joined me at the table I had secured at the Montmartre. After a cheerful greeting he darted curious glances at the occupants of the various tables in the dining place.

"Well, what luck did you have?" I finally ventured.

"Splendid—splendid!" Brooke replied absent-mindedly as he continued to look about. "Say, Greg, isn't that Mary Bicknord over there—no, I guess I'm wrong. It's a little girl with her Momma. You know, I believe there are more little girls here with their Mommas than there are film stars. No, there's Ima Faire and John Milbert! And isn't that girl over there—the dark one—the promising young star you told me about, Janet Faynor? Well, what I was about to say when I interrupted myself was about these little girls and their Mommas. It looks to me as though each little girl is togged out to represent the movie star she most resembles—sort of a hopeful masquerade, you know. In other words, that these fond Mommas regard this place as a show-case in which to exhibit their wares to the dining producers and directors. Isn't it the case that the less imaginative producers are always looking for a new face and trying to find one that resembles another which has proved its worth in curls at the box-office? Am I right, Greg?"

"Alas—yes! And you're very observant. But tell me, Clay, what happened after I left you?"

"You would spoil everything, wouldn't you!" he replied smilingly. "And just while I'm enjoying an opulent eye-full! Well, my relative—or rather, Barbatti's relative—appeared. And he was the chef! Uncanny, my prediction? Well, a good guess come true, to say the least! But to begin, I arranged matters with the officer at the door to admit any one who should put in an appearance. The first one was the chef. He was terribly wrought-up over the tragedy—bellowed about in Italian, and all that, and it was some time before we could quiet him. Finally I was able to convince him that I was there to help him secure his vengeance, and that, naturally, made a great hit with him. Well, I secured information from him which would drive poor old Rawson wild with envy. He told me his life history as well as that of Barbatti, who was his brother-in-law, by the way—a sort of relative, you must agree."

Clay Brooke paused for a moment to light a cigaret.

"The story begins in New York," he continued slowly, "where Barbatti and this brother-in-law, Guglielmo—or Gugli-something—kept a speak-easy on 41st Street, across from the stage-door of the Amsterdam Theater. Does that suggest anything to you? Well, it did to me, and before many minutes passed I learned that among Barbatti's customers were Berylyn Bovary, Frank Wagner, and Carleton Dazian. Now perhaps you'll see the connection with which I took such a delight in torturing poor Rawson. Well, Bovary and Wagner hung out in Barbatti's for a long time, then Wagner dropped out of the picture, and before long Dazian appeared on the scene with the girl. Barbatti knew them all, of course. It was around this time that Berylyn had some of her best photographs taken, and, as chorus girls will, she exhibited them in Barbatti's and the proprietor asked for one, either because he wanted it, or because he was being polite and thought he had to. That's that—but it ties up with my general scheme of things.

"The next event of importance happened when Guglielmo, the chef, pulled out of the business and went to California to try his hand in the grape-into-wine industry. He tried for a long time to get his brother-in-law out here, but without success. Then Barbatti's life became one raid after another, so he decided to pack up and join Gugli in the land of sunshine, flowers, and grapes. After a time they opened the speak-easy on Vermont Avenue and modeled it along the lines of the old one in New York. Do you follow me?"

"Yes, go on," I nodded eagerly.

"One of their first customers," Brooke continued, "was Wagner, who renewed his friendship with Barbatti and the chef, and began to patronize the place pretty steadily. Wagner, however, wasn't much of a drinker, according to Guglielmo's statements. He knew when he'd had enough and then he'd pay his check and go home. He and Barbatti appeared to be friendly, and the chef has no reason to think that Wagner was mixed up in the affair. Sometime afterwards, Carleton Dazian appeared on the scene and renewed his friendship with the Italians; and a few nights later he came again bringing Berylyn Bovary with him. This time there was a real reunion, and after the usual crowd went, Barbatti celebrated by opening a few bottles of champagne. Dazian and Bovary patronized the place from time to time after that, singly or together, and one night Wagner entered and saw them there. He stopped at their table and spoke with them for a minute, but nothing out of the ordinary passed between the three. After that, Wagner didn't come around so often. Now the only members of our precious family of suspects who have not visited this place are Charles Gilbert and his son. Now, tell me what you think of my recital, Gregory?"

"It makes me bromidic," I replied. "I am forced to state that 'it's a small world'."

"Isn't it!" Brooke agreed. "Now, I tried my best for Rawson's sake to tie Barbatti up with our mysterious stranger who lurked in the shadows of the studio and killed Berylyn Bovary, but the chef informed me that he knew very little about the studios—with the exception of the people connected with them who frequented his place. I checked up on the night of the murder of Bovary and learned that Barbatti had been at his restaurant all afternoon and evening. In fact, he seldom left it during those hours. I jolly well knew that Rawson was wrong, but when a man is as worried as he is, one might as well encourage his favorite theories."

"Then, when you suggested that he announce to the reporters that Barbatti was the murderer of Bovary, you knew Barbatti hadn't committed the crime?"

"Of course!" Brooke laughed softly. "I encouraged Rawson in the act for two excellent reasons. One to relieve his mind, as I just said, and the other so as to encourage the real murderer to come out from under cover. You see, in that way, the man we are after will be relieved of his own worries the same as Rawson."

"Do you know who the real murderer is, Brooke?"

"Why—bless my soul, Gregory!" the criminologist smiled. "You very nearly caught me off my guard! To that I can truthfully answer in the conservative manner of the native Philadelphian, 'Yes and no'. I have arrived at certain conclusions, but I am not sure enough. But it's only a matter of time before I'll be very sure."

"Will you tell me this," I ventured, "will you tell me what you meant when you told Rawson that there is a connection between the murder of the movie queen and the murder of Barbatti?"

"Well—yes, I'll endeavor to satisfy your curiosity," Brooke replied, reaching in his pocket and drawing out a torn newspaper clipping. "You see this? This is what I tore out of the paper in Barbatti's room. It's a portion of the personal column and you will note that Barbatti had drawn a pencil mark around each of the advertisements we inserted. This gives me further proof that he was our mysterious F.B., and also that he was interested in disposing of more Monte Cristo stock. The latter part of my argument is backed up by the certificates we found in his trunk. I saw no reason why I should confuse Rawson by letting him entirely into my confidence. He'll be satisfied when I bring the case to its conclusion."

"But what do you make of it, Brooke?" I queried. "Do you think that the same person that killed Berylyn Bovary killed Barbatti?"

Clay Brooke looked meditatively at the ash of his cigaret. Then he returned my gaze and spoke with his usual candor.

"Yes, I'd say so—with reservations. I'll admit that it is a confusing affair. According to what I've learned from Barbatti's brother-in-law, a lot of past history dovetails into present history. That is, we have the same characters involved in our drama. Somebody killed Berylyn Bovary. Barbatti had her portrait, which means little, but she had purchased stock certificates which we know he owned—which means more. A slip of paper with initials, which we assume to be Barbatti's, was found near the scene of the first tragedy. Then Barbatti sees our advertisements, answers them, and was murdered shortly after. But—but—"

The criminologist hesitated and the corners of his mouth twitched slightly. All trace of a smile had vanished from his features.

"But what puzzles me, Greg," he began again slowly, "is the fact that it isn't one man at the bottom of the affair—it's two—I am sure of it. And I can't seem to pair any two off together. I would wager that two people were on hand when Bovary met her end. If you remember, I rather jokingly remarked that to Rawson at the studio the night of the murder. Yes, I'm pretty sure of this. But I'm positive that two—two men called on Barbatti and that both were instrumental to his death."

"But what motives do you apply to these two cases?"

"Ah—there you nearly have me! You know, I was pretty well satisfied with myself and was about to tell all to Rawson when I suddenly came to the conclusion that two people are mixed up in the case. I fought this theory, but it was no use. It isn't difficult to dispose of the matter as far as Barbatti is concerned. In this case, the culprits were confronted with the fear of disclosure—they know we know about the stock certificates, and about the initials, F.B. They also may have known that Barbatti answered the advertisements we inserted and was about to play them into our hands.

"But as far as the Bovary girl is concerned, you're going to laugh at a rather morbid theory that persists in coming into my mind. I keep thinking of an incident in Dumas' *The Three Musketeers.* Do you recall the bloodthirsty murder of Milady which was performed near Armentieres, later famous in A.E.F. balladry? Anyway, Milady was tried for her life by D'Artagnan, Athos, Porthos, Aramis, and Lord De Winter because she had brought misfortune to each one of them, and death to others. She was judged by each one according to her crime, and when she was found guilty, the executioner of Bethune polished her off in his characteristic fashion. Now what I'm driving at, is that Bovary—though it isn't the chivalrous thing to say at this time— might be called a reincarnation of the fictionary Milady. I'll admit that the comparison is unfair because one is real life and the other is fiction—and Dumas' fiction can be pretty hardboiled when compared to modern life, even in the raw. See what I mean?"

"Then, by your comparison, you mean that we know of four men who have had reasons to want to destroy Bovary?"

"Yes," Brooke nodded hesitatingly. "Not that I can for one moment make myself think that all four had a hand in it. One of them did, assisted by another of whom I am not sure. He doesn't fit into the continuity—fit into the Barbatti affair—if you know what I mean. So now you can see why I hesitate to impart my theories to John Rawson. He'd be jolly well apt to have me locked up and put under observation, and I can't say that I'd blame him. Would you?"

"No—I might if I were Rawson, though."

Clay Brooke threw his head back and laughed gleefully. Then he reached for the check and paid for it over my protest.

"What have you got on for this afternoon?" he asked.

"Nothing—of course, there are a number of scenarios I should be thinking about, but we've put them off for so long now that they can wait."

"I suppose you've been excused from the studio by your chief—gathering atmosphere, eh? That's always a rather good thing to be doing. Well, he can have you back soon. Today we're going to gather some more atmosphere—we're going to make a few calls this afternoon, just to see what we might stumble onto."

We rose from our chairs and made our way between the crowded tables to the door. On reaching the entrance, I discovered that Clay Brooke had lagged behind, and looking back I saw him in an animated conversation with a couple whom I could not identify at a side table. In a moment he smilingly rejoined me.

"That was Evelyn Halloway and young Gilbert," he explained cheerfully. "Thank heavens, they've forgiven me for the rather rough way that I once handled them. A very charming couple—they haven't the slightest realization, Greg, that they are both going to play important roles in the denouement of our mystery."

I looked back curiously while Brooke was securing our hats from the check-room and saw the two young people in what seemed to be a most agitated conversation. Suddenly the girl glanced over her shoulder in our direction with a half-frightened look; then, as Brooke approached me, she quickly turned back to young Gilbert.

XVIII. The Face in the Mirror

"He's a lucky young fellow—Mitchell Gilbert, I mean," Brooke continued, as we walked to the place where my car was parked. "Now if I were only a little younger—h'm, what is it about a fellow of my age, Gregory, that makes him utter bosh like this? I'm neither old nor young—I'm just in the—shall I say, the interim? And here I find myself on the verge of chanting the lyrical bromide about December casting longing eyes at May!"

"But, Clay," I cut in impatiently, "what did you—"

"I have it!" he exclaimed, interrupting me. "I have it! It's your beastly climate—that's what's affecting me! It's your climate and a pair of very charming gray eyes. But Claire Demoset's eyes are blue, aren't they? Come, come—where was I going to ask you to drive me? Oh, yes—to Cahuenga Avenue."

"Why to Cahuenga?"

"Because that's the address of a gentleman whom I desire to see. When I want assistance in this Hollywood puzzle, I seek him because he seems to stimulate me. These bloodhounds of Rawson's pack, lathered in officialdom, irritate me; but this minor sleuth gives me a soothing urge. I am referring to our friend, Taylor."

"I was surprised we didn't see him at Barbatti's," I remarked. "He struck me as one of those fellows who is quick to appear on the scene."

"Well, this new crime is hardly in Taylor's province," Brooke commented. "After all, he's only a studio sleuth, a glorified watchman, and not, as I just remarked, one of Rawson's whippets. Hello, here's—"

"Hello, Mr. Brooke!" cried a voice suddenly, and looking up I beheld Carleton Dazian stepping out of a roadster which was drawn up to the curb just ahead of my car. A small dark-haired girl sat behind the wheel and smiled in our direction.

"I'm glad I had the good luck to run into you, Mr. Brooke," Dazian said as he greeted us. "I called at your bungalow last night, but you were out. I thought you might enjoy a ride into the far open spaces."

"Oh, is that so? Sorry I missed you!" the criminologist replied pleasantly. "Black and I were taking in the concert. I managed to lure him away from his typewriter long enough to listen to some good music. I imagine," he added, with a glance in the direction of the girl in the car, "that you found an excellent substitute, for me."

"Oh, yes—the woods are full of 'em!" Dazian laughed. "But how is the case progressing—and what do you think of poor Barbatti's finish! I knew him in New York when he kept a speak-easy right off of Broadway."

"Is that so?" Brooke asked innocently.

"Yeh—I used to drop into his place now and then when I first came out here. Nice sort of fellow. What do the police think of it?"

"They're inclined to believe he was mixed up in the studio affair in one way or another. Do you think there can be anything in that theory?"

"No; I can't see it," Dazian remarked thoughtfully. "However, you never can tell how the picture'll look from where you sit, can you? Well, my sweet mama'll be getting fidgety, so I'll be chasing along. Sorry I missed you last night—I'll try again some time."

"Yes; I wish you would," Brooke nodded.

Carleton Dazian left us and climbed into the roadster, then he waved his hand as they swerved into the traffic. Brooke continued to stare after him as I was unlocking the door of my coupe.

"Amazing fellows, that kind," he remarked. "Off with the old, you know. But that was a lucky meeting. I wanted to question Dazian about Barbatti and he volunteered most everything I wanted to know. Still— well, we can reach him easily enough if it's necessary.

Let's see, weren't we going somewhere—oh, yes, to Cahuenga Avenue!"

When we reached our destination, Brooke rang the door-bell of a dwelling which seemed to be half rooming-house and half hotel. The place was quiet and appeared to be deserted; but after a few minutes a dowdy, yellow-haired woman answered the bell.

"Good afternoon, madame," Brooke bowed courteously, "I'm sure you must remember me—Mr. Brooke? I. came to see if Mr. Taylor is in."

"Oh, yes; I remember you, Mr. Brooke. Mr. Taylor was only speaking to me about you the other night. But I'm awfully sorry, he's out of town right now."

"Out of town?" the criminologist repeated. "Now that's too bad. And I needed his assistance so much today."

"Let me see—let me see," said the woman, "there's a telegram here he sent me. Just a moment and I'll see if I can find it."

She disappeared inside and then returned, waving a folded yellow sheet of paper.

"Here it is!" she said, eyeing Brooke coquettishly. "I knew I'd find it! It's from Mr. Taylor and he sent it from San Bernardino. You can see that he says he won't be back to Hollywood until tomorrow morning. I saw him yesterday afternoon before he went and he explained that he was called there suddenly, but that he'd wire me when he'd be back."

She handed the telegram to the criminologist.

Brooke glanced at it rapidly. "Then he left yesterday afternoon, and won't be back until tomorrow morning. I wanted his assistance on the murder that took place last night."

"Oh, yes!" the woman said, growing serious. "It was terrible, wasn't it! I—really—I don't know what's coming over this place. It's always been so sorta peaceful, you know. Well, shall I tell Mr. Taylor you called, Mr. Brooke?"

"If you please. And ask him to 'phone me when he returns—or else I'll get in touch with him. And thank you very much, Mrs.—"

"Mrs. Cordoba," smiled the landlady before disappearing inside.

"Cordoba!" Clay Brooke repeated as we approached my car. "Is the Latin influence even reaching into landlady circles, Greg? She has the face of a Rafferty!"

"Probably her professional name," I remarked. "I don't doubt but what she does screen work—or at least hopes to—between the hours of landladying."

"I see," Brooke smiled as he took his seat beside me. "Well, I suppose I'll be bitten by the celluloid bug sooner or later—but for heaven's sake, stop me, Greg! Bundle me up and send me home! They'd be sure to cast me as either a dignified father or a roue."

"I'll promise that I won't let them get you until you solve this mystery," I replied, laughing. "When do you think that will be?"

"Probably tomorrow," Brooke calmly replied, "if things continue to run smoothly. Now, let me see—where are you taking me to, Greg? I want to look up our friend, Wagner, and find out what he can tell me of Barbatti. Just a minute, now." He drew out his address book and consulted the pages. "Wagner lives on Melrose Avenue— oh, but he's taken unto himself a bride! Well, let's hope he hasn't already sought larger quarters. I'll be owing you money for gas after all the driving you're doing today, Greg."

When we drew up to the small apartment house on Melrose Avenue the first thing that caught our eyes was a moving van which was backed up to the curb, and a number of pieces of furniture piled on the sidewalk. We were about to step to the entrance when Wagner suddenly appeared in his shirt-sleeves, gingerly carrying a well-inhabited goldfish globe.

"How d'ye do, Wagner," Brooke smiled, eyeing the globe. "I trust that none of your finny fellows is goldplated—all eighteen karat?"

The picture director appeared to be somewhat startled at the sudden appearance of the criminologist and me.

"They're my wife's," he confessed, sheepishly putting them down on the gravel walk. "She loves animals, you know—goldfish, canaries, and those kind of things. Well, they aren't so much bother as a police dog, so I've got no kick."

"Moving?"

"Yes; we. are. I bought a bungalow out toward Culver City. There's plenty of work out that way right now. Anyway, with my bus it's easy enough to get back into the center of things."

"Wagner," Brooke began, becoming serious, "I suppose you know why I've come to see you. I want you to tell me what you can about Barbatti and where you were last night."

There was a dangerous flash in the director's eyes. Then he caught himself and returned the criminologist's gaze calmly.

"Trying to hook me up with that affair, too? Well, you can't do it, Mr. Brooke, because I've got a real alibi this time! I was here in the apartment all last night. George Cline, my cameraman, and his wife were over while we were packing, and after we finished we played bridge till about one o'clock."

"Yes?"

"Yes—and if that isn't enough for you, the boy at the drug store can back me up as he came here plenty with ginger ale and seltzer."

"Oh, I don't doubt your word, Wagner—not for a moment!" Clay Brooke protested. "I happen to know you were once acquainted with Barbatti, and I'd like all the information you can give me about the man."

Wagner, after a moment's reflection, appeared to be mollified. "Come on in the house where we can talk," he said. "I've sent my wife ahead to meet the van—you know how women can get in the way of things. Just, a minute— I'd better put these damn fish in a place where they won't get tipped over." He picked up the globe carefully and deposited it in a far corner of the van, surrounding it with blankets.

"I hope they won't smother where I put 'em," he said returning to us. "All right, let's step into the house. I guess it'll be about fifteen more minutes before they'll have the rest of the stuff loaded."

Wagner led the way into the front apartment on the first floor where we almost collided with three moving men grunting over a huge cabinet they were trying to get around a corner.

"There's a real antique for you," the director grinned. "It's a folding bed—one of the last of the herd, I guess. My wife don't like it, so I've got to get rid of it. She thinks it's going to fold up with both of us inside. Maybe I can sell it to one of the studios as a comedy prop." He waited for a moment until the folding bed disappeared out the door, then he added, "Sorry I can't ask you gentlemen to have a comfortable chair."

"That's all right," Brooke assured him. "Now then, I want you to tell me all you can about Barbatti."

"Well, it won't be much because I don't know much. I've known him since he opened his speak-easy out here. Used to go to it a lot and then cut it out pretty much."

"Wagner, why don't you tell me the truth?" Brooke asked good-naturedly. "It would be just as easy for you."

"What the hell do you mean!" growled the director.

"Just what I say," Brooke answered calmly. "I know a great deal about you, you know, and it's aggravating when you go off on a tangent like this. It's a bad habit, old fellow, and you should get over it—especially now that you're a married man and have a wife who will be on needles and pins continuously if you persist in weaving fantasies about yourself."

"Well, what do you want to know?" Wagner replied sullenly.

"It might be easier for you if I told you what I do know," the criminologist smiled. "Then we can reach an agreement. To begin, I dislike appearing disagreeable and bringing up the unpleasant past, but I know that you and Berylyn Bovary used to frequent Barbatti's joint in New York. Know where the expression 'joint' comes from, Wagner? From the joints of the bamboo that makes the stem of an opium pipe. It's an expression from darkest Chinatown. Here I am off the subject again! Let's see— you and the Bovary girl used to frequent Barbatti's joint when it was on 41st Street in New York. Then you and the lady split and she continued to sip Barbatti's red ink in the company of Carleton Dazian. Am I right thus far?"

"Yeh."

"You see, Wagner, I know. A movie director shouldn't ever attempt to invent an untrue background. Leave that to the scenario writers. Anyway, you dropped out of the picture. Then you came to the Coast and when Barbatti opened a speak-easy here you sought recreation within its homey portals. Then Bovary arrived, and then Dazian, and the place didn't look so good to you. Am I right? Then somebody murdered Barbatti. Sad, isn't it, Wagner?"

"Damn it all! I tell you I've got an alibi!" Wagner ejaculated furiously. "And you haven't got a damn thing on me! Not a damn thing!"

"Of course, I haven't!" Brooke agreed amiably. "Really, you weary me! You say you have an alibi—good enough! I'll let the District Attorney and the men from headquarters check you up if they're interested. Personally, I don't believe they are even aware of your friendship and past acquaintance with the dead man. I am probably the only one who knows, and I see no reason for telling them. Can't you see, Wagner, that what I'm after is information? And if you've got any, for God's sake give it to me and tell me the truth!"

The director surveyed the floor thoughtfully; then he raised his head and looked at the criminologist.

"Mr. Brooke," he said, "I can't tell you a thing. What you've told me about Barbatti's joint and where I come in is the truth—both in New York and out here. But I can't tell you anything about the murder because I don't know anything."

"All right," the criminologist smiled, "that's what I wanted to hear you say. I don't believe in swearing out warrants indiscriminately just because a crime has been committed. It's—it's embarrassing, especially when one is a bridegroom. But tell me this, Wagner, when were you in Barbatti's place last?"

"Oh, months ago—two or three months, anyway."

"I see. Well, from what I can learn, Barbatti was a pretty nice sort of a chap for a fellow in his particular industry—no enemies, or anything?"

Wagner nodded.

"I don't suppose Barbatti ever frequented the studios?"

"Not that I know of. Those wops are always pretty close to their places of business, you know."

"I imagine so," Brooke smiled. "I think their patrons usually imagine them jumping around on grapes in their bare feet. Perhaps you can tell me this, Wagner—when did Berylyn Bovary give Barbatti her photograph?"

The motion picture director appeared startled at Clay Brooke's question.

"Berylyn gave him her picture?" he repeated slowly. "I didn't know that she did—not while I was with her."

"Probably when she was going with Dazian," Brooke remarked.

"I wouldn't be surprised—the dirty little pimp!" Wagner muttered, half to himself.

Brooke paused before continuing. Then:

"Wagner, do you believe there was any kind of friendship between Bovary and Barbatti?"

"No. Barbatti couldn't have done her any good—only sold her drinks. Get what I mean?"

"Then, there's nothing else you can tell me?"

"No, Mr. Brooke, I've told you all that I can," Wagner replied wearily. "God knows this mess has brought plenty of grief to me, and I'd tell you anything—but I don't know anything. That's that—I don't know anything!"

The criminologist smiled affably. "Well, we won't keep you any longer, Wagner. Sorry to have disturbed you, and—and I hope the fish reach your new home safely."

"Oh, those damn things!" the director replied rising. "When do you expect to reach the finish of this case, Mr. Brooke?"

"Sometime tomorrow. Oh, by the way, better give me your new address. You'll want to be among the first to get the news, I'm sure. Here—write it in this book beneath your old address. H'm—quite a distance from here. Well, we'll be running along now."

Wagner followed us to the door and stood watching as we drove away.

"Really, that young man should change his ways," Clay Brooke remarked. "He's such a fluent-liar. It's a habit—just like a person who continually forgets things. Let's see, where are we going now—oh, yes, we're going to pay a brief visit to a lady."

"A lady?" I repeated.

Brooke gave an odd smile. Then:

"Well, a—a sort of a lady. We're going to call on Margaret Hagney. I hope you haven't forgotten her! Goodness knows, old Rawson has! Let's see now," Brooke added, consulting his book, "she lives on North Wilcox. Is that far from here?"

The criminologist was silent as we drove across town, only becoming interested for a moment when we passed a group of pretty "extra" girls on their way to one of the large studios.

"Cunning chicks," he remarked to me. "Didn't you tell me that that kind makes around seven-fifty a day? When they're lucky, I suppose. I imagine that each one of them hopes to be a star—pretty slim chances, I'd say. There are altogether too many pretty women to the cubic foot out here, Gregory. Not the style of our New York women—but they make up for it with their natural beauty. You may quote me on that remark to your blessed Chamber of Commerce, if you like. Speaking of New York, I always fancied the old saying to the effect that there are a million bulbs on Broadway, and a boob for every bulb. Rather good, eh? I've forgotten who originated it—it was either O. Henry or Richard Harding Davis."

When we arrived at our destination we found a small rooming house, not unlike the one we had visited an hour or so before. Clay Brooke rang the bell and after a moment the landlady answered. Yes, she thought Miss Hagney might be in. That was her door on the first floor directly at the bottom of the stairs. The landlady obligingly knocked for us, then disappeared in the rear. No answer came; so, Brooke knocked again.

"Who is it?" came a voice after a moment.

"Miss Hagney?" the criminologist said pleasantly. "This is Mr. Brooke—you remember me, I hope? I'd like to see you for a minute, if I may."

There was a pause. Then:

"Oh, yes, Mr. Brooke. If you'll just wait, please."

"I always enjoy trying to imagine," Brooke whispered to me, "what a woman is doing on the other side of the door when she tells a gentleman caller to wait a moment. Of course, my imagination enjoys more play when it is concerned with a really pretty woman—if you, know what I mean."

The door suddenly opened and Margaret Hagney peered out at us.

"Oh, how do you do, Mr. Brooke," she said mechanically. "I'm sorry I had to keep you waiting. I wasn't expecting any one."

"And I'm very sorry to have burst in on you in this fashion, Miss Hagney," Brooke apologized courteously.

"May we come in for a moment or so? There are a few questions I should like to ask you."

The woman gave a rapid backward glance; then she opened the door for us to enter.

"Things are a bit messed up, Mr. Brooke," she explained. "I'll have you know I'm not usually this dowdy. It's just that I'm still out of a job and—well, you know how that is."

The criminologist nodded sympathetically as we entered. It was a parlor-sized room furnished in conventional boarding-house style, with two windows looking on the street. The furniture was decidedly Grand Rapids and there were a number of gaudy pillows scattered about. On a table were a few motion picture magazines. Toward the rear were opened folding doors which led into a small bedroom.

"So you're having difficulties getting another position?" Brooke asked. "Now that's too bad! Gregory, do you know any one among your many lady acquaintances that needs a good maid? We'll certainly have to see what we can do for you, Miss Hagney."

"I'm—I'm afraid the tragedy of poor Miss Bovary is what prevents it, sir," the woman said sorrowfully. "Have you found out anything, Mr. Brooke? And now I see there's been another murder! What are things coming to!"

"Yes, there's been another," Brooke nodded. "Tell me, Miss Hagney, was Miss Bovary friendly with Barbatti? Wait a moment before you answer—you see, the reason I ask is because he seems to fit the description you gave of the stranger who waa hanging around the studio."

"Oh, I never thought of that!" Margaret Hagney replied slowly. "But it couldn't be—yes, it might! Mr. Brooke, he might have very well been the man. I never thought of it before, but now that you speak of it, the stranger I saw looked a lot like Barbatti."

"You knew Barbatti, then?"

"Oh, yes—well, in a way. I've been to a lot of rackets at his place—parties, you know. Yes—come to think of it,

Miss Bovary used to get hooch from him. And she used to go to his place for wop food with Carleton Dazian when Mr. Gilbert wasn't on the job. I wonder—say, it looks like he might have killed her, doesn't it?"

"It's a perplexing question, Miss Hagney," Brooke admitted. "You see, we found Miss Bovary's picture in his room."

"No! Was she stringing him along, too! Well, I should think that would make it pretty clear that he done the murder. I don't like to say things about people, but I guess there's no harm after one of 'em is dead. Yes, I'm almost sure that Barbatti was the man hanging around the studio. Of course, there's no real sign that he done it, and I may be wrong, but it certainly looks like he was the one."

"But you aren't sure, are you? You aren't positive that Barbatti was the man you saw?"

"How can I be sure, Mr. Brooke, when I didn't get a real good look at him! I wouldn't swear it on a stack of Bibles, but it seems to me that he might have been the one."

Brooke nodded. "Of course, if you had been sure you would have told us long ago. Then you really know nothing of any friendship between Barbatti and Miss Bovary except that she bought wet goods from him, and occasionally went to his restaurant?"

"That's all I know, sir," she replied thoughtfully. "And you can't think of anything else—tell me this—oh, well, it doesn't matter."

Clay Brooke rose nervously to his feet and walked slowly toward the bedroom.

"Nice little place you have," he remarked. "Have you a kitchenette?"

"Oh, no," the woman replied, rising from her chair. "No—I use an electric grill to get my meals on."

The criminologist's glance covered the bedroom searchingly and then he returned smiling nervously.

"Well, Greg," he said suddenly, "we'd better be getting on if we're going to keep our appointment. Thank you very much, Miss Hagney, for so kindly submitting to an informal interview. Next time I'll give you fair warning of my coming."

"Oh, that's all right, Mr. Brooke," she murmured. "I'm just sorry the place isn't fixed up more. If I'd known you were coming—"

"It's quite all right—quite all right, Miss Hagney. "Well, good day, and thank you again."

Clay Brooke fairly pushed me out of the door and onto the sidewalk. Then he rapidly glanced at the buildings on either side of the rooming house.

"It's not much use," he murmured. "All of these buildings seem to be connected."

"What in the world are you talking about!" I asked.

"Well, it couldn't have been a vision, Greg," he replied slowly, "I distinctly saw a man in the mirror in the bedroom. He was in a closet and I saw him come out—couldn't make out who he was. And before I recovered my wits he managed to get out by a door which doubtless leads to a back door in the rear of the hall. It's none of my business, perhaps, but who in the devil do you suppose he could be?"

XIX. JOHN-DOE WARRANTS

Clay Brooke was up bright and early the next morning, and directly after breakfast we started in my coupe for the office of the District Attorney. The night before, Brooke had shut up like a clam and absolutely refused to discuss anything pertaining to the murder case, or any of the people involved.

Sensing that he was in need of relaxation, I had begged him to go with me to the gala opening of a super-special photoplay at the Pyramid Theater, and now, as we drove to the Hall of Justice, he commented amusingly on the showiness of the opening—the throngs of fans who had crowded the sidewalks hoping to see their favorite stars in the flesh, the stars themselves in evening array and glittering jewels, the flashlights that boomed, and the huge trucks lined up in the streets with powerful searchlights playing on the theater entrance.

"Simply amazing, Greg—simply amazing! Do these events occur often?"

"As often as a producer makes a picture which he can't cut down to less than ten reels," I informed him jocularly.

When we reached the Hall of Justice the District Attorney greeted us most enthusiastically. Indeed, he seemed in excellent humor. Clay Brooke tossed his hat on John Rawson's desk and then slumped into a chair.

"Have you seen the morning papers?" Rawson asked cheerfully.

"No, I haven't," Brooke smiled. "I suppose there's lots about the opening last night. Was I mentioned as being among the celebrities present?"

"I am referring to this confounded murder case!" the District Attorney replied in an annoyed manner. "I followed your advice, and the papers are filled with an account of the solution of the Bovary affair naming Fiore Barbatti as the murderer."

"Oh, indeed?" the criminologist asked, lifting his eyebrows. "Well, that should quiet your persecutors and make your life more peaceful. But cheer up, Rawson, I'll have the real murderer for you before the day is over."

"What are you talking about, Brooke?" Rawson gasped.

"I thought I spoke distinctly," Brooke smiled. "But, really—I shouldn't have said that! There's deep color rushing to your face, my dear fellow, and it's bad for your high blood-pressure. Now if you please, may I see the letters that came in answer to our advertisements?"

"Brooke, I wish you'd explain yourself!" Rawson blustered. "You've kept me in the dark long enough!"

"I'm not entirely out of it myself," the criminologist replied with a shrug. "I am merely making you a sort of a promise which I hope to keep. Please don't ask any more because I've got a number of important affairs to attend to today. May I see the letters, please?"

The District Attorney stared at Clay Brooke for a few seconds, then snorted and pressed the button on his desk. The door opened and his secretary entered.

"Shapiro, I want you to bring in those letters you have on file—I am referring to the ones answering our advertisements."

The secretary nodded, disappeared for a moment, and then returned with two bundles of letters. With an impatient gesture, John Rawson handed them to the criminologist who rapidly began running through them.

"H'm!" he murmured. "There are plenty answering our request to write if they are in need of money! Not so many who have Monte Cristo mining stock, but a number of other offers. Hello—here's our Monte Cristo fellow, poor Barbatti! We might almost call this his death warrant."

Clay Brooke laid the letter aside and then began running through the entire lot again, glancing now and then at the one he had laid aside, frowning deeply as he did so.

"Here we are!" he said after a moment, comparing the one with the other. "I'd like to borrow both of these, if I may, Rawson. I'll give you a receipt for them if necessary. No? That's awfully good of you!"

The criminologist rose from his chair and walked over to the window where he pressed each of the letters against the pane and scrutinized them carefully.

"Not much help—no, not much," he commented. "However, I'll take them, Rawson, if only to prove that I appreciate your generosity. Come, Gregory, let's be running along!"

"But—but," stammered the bewildered District Attorney, "where—when am I going to see you again, Brooke?"

"In a very short time, my dear fellow," Brooke replied, reaching for his hat. "I'll keep in touch with you and—better than that, I'll return here early in the afternoon. See you anon, Rawson."

The District Attorney stared at Clay Brooke with troubled eyes as we departed. The criminologist chuckled to himself as we walked down the hall toward the elevator.

"It's really nasty of me," he confided, "to give Rawson so much anxiety. But great heavens—suppose my theory should be all wrong! No, that can't be, Gregory."

When we reached the street, Clay Brooke's manner changed abruptly. He seemed to have put all thought of the two murders out of his mind. A peculiar smile played about his mouth.

"Did you see Claire Demoset at the opening last night?" he asked suddenly. "Oh, that reminds me, I've got to make a 'phone call. Mind waiting for a minute, Greg?"

I stood outside the cigar store while the criminologist entered and disappeared in the 'phone booth. I wondered whether Brooke's sudden thought of the girl had inspired his telephoning. In a moment he emerged.

"Now, Greg," he said, "I'm going to do you a great favor. I'm going to excuse you from active duty for a few hours and permit you to return to your bungalow where you can get in some deep concentration on your blessed scenario. And take heed to my criticism over the shortcomings of the super-de-luxe-special we saw last night."

"Well—when shall I see you?"

"I'll telephone—no, better yet, I'll meet you for lunch. How about the Montmartre about one o'clock? Is this the day that they hold the fashion show when tables are at a premium?".

"No—then I'll see you at one," I replied.

Clay Brooke hailed a cab and was off. I climbed into my car and started toward my bungalow filled with thoughts which mingled the name of Brooke with Claire Demoset. That he was dazzled by the film star, there was no question; and I was convinced that Claire more than admired him. However, he had said nothing to me which could make me believe his intentions were serious. But, on the other hand, why should he tell me everything?

I was in a state of perplexity when I reached home, over the many angles of the case, and in that condition I attempted to work out some situations in the scenario which Brooke had outlined. I had been working an hour or so when the ringing of the door-bell interrupted, and leaving the mass of typewritten sheets, I hastened to answer it to Brooke's assistant, James Taylor.

"Is Mr. Brooke home?" he asked, after we had exchanged greetings.

"No—he isn't."

"I found a message saying he wanted to see me," Taylor explained. "Will he be back soon?"

I informed the caller that the criminologist had planned meeting me for lunch and that I didn't expect him to return before that time.

"I suppose," Taylor said after a pause, "that he wants to see me about this new murder—the murder of Barbatti. I just heard about it when I got back this morning. I had to run up to San Bernardino to help my sister out of a fix over some property."

"Yes," I answered. "Mr. Brooke stopped at your boarding-house the morning the crime was discovered. The landlady showed us your wire, and Brooke was disappointed you weren't around. He told me that he enjoyed working with you very much."

Taylor grinned his evident pleasure at my remark.

"Mr. Brooke's a mighty clever man—a mighty clever man! I only wish I had his brain! There's something up in that head of his—not just sawdust like most people."

"Yes, he's clever," I agreed. "Don't you want to come in and wait? He might 'phone me."

"No, thanks. I guess I won't do that. Just tell him I got his message and dropped around as quick as I could. I've got to go to the studio and report. Mr. Brooke can reach me there if I'm not at home."

Shortly after Taylor departed the telephone rang. It was Brooke. I informed him that the studio sleuth had called to see him and Brooke appeared sorry to have missed the man, although I fancied I could detect a chuckle of amusement in his voice. The criminologist then said that he had changed his mind and wanted me to meet him at the District Attorney's office. We would all go to lunch from there.

"I'm going to give Rawson the fun of having a warrant sworn out," he finished. "Well, see you in a few minutes, Greg."

Before I could question him he had hung up the receiver.

Clay Brooke reached the Hall of Justice before me, and I found him nervously pacing the reception room of the District Attorney's office.

"I just missed Rawson," he announced impatiently. "He left for lunch earlier than usual—isn't that just like him? Now where can the fellow be? I've had his secretary calling his clubs and every other place where we'd be likely to find him. Isn't this a pretty pass, Greg—just when I was all steamed up to slap a joker on the table?"

"Who's the warrant for?" I asked.

"John Doe," Brooke smiled. "Simply, John Doe. That's my favorite method. And it's a good one in this case where there are two elusive gentlemen to be brought to justice."

"Why not two warrants?"

"A very good idea!" Brooke replied slyly. "I'll make a mental note of that suggestion. Well, there's no use waiting here any longer. Let's run over to the Montmartre and have a bite. By that time Rawson should have returned. I suppose your car is outside, Greg. Really, I shouldn't be surprised to see you wearing it to bed! Now there's an idea—if some mechanically inclined Burbank could construct Hollywoodians with cars attached he would receive a honking vote of thanks!"

On the way to the popular Hollywood rendezvous, I endeavored to pry the secret from the criminologist, but he refused to name any culprit except his mysterious John Doe. As I had had the foresight to 'phone and reserve a table, we were seated at once. Clay Brooke ordered a huge lunch while I contented myself with a salad and iced tea.

"You know, Greg," the criminologist began, "this case is a most curious affair. Most curious and complicated— Hello! isn't that old Charles Gilbert getting up from the table and leaving? Right over there— the smug, elderly gentleman with the blonde siren in the red hat following him."

I turned in my chair and looked in the direction that Brooke indicated. As the object of the criminologist's gaze stopped and turned to permit someone to pass I could see that it was without a doubt the millionaire.

"As Carling would say," Brooke commented in an amused manner, "'he ain't lettin' no grass grow under his feet!' I wonder who the girl is—know her, Greg?"

"Can't say that I do—probably an 'extra' girl."

"And quite probably a star of the future," Brooke added with a strange smile. "Can you put yourself in that old boy's place? The light of his life was foully murdered only a few days ago—and look at him now! He must be a hard-shelled old fellow! Remember the way he broke down and confessed how much he loved the Bovary girl? Queer, isn't it? Or else he's frisking about so shamelessly to show the world at large that he wasn't greatly interested in his Berylyn. What was it Shakespeare said—oh, it doesn't matter. I'd only misquote the merriest villager of Avon."

"'The-way of the transgressor is—'"

"Oh, but it isn't!" Brooke interrupted. "If he's careful! Besides, that's from the Bible. Let's get the check."

When we returned to the Hall of Justice we were informed that the District Attorney had arrived. We were immediately ushered into his office.

"Where the devil have you been!" Brooke demanded of Rawson. "I scurried up here an hour or so ago to invite you to go to lunch. If you'd have waited for us you would have had the pleasure of seeing Charles Gilbert dining with his latest cutie."

"Huh?" sniffed the District Attorney lifting his eyebrows. "Has he got another already? Well, to tell the truth, Brooke, I've been engaging myself in following certain theories of my own. I visited the mortuary where Dr. Jeffreys completed his autopsy on Barbatti; and Carling and I made a discovery which rather convinces me that the Italian is the victim of a vendetta."

"Oh, is that so?" Brooke nodded politely.

John Rawson leaned toward the criminologist and. gazed at him intently.

"Yes," he said, after a short pause. "We discovered a design tattooed on Barbatti's arm—a design with the appearance of a tower with an arched gateway and three pointed turrets. I am sure that you will agree that these tattoo marks rather prove that Barbatti was a Camorrist."

Brooke smiled pleasantly. "I agree with you perfectly. In fact, I made the same discovery during my examination of the body. I would certainly have called your attention to it at the time had there been a knife slash on the unfortunate man. A knife slash, you know, is the mark put on traitors of this select criminal fraternity and it is usually carved on the victim's cheek. If there had been a knife wound, I certainly would have called your attention to the tattoo mark."

The District Attorney's crestfallen face betrayed his disappointment.

"Then—then you refuse to believe that there is any kind of a feud connected with the murder of Barbatti?"

"Yes, I do," Brooke said seriously. "I'll qualify my statement and say that it could be a sort of a feud—not an Italian feud, mind you, but an act of vengeance, an act to prevent a betrayal. No, Rawson, my dear fellow, I fear you are romancing when you place your theory that the man was a victim of a vendetta because of the tattoo marks."

The District Attorney was nettled by Clay Brooke's calmness. His look shifted from the criminologist and he gazed dejectedly out of the window.

"Oh, come now—cheer up, Rawson," Brooke chided. "I think it would do your heart a lot of good to order a warrant drawn up—say a warrant for the arrest of the murderer of Berylyn Bovary."

John Rawson shot a quick glance at the criminologist.

"What do you mean!" he demanded.

"Just what I say," Brooke continued, calmly lighting a cigaret. "Or better than that, let's have two warrants— one for the murderer of Bovary and one for the murderer of Barbatti."

The District Attorney smiled at Clay Brooke indulgently.

"Brooke," he said wearily, "a moment ago you scoffed at me for romancing, and now you—"

"Nonsense, my dear fellow! Please do as I say! I suggest two warrants, John-Doe warrants, if you don't mind. Is your car outside? Oh, yes; I noticed it when I came in. Gregory has his here, too, and he's such a splendid driver I suggest that you risk your life and come along with us in his car. You can give orders to your chauffeur to follow us with Carling and a number of his henchmen. We may need them."

John Rawson stared at the criminologist in amazement.

"Are you serious?" he demanded. The expression on Clay Brooke's face apparently assured him, for he immediately pressed the button on his desk and summoned his secretary.

"Get Carling!" he ordered. "And I want him to get me two John-Doe warrants immediately. Understand that? And have Carling shake it up!"

"Yes, sir," the secretary replied, leaving the room hurriedly.

"Well, who are we after—and where are we going?" Rawson demanded, turning to Clay Brooke.

"Tut, tut, Rawson! Your blood-pressure!" the criminologist cautioned, wagging his forefinger at the District Attorney. "We're going to—well, first I want to stop at Cahuenga Avenue. I want to pick up Taylor. I think he'll be helpful to us. Then—well! here's Carling already!"

The captain of detectives entered the office breathlessly, a questioning expression on his face.

"What's up!" he demanded.

"Get two John-Doe warrants immediately!" Rawson snapped. "Then get three of your men and pile into my car—it's down in front. My chauffeur will be instructed to follow me closely. I'll be with Mr. Brooke in Gregory

Black's car. Understand that? And these John-Doe warrants are for the arrest of the murderer of the Bovary girl and the murderer of Fiore Barbatti."

"Holy tripes!" Carling exclaimed. "Who are the birds?"

"Never mind that now, Carling! Get those warrants and your men and shake it up!"

Carling gulped and nodded, then hustled out of the room.

"Now then, Brooke—come on!" the District Attorney snapped impatiently. "I don't know where you're taking us, but let's not waste any time!"

Clay Brooke reached for his hat and stepped over to John Rawson's desk, carefully extinguishing his cigaret in the ash tray. Then he slowly drew another from his case, lighted it with his briquet and followed us out of the room.

XX. SECOND FLOOR REAR

"Rawson, my dear fellow, your patience is amazing!" Clay Brooke smilingly remarked over his shoulder to the District Attorney when we were speeding in my coupe toward the address on Cahuenga Avenue. "Really, I'm beginning to have the profoundest admiration for you!"

John Rawson's reply from the rear seat was a grunt of annoyance.

"Come, come!" the criminologist chided turning about. "That's no kind of an answer after my compliment! Just fasten your optics on that exceedingly pretty girl approaching us. She looks as though she's ready to walk into a camera's close-up—and a very pretty picture she would make, too! Doesn't a glimpse of beauty like that cheer you, Rawson—make your heart glad that your eyesight is good, and all that sort of thing?"

The District Attorney sniffed peevishly.

"Dear, dear!" Brooke murmured, shaking his head sadly. "Is there nothing I can do, Rawson, to brighten your outlook on life? Now, what would you say if I were to tell you that we are on our way to arrest Mr. Charles Gilbert?"

"Charles Gilbert!" exploded the District Attorney.

"Yes," the criminologist smiled. "What would you say if I were to tell you that—well, you've said it already, haven't you? You repeated the name of Charles Gilbert after me like an automaton, a piece of mechanism, with an exclamatory punctuation after it. No imagination at all in your reply. Just for that I don't think we'll arrest Charles Gilbert. We might, though—we might. One can never tell."

"For heaven's sake, Brooke, stop this nonsense!" Rawson blustered with irritation. "I'm a nervous wreck already over this affair and you seem to be trying your best to bring on the final collapse."

"Nothing of the kind—nothing of the kind!" Brooke laughed. He lapsed into silence for a minute or so, then stole a glance over his shoulder at the District Attorney.

"Yes, I'm still here!" Rawson grunted. "Well, here we are on Cahuenga Avenue—does your man live in this neighborhood?"

Brooke peered ahead through the wind-shield. "Just a short distance—we'll be there in a moment. Hello—did you see that car that just whizzed by us?"

"No—who was it?"

"Carling and his huskies in your car. If they aren't careful they'll be arrested for speeding. Ah—they noticed that they passed us and now they're slowing up. Step on it, Gregory! You know, Rawson, you have the most amazing speed limit out here! I rather like it—in fact, it's one of the many pleasant recollections I will have of Hollywood."

"Isn't this the place, Clay," I interrupted, "Taylor's boarding house?"

"Yes—here we are! Suppose we wait until the other car pulls up. We can send one of Carling's men to ask for Taylor."

As he finished, the District Attorney's limousine drew up behind us and Carling alighted. Rawson instructed him to have one of his men ring for the studio detective. Carling selected Leahy, and that worthy started for the door of the boarding-house.

"My kindest regards to Mrs. Cordoba!" Brooke called after him.

Leahy rang the bell and presently the landlady appeared. After a moment he returned to our car while the proprietress lingered in the doorway.

"Taylor isn't in, according to the dame up there," Leahy reported.

"Maybe he wasn't expecting us."

"Oh, but he was!" Brooke cut in impatiently. "I 'phoned and told him I was coming and to be sure and wait."

"He's probably gone to the studio," Rawson remarked.

"No, he was going to be here!" the criminologist persisted. "Let me have a word with the landlady. She must be mistaken."

Clay Brooke left the car and approached the woman. After a brief exchange of words he returned to us.

"I'm going up to his room, Rawson," he said. "He's probably fallen asleep. Won't be but a minute."

The District Attorney nodded and Brooke left us and entered the rooming house. Rawson snapped his fingers impatiently while Carling paced the sidewalk, stopping now and then to glance in the direction of the door. In a few moments Clay Brooke appeared. There was a disquieting expression on his face.

"Something funny has happened in there, Rawson," he declared. "I—really, I don't like it at all. Taylor's door is locked and I peered through the keyhole. Quite an unpleasant sight inside, if you know what I mean."

"Good Lord! Not another tragedy!" the District Attorney groaned. "Good Lord! What does it all mean, Brooke! One after the other—one after the other!"

"Let's not waste any time," Brooke replied curtly. "The first thing to do is force that door and see what has happened at close range. We mustn't alarm the landlady any more than necessary. She's a pleasant soul and we'll certainly want to question her. Better have Carling leave one of his men with her. Leahy would be a good one."

Carling was listening to Clay Brooke in open-mouthed amazement, and when John Rawson nodded feebly in his direction he hastened to give instructions to Leahy.

"Oh, Carling," Brooke called after him, "have your men examine the outside of the house—Taylor's room is on the second floor rear. Better take a look in the back-yard. Now, gentlemen, if you are ready," he added, turning to Rawson and me, "we'll force that door. Yes—

you come with us, Carling. I'll handle Mrs. Cordoba, she's really quite attached to me."

The landlady watched, with startled eyes, as John Rawson, Carling, and I followed Clay Brooke to the door of the boarding-house.

"Goodness gracious!" she exclaimed. "What has happened, Mr. Brooke?"

"Nothing to be alarmed at, Mrs. Cordoba," he assured her pleasantly. "You see, it's necessary that we have a look into Mr. Taylor's room. You have a pass-key? That's splendid! Now I'll be very grateful to you if you'll remain here with this gentleman. This is Mr. Leahy, Mrs. Cordoba—now, you've been properly introduced. We won't be upstairs long."

With puzzled alarm the landlady watched us pass through the door and continue up the staircase, with the criminologist leading the way. When we reached the landing on the second floor, Clay Brooke approached a door in the rear, and after fumbling a moment with the key, he unlocked the door and opened it.

A most amazing sight met our eyes. The chaos we had beheld in the room of Fiore Barbatti was nothing compared to the upset condition of the quarters of the studio-detective. The bed was in disorder, chairs were overturned, bureau drawers were pulled out and, on the floor, papers were strewn about in confusion, in every direction that the eye could see. On the floor lay a rumpled suit of clothes which had the appearance of being hastily discarded; and, nearby was a blue shirt, which I remembered as Taylor's, spotted with blood.

"Good Lord! Good Lord!" the District Attorney murmured gazing about. "This completely does me up, Brooke! But where's the body?"

"That seems to be something we've got to find!" Brooke replied sharply. "Rawson, I suggest that you and Gregory remain in the doorway, if you don't mind, while Carling and I make a hasty inspection of the premises.

We can get about without disturbing things much easier than either of you."

I stepped aside to permit the captain of detectives to enter, and Carling first walked directly to the bed and peered under it. He rose and shook his head negatively. Brooke had been examining a half-opened window; then he stepped to a closet in the corner of the room and looked in, moving the scanty number of garments about as he did so.

"Peculiar," he remarked after a pause. "We seem to be confronted by a murder, and yet there doesn't seem to be any corpse! This savors of Dickens' *Bleak House,* in which an unfortunate gentleman died of spontaneous combustion. Carling, what do you think of it?"

"I'm damned if I know, sir!" the captain of detectives replied, removing his hat and scratching his head. "There certainly should be a victim on the premises after all the blood that's been spilt. The dead man couldn't have walked out by himself. Well, so far there's no need, to send for Dr. Jeffreys."

Clay Brooke returned to the window. "They couldn't have very well lowered him out of here without leaving signs of it. No blood-stains on the window ledge, nor anywhere nearby. H'm! I remember this suit of clothes belonged to Taylor, and I believe this shirt was his."

"Yes," I put in, "he wore that shirt when he called to see you this morning. I'd swear he was also wearing that suit."

"Very good, Greg," Brooke complimented. "Now, let me see—" he examined the shirt carefully— "a knife stab through the pocket on the left-hand side— and blood stains. Pretty close to the heart, I'd say. Hold on, now!" he exclaimed, causing Rawson and Carling to stare; then, regaining his composure quickly, he added, "Curious thing—h'm, very curious. Have you found any kind of a weapon, Carling—knife, or anything else?"

"Not a damned thing, sir!" the captain of detectives replied emphatically. "There certainly ought to be a weapon about and I'm not through looking for one—I'm telling you!"

While Carling resumed his search for the implement of the crime, Clay Brooke approached the door leading to the hall and examined it carefully. "Locked from the outside," he remarked. Then he sank on both knees and investigated the floor. Then, borrowing Carling's electric torch, he played it on the floor outside of the door and in the hallway. His attention became focused on the two other doors in the hall, and, approaching them, he tried the knobs. Both were locked.

"Brooke," Rawson put in suddenly, "hadn't I better send for the finger-print experts?"

"If you want to," the criminologist replied without enthusiasm. "I have an idea that there won't be much use in it—but do as you like. By Jove, there's something very peculiar been going on here—very peculiar! No, I shouldn't send for the finger-print squad. We can get along without them. Find any weapon yet, Carling?"

"No, sir. Funny, isn't it?"

"Very! Do you happen to have a glass with you, Carling—some sort of a magnifying glass. Thanks—this'll do nicely."

Brooke took the glass which Carling offered, polished it, then dropped to his knees and investigated the blood-stains on the carpet and floor. Then his eye fell on the blood-stained shirt, and picking it up he walked to the window and gave it a most pains-taking examination by means of the magnifying glass. A faint smile played about his lips, and he placed the shirt carefully upon the bureau. Then he returned the glass to Carling.

"I may want to borrow that piece of wearing apparel, Rawson," he remarked, turning to the District Attorney. "Might want to make a microscopic examination—unless something turns up which will convince me that it is unnecessary."

"You can have the entire room, if it'll help any!" Rawson exploded, giving Brooke a glance of impatience.

"Thanks—I won't need it! Now, then, Carling, I think it would be wise for you to step downstairs and instruct your men to continue their search for the body—a thorough search, mind you. And I wish you'd also be good enough to send up Mrs. Cordoba."

"Yes, sir!"

As Carling left the room, Brooke paced to the window and back, then suddenly uttering a faint exclamation he drew his address book from his inside pocket and searched through the pages. After a moment he darted a glance at the District Attorney.

"I'll be right back, Rawson," he said. "Going to run downstairs and make a 'phone call. Please hold Mrs. Cordoba here until I return."

The District Attorney grunted his reply and watched Brooke hurry from the room and down the stairs.

"Now, what in the devil is he up to!" he snorted. "He always seems so sure of himself—as if he knows exactly what's behind the whole horrible case. Well, I give up! I'm blessed if I can see what connection these three murders have—one right after the other, too!"

There was a noise outside and Carling appeared, followed by Mrs. Cordoba. There was an expression of fear on the landlady's face which turned to absolute horror when she beheld the terrible scene in the room. She uttered a muffled cry and clutched at her face with her hands in such terror that I feared she was going to faint.

"Oh—oh! What has happened!" she cried. "Oh—poor Mr. Taylor! Poor Mr. Taylor!"

"Steady, ma'am—steady!" Carling said, taking her by the arm. "There's nothing to worry about yet—we ain't been able to find the corpse even!"

"Oh, but—"

She was interrupted by the sudden appearance of Clay Brooke.

"What luck?" Rawson asked.

"Very little," Brooke replied drily. "The party I telephoned has moved—bag and baggage."

"Oh, Mr. Brooke!" Mrs. Cordoba cried. "You must tell me what has happened here!"

"Haven't these gentlemen told you!" the criminologist exclaimed, in mock surprise. "Well, all I can say is that there is every evidence of murder except the dead man. Now, Mrs. Cordoba, I want to ask you a few questions. To begin, you have said that you did not see Mr. Taylor leave the house. Then, so far as you know, no one has been here to see him?"

"Oh, no—no one's been here!" the landlady replied nervously. "Of course, Mr. Brooke, I don't see everyone that comes and goes, but I do my best, and no one can accuse me of not running a respectable house."

"I understand," Brooke nodded. "Now tell me this—do you serve dinner for your roomers?"

"No, sir. All of my lodgers eat out. There are several reasonable restaurants nearby, you see. I tried to run a table once, and serve good vittles, but it didn't pay me."

Brooke paused before continuing.

"Then I don't suppose you keep many servants, only a woman to clean the rooms and throw out whatever refuse there might be?"

"That's right, Mr. Brooke," Mrs. Cordoba nodded. "I do most of the work myself, but I have a woman who takes care of these upper floors—just for the daily cleaning, you know. I take care of the linen myself."

"I understand. I'd like to step downstairs with you for a moment, if you don't mind. Rawson—"

Brooke was interrupted by the sound of someone hurrying up the stairs; then Carling rushed breathlessly in the room. In his hand he carried a large knife.

"I—I found this in the yard!" he puffed.

"Oh—may I see it?" Brooke asked eagerly. "H'm— looks like a new one! And no signs of blood on it, either—

yes, there's a slight stain where the blade fits into the handle. Mrs. Cordoba, have you seen this knife before?"

"No—no!" the frightened woman stammered. "It isn't like any I've got!"

"It looks as if it's been recently purchased," Brooke went on. "Oh, well, keep that with your collection of exhibits, Carling. I'll be back here in a moment or so. Come along, Mrs. Cordoba!"

Clay Brooke and the landlady disappeared down the stairs while the District Attorney and Carling watched him with mystified expressions. Then the detective-captain shifted uneasily and turned to John Rawson.

"This is the strangest case I've ever heard of!" he said. "This here knife is the thing that did it—that's plain enough. But where in hell is the body? It certainly isn't on the premises, and I can't figure how they could have gotten it out of here. What do you think Mr. Brooke thinks about the case?"

"I haven't the slightest idea," the District Attorney answered wearily. "Brooke has an annoying habit of seeming to know exactly what has happened and keeping it devilishly close to himself. It's a maddening way he's got—but I have faith in him. Brooke knows what he's about."

"Yes, I suppose, but—"

Carling was interrupted by the appearance of Leahy.

"Mr. Brooke suggested I take these keys here," he said, indicating the bunch of pass-keys hanging in the keyhole of the door, "and go through the other rooms on this floor and the floor above. I've already been through all the rooms that are unlocked and haven't found anything yet."

Leahy took the bunch of keys and Carling followed him as he began his inspection of the other rooms on the floor. After making an inspection on the floor above, they returned and reported their search to be fruitless. They had found no clues pertaining to the tragedy, and the disappearance of the victim was still a mystery.

"Where th' hell do you think this corpse is, Carling!" Leahy demanded. "This is the first time one ever got up and walked out on us!"

"Somebody must have gotten it out of here," the detective-captain commented shaking his head, "but I can't see how they done it without being seen."

There was a sound of footsteps on the stairs and Clay Brooke entered.

"You'd better go down and comfort Mrs. Cordoba," he told Leahy. "She's in a frightful state over this affair. I think she likes you, Leahy—in fact, I scent a budding romance."

Leahy looked at Clay Brooke with a peculiar expression and reluctantly started down the stairs.

"Well, did you find anything, Brooke?" Rawson asked eagerly.

"A rather amazing thing!" the criminologist smiled. "Or, I should say, ingenious! But what will interest you more, Rawson, is that our friend with rubber heels—you remember the rubber-heel marks in Barbatti's room— well, he's been on this job, too."

"Then you think," Rawson ventured, "that the same man who killed Barbatti has done away with Taylor?"

"That's exactly the way I should put it," Brooke smiled, "exactly the way. Oh, by-the-by, I won't want to borrow the blood-stained shirt, so Carling can take it along. But come now, we musn't waste any time. If you want to accept any advice from me, let me suggest that you make a very thorough search for the missing man. I don't believe the clue of the rubber heels will come in very helpful, although it might."

"Do you think," Rawson began, "that—"

"Oh, yes!" Brooke continued. "And it would be an excellent idea to post two of your men at this house the rest of the day—front and rear. Leahy didn't find anything in the upper rooms, did he? I thought not. Well, it won't do any harm to go over the rooms again. And now let's get out of this. I've a puzzling theory that I want to follow up and it won't do to waste any valuable time. I suppose, Rawson, I can reach you at your office the rest of the day, and later at your house? Good!"

"But—but—"

"Can't wait now—come on, Gregory! Oh, Rawson, I'd keep quiet about this affair. Carry on as though nothing had happened—it's best that we do so. I've sworn the landlady into secrecy and I'm sure she won't talk. Well, I'll 'phone you later—and keep those warrants in a handy place where you can reach them at a moment's notice."

The District Attorney watched in bewilderment as Clay Brooke hurried out of the room and down the stairs. He nodded pleasantly at Mrs. Cordoba as we passed her in the hallway and pressed his fingers to his lips.

"There's nothing to worry about, I assure you," he told her. "Just carry on as though nothing had happened."

"And now, Greg," Brooke said when we approached my car at the curb, "I'm going to leave you, but before doing so I want to encroach on your hospitality once more. Are you in the mood for a party? Well, I'd like you to give a-party tonight. Invite any one you want—lots of people. And try to get Claire Demoset—I like that woman immensely. Invite everybody except John Rawson. I'm going to take the liberty of asking a number of guests myself. Oh, and I wonder if you can fix up a mystic chamber?"

"A what?"

"A mystic chamber—a sort of a dark room draped in black cloth—sort of mysterious, you know. Your study would do splendidly. I have it! Get one of your men from the studio and have him trick it up—you know, kind of spooky. We aren't going to tell ghost stories, but that'll help you get what I mean. And, Greg, let's not make this one a kiddie party. Well, see you later—I'll be with you around dinner time. Never miss a meal—that's me! Pardon the grammatical irregularity," he laughed. "And don't forget—I must see Claire tonight!"

Before I could reply to Clay Brooke's rapid-fire instructions, he had hailed a taxicab and was speeding down Cahuenga Avenue.

XXI. Evelyn Halloway Assists

At six-thirty Brooke had not yet put in his appearance, and I was about to give orders to Fuji to delay the dinner when the criminologist suddenly arrived. He flung his hat upon the couch in the corner, then dropped into a chair with a deep sigh.

"Well, old man," he said, "I feel as if I've been half-way around the world! But what luck—could you get anybody to come tonight?"

"Oh, yes—it isn't difficult to get people to come to a party. But—"

"How about Claire Demoset—is she coming?" he asked eagerly.

"Yes: if she can possibly make it—I think Claire likes you," I smiled. "You see, I 'phoned her and said I was giving a little party for you, and she was frightfully cut up because she has to stay at the studio tonight and make voice tests for her new picture. She promised to come as soon as she can, if she isn't kept too late. But where've you been this afternoon?"

"She was cut up, was she?" Clay Brooke asked ignoring my question. "I hope she'll be able to make it. I've got to see her, Greg!"

"What's going to happen, Clay?" I asked curiously.

"An interesting experiment, I hope," he smiled. "But show me what you've done to your library."

The criminologist followed me into my study and ejaculated with enthusiasm at the transformation that had taken place.

"Splendid, Greg, splendid! Did some of the boys from the studio help you? The black cloth draped about is very effective. I like your gold and silver stars and half-moons, too. Now, if we only had a black cat that would oblige us by posing with its back arched! H'm—we've got to have a crystal ball—you haven't got a goldfish globe, have you? We could put it upside-down on the table, then, with a small amount of black velvet around the base, and a blue light on it, I think it would pass muster."

I laughed and told Brooke that I was not the possessor of such an object, but I promised to send Fuji for one as soon as we had finished dinner. At that moment my Jap entered and announced that dinner was served. Clay Brooke hastened to make his toilet and soon joined me in the dining-room.

"Who's coming tonight, Greg?" he asked as he seated himself.

"As many stars as I could get on short notice. There's Dolfo Mendez, Carol Grant, Harry Gibbs, June Moran, Gilbert Arden, Betty Duane, Dolores Fenton, and a number of others—and, of course, Claire Demoset if she can make it. Oh, I also managed to get Johnny Dines, the comedian. He's a great one to keep a party going."

"He is—that's good!" Brooke commented. "Is he a pretty good friend of yours? I'll probably want you to run out of your party with me, and should this happen you can turn the festivities over to your comedian. Better tell him that as soon as he comes so he'll be prepared if he misses you. Make some kind of a good excuse."

"What's this all about, Clay?" I ventured. "I wish you'd tell me what you've been up to today and what's going to happen tonight. I don't like working in the dark this way."

"It'll soon be over, Greg," the criminologist chuckled. "You see, when I'm working on a case I don't confide in any one. That's what drives John Rawson wild. I form my theories, make my suppositions, and follow up my clues with maddening secrecy. I'm my own confidant, in other words. I can work better that way and at the same time I have my friends and associates working most efficiently for me without their knowing it. You probably aren't aware of the fact, Greg, but you have helped exceedingly a number of times when you hadn't the slightest idea you were doing so. Don't look so astonished—I mean it!"

"But—but—"

"What's the reason? Is that what you were going to ask? Well, I'll tell you. The most intelligent people—including myself—are very bad actors. When they know they've got a duty to perform which is intriguing and depending on secrecy, they're exceedingly self-conscious. They can't act natural to save their lives. They're very apt to give the game away—do you see what I mean? Now, if they don't know what's happening, or going to happen, they act their natural charming selves. And that's what I want them to do. I've let Rawson babble about his vendetta because it interested him and kept him out of mischief. If I'd told him all that I know, he'd have made a couple of arrests before I would have sufficient proof for a conviction, and the entire case might be bungled. As it is, I'm taking the greatest delight in being a strong, silent master-mind. That's a role I take a singular delight in. Curious, is it not?"

"And you mean to say you've had me acting for you—when?"

"Oh, numerous times," Brooke smiled blandly. "You've done a number of services for me—some of them when I've been out of sight and hearing. This is excellent salad—did you make it? Now as far as tonight's performance is concerned, I must tell you that I'm expecting—or rather, I'm sincerely hoping that I will have to leave this house rather suddenly. If that is the case, I want you to come with me. Have your car parked in the drive inconspicuously with the lights out, and get ready to run for it when I give the word."

"This is all very mystifying," I murmured.

"Isn't it, though!" nodded the criminologist, rubbing his hands together. "I love it, Greg—I love it! In fact, I'm so excited I'm afraid I can't eat my dessert. Oh—I almost forgot to tell you that I took the liberty of inviting a few guests to your party—Evelyn Halloway and her young friend, Mitchell Gilbert. I also invited the boy's father, but I doubt if he will come. He's probably afraid we'll have him carrying a dummy in and out of doorways. Carleton Dazian is coming, too. I suppose he'll try to talk himself into a job in the movies while he's here."

"How about Wagner?" I asked. "If you're planning on some kind of a show-down, he certainly ought to be present. He could furnish the goldfish globe, too."

Clay Brooke chuckled softly. "Getting curious, aren't you? To tell the truth, I tried to reach Wagner, but he hasn't a 'phone in his new house. I sent a message and if he comes so much the better. Finished eating? Well, I suppose we'd better dress—some of your Hollywoodians are sure to come in formal array and we must make them feel at home. Oh, I very nearly forgot something. We've got to have a costume for our fortune teller—some kind of a black robe, or a—"

"How about my black silk Japanese lounging robe?"

"That's great! Thank heavens you've got what the well-dressed man should wear while lounging! And don't forget to send your man for the goldfish globe."

Half an hour later Clay Brooke and I were in evening attire waiting the arrival of the first comers. The criminologist had put the finishing touches on the make-shift clairvoyant studio and carefully arranged the goldfish globe to suit his needs. He took unusual care with what he professionally termed the "lighting effect", and by pressing my drop-light into service and substituting a blue bulb for the white one, managed to secure an eerie effect with the blue light shining down on the globe while the rest of the room was in darkness.

"Oh, there's one more thing I want you to do for me," he suddenly said. "Shortly after the guests arrive, 'phone for a taxicab and have the driver stop a short distance down the street, headed toward town. Tell him he's to wait and not to accept any fare unless it's someone leaving this house in a great hurry. He can pretend he's sleepy, drunk, or got a fare already, I don't care which, just so he waits and gets the right man. Now, here's something else important. When he gets his man, he mustn't hurry too much. He's got to be slow getting started and travel at a speed so that we won't lose him in your car. Can you get a man to fill this order?"

"I think I can find the very one for us," I said. "I'd better 'phone now and reserve him for the next hour and a half. His name is Kranz, and he used to drive a truck at the studio. I'll get busy right away."

"Fine! And can you remember all of those instructions? Good!"

I immediately began telephoning and was lucky enough to locate Rudolph Kranz, who had graduated from driving a truck loaded with props to distant camera locations to owning his own taxi. I explained what Brooke wanted without going into details, saying I would slip out of the house when the time came and give him instructions in full. Kranz promised to have his car parked at the proper spot within an hour and a half. When I returned to the living-room, I found the criminologist sitting by the fireplace in my easiest chair, idly puffing a cigaret.

"You are a very useful chap, Greg," he smiled at me. "Do you know that?"

"Useful—how do you mean?"

"Oh—lots of ways. Knowing taxicab drivers, and so on. I fancy your, friend, Kranz, will come in very handy before the night's over. Hang it all—why doesn't somebody hurry up and come to our party! Isn't it maddening? I always feel like a perfect boob when I'm sitting around waiting for something to happen!"

The ringing of the telephone interrupted my reply and I hastened to answer it. The call was for Brooke and it was a feminine voice that came over the wire, a familiar voice, and yet I couldn't place it. The criminologist rose lazily and walked to the telephone in the hallway. In a few minutes he returned, his face wreathed in smiles.

"Guess who, Greg? Claire Demoset. She called to tell me personally what you told me—that she has to work at the studio tonight, but she'll be over as soon as they finish. I hope she makes it on time—probably not. I can't take any chances at this stage of the game. What do you think I'd better do about it, Greg? I fancy, though, that the husband of a movie star leads a dog's life—everywhere I'd go I'd be known as the husband of Claire Demoset. Don't worry, old fellow, I'm not serious—yet."

Suddenly there was a ring at the door-bell and Clay Brooke's eye lighted expectantly. He rose and followed me to the door. Our first guests were Evelyn Halloway and Mitchell Gilbert.

"Oh, are we the first ones!" the girl laughed. "It's your own fault, Mr. Brooke. You insisted that I come early."

"Oh, but it was very nice of you to do so," the criminologist smiled. "Where's your man, Greg—he ought to be here to show these people where to put their things."

Fuji silently appeared and I instructed him "as to the rooms where wraps were to be deposited. Clay Brooke watched the girl with admiration as she left the room followed by young Gilbert. In a moment they both returned.

"Miss Halloway," Brooke began, when amenities were over, "I have a special role for you to perform tonight. That's why I wanted you to come early. I'm sure you won't mind, Mr. Gilbert. You know, every party has to have some sort of a novelty these days to keep people from talking about the host, and while I'm no great shakes as a cotillion leader, I've devised what may be a different stunt from the usual. Greg has rigged his study into a clairvoyant studio, a mystic chamber—crystal ball, and everything—and I want you to read our guests' pasts and futures in the crystal. There's really no harm, because the crystal is only an inverted, uninhabited goldfish globe. Will you do it?"

The girl smiled hesitatingly. "Why—why, really, I don't think I could."

"Oh, sure you can, Evelyn!" Mitchell Gilbert put in. "There'll be a lot of film people here and all you'll have to do to satisfy them is say that their next picture will be their best, and that they're going to be given a better contract, and all that sort of rot."

"Exactly!" Brooke laughed. "You can see how simple it is! Really, there isn't anything to it! The room is almost in darkness, so nobody will know who you are. Come—let's have a look at it! And, Greg, would you mind getting that gorgeous robe of yours?"

I ran upstairs to get my dressing-gown and when I returned the criminologist was showing the girl and young Gilbert the intricacies of our mystic chamber.

"Ah, here we have it!" Brooke exclaimed as I entered. "Just see what Gregory is going to let you wear! Really, half of the women in Hollywood would die for the privilege! Now the idea is this—you are to sit in this chair in gala attire, and as each one enters you are to stare into the crystal and tell them whatever you think will please them most. H'm, I've got it! To make it easier, I'll be on hand and tell you who your customers are and give some hint about them just before they enter. I won't always be right, because I don't know them very well, but that won't matter just so you tell them pleasant things."

"But hadn't I better have something to put over my head?" Evelyn Halloway asked.

"Then you'll do it!" Brooke cried jubilantly. "Of course, you can have something to put over your head! Gregory, what have you got to put over the lady's head? I have it— I mean I really have! I've got a black silk scarf which I'll sacrifice for the occasion. We can cut eye-holes in it and it'll be just the thing. Just a
moment—I'll get it."

Brooke scurried upstairs and returned, gleefully waving his black scarf, while in his other hand was a pair of shears.

"Now I'll transform you into a first-class medium," he said gaily, and, draping the scarf over the girl's head, he snipped out slits for eye-holes. "Now then," he added, turning to Mitchell Gilbert and me, "I have some very confidential information to give Miss Halloway, so we will be delighted if you will excuse us for a few minutes. I must coach her in her role; for, there is considerable importance attached to one or two of her readings."

Young Gilbert and I left them and returned to the living-room. The millionaire's son was greatly intrigued by Clay Brooke's novel idea and appeared to have no suspicion of the criminologist's reason for the unusual form of entertainment.

Hardly had we seated ourselves with fresh cigarets when the doorbell rang. The arrivals were June Moran and Johnny Dines. After introducing them to Mitchell Gilbert, I drew the comedian aside and quietly informed him that he was to consider himself host, should I happen to be called away suddenly. I carefully explained the possible conference with one of our directors over the story of a forthcoming photoplay.

The next arrival to my surprise was Charles Gilbert, and as he entered, Clay Brooke and Evelyn Halloway appeared from their conference in the mystic chamber. The criminologist spoke to the millionaire cordially and then left him to greet a number of other guests who trouped in, followed by Carleton Dazian, looking more dapper than ever.

"Glad to see you," Brooke said, greeting the latter. "If you don't know all of these people you'll have to ask Greg to introduce you. I can't remember all of their names to save my life."

Suddenly the telephone rang and Clay Brooke signified that he would answer it. In a moment he returned and approached me, smiling.

"That was the lovely Claire again," he whispered in my ear. "She 'phoned from the studio to say she might be kept rather late. She is going to call again when they are through to see if the party is still on." He gave me a dig in the ribs and walked over to where Evelyn Halloway was talking with Johnny Dines.

The large living-room was now filled, and all were apparently enjoying themselves, utterly unaware of the fact that the criminologist was staging a mysterious drama in their midst. Harry Gibbs was playing softly on the piano in the corner of the room, while June Moran gave pantomimic imitations of various screen celebrities. I glanced at my watch and saw that it was a few minutes after nine. Suddenly I felt a tap on my shoulder. It was Clay Brooke. He signified that I was to follow him into the hall.

"Better go out and make sure that your cab driver has arrived," he whispered. "You're sure you've got the instructions correct? All right. Now tell him this—tell him to stay parked at his destination until we get there. His fare may want him to wait anyway. But don't let him give the game away whatever you do."

I nodded and quietly left the house. The gleam of a red tail-light a short distance down the street told me that Kranz had arrived. So, hastening to the taxicab, I gave him Clay Brooke's instructions. Kranz repeated them after me in a bewildered manner, but I was sure that I could trust him to carry "them out to the letter. When I returned to the house, the criminologist's eyes were on me. I nodded that all was in readiness. Brooke immediately sought Evelyn Halloway, and together they left the room for the mystic chamber. In a few moments he returned and approached me.

"I rather hate to interfere with the fun that everyone seems to be having," Brooke confided, "but business is business, and we've got to begin our fortune-telling. Can you do a bally-hoo act, Gregory? Hit your dinner gong to get attention. Then turn your silver tongue loose and lure your unsuspecting guests into the big tent to have their fortunes read."

"I think I can," I murmured, "but to tell the truth, I'm nervous as hell."

"So am I—but let's not be!" Brooke smiled. "Now remember this, Greg—you're to watch and follow me when I leave. Your car is ready, I suppose? Good! All right—let's start the big show!"

Clay Brooke saw me hesitating, so he seized the Chinese gong and beat upon it furiously. The music and gaiety suddenly stopped and all eyes were turned in our direction.

"It was only me," Brooke smiled. "Our host has something to announce."

He darted an encouraging glance in my direction, so I began an extemporaneous bally-hoo.

"La-dees and gen-tul-men! We have for this aus-pic-ious oc-cai-shun one of the won-dahs of the age for your en-tuh-tain-ment! We have at great ex-pense secured Mam-selle Fi-fi, the girl mah-vul, a pret-ty lit-tul la-dee who wants to see you one and all! Step into the side-show tent—into the cham-bah of mys-ter-ee, and let the lit-tul la-dee tell your past, present, and future! She will am-aze you! She will fas-cin-ate you! She will fore-tell as-toun-ding wealth and rich marriages for you one and all! Don't crowd, la-dees and gents, but step one at a time into the cham-bah of mah-vuls and consult Mam-selle Fi-fi!"

Enthusiastic cries and applause followed as I finished, and I noticed that Brooke had rushed Mitchell Gilbert to the head of the line which was forming, doubtless to give the girl an easy candidate for her first reading. As young Gilbert stepped into the dark room, June Moran became the first in line, followed by Johnny Dines, then Carol Grant, Betty Duane, Carleton Dazian, Dolores Fenton, Charles Gilbert and Harry Gibbs. Others who were far in the rear, seated themselves to await their turn.

After a few minutes Mitchell Gilbert stepped out smiling broadly, apparently pleased with what the fair seeress had told him. Clay Brooke disappeared into the mystic chamber for a moment, then motioned for June

Moran to enter. He repeated the same performance as Johnny Dines' turn came, and the others who followed in line.

"It's great, folks!" the comedian announced when he emerged. "I was told that I'm going to marry the leading lady of my next picture. I've got a contract ready, so step up girls, but don't knock me down in the rush."

Clay Brooke approached Johnny and whispered something in his ear. The comedian smiled and nodded, then going to the piano he began ragging oriental music. Those who had been sitting awaiting their turn rose and sought dancing partners, trying to keep their places in line all the while. When Betty Duane emerged giggling from the dark room, Carleton Dazian entered. Dolores Fenton was chatting with Charles Gilbert as she waited her turn, while Clay Brooke continued to remain at his station at the entrance. When Dazian emerged, Brooke stepped in quickly and then reappeared and admitted Dolores. The criminologist nervously drew a cigaret from his case and lighted it, then walked over toward the piano and carefully surveyed the room. He had permitted Charles Gilbert to enter the dark room unannounced, probably because the girl knew her role well enough in this case.

"Con-stan-tin-o-ple! Tummety - rum - tum - tum!" Johnny sang, continuing to beat upon the keys and giving a drumming syncopation to the oriental number.

When Charles Gilbert emerged from the chamber of mystery, he approached Clay Brooke smilingly and offered a cigar, but the latter refused it and continued to puff nervously on his cigaret. Then Brooke glanced in my direction with a perplexed expression, and leaving the millionaire he walked slowly out of the room toward the kitchen. After a moment he returned rapidly and glanced about the room. Then, quickening his pace, he hurried out the front door. He was just gone for a second, and as he hastily returned he motioned to me, then slid out of the side door while I followed as quickly as I could without attracting attention. Brooke was already in my car when I arrived.

"Now's the time, Greg!" he murmured calmly. "Our man has skipped! Put out your lights and get started as quietly as you can. And for God's sake don't lose sight of the red tail-light of that cab!"

XXII. The House on Temple Street

We rounded the corner of the drive that led to the street and followed the taxicab as cautiously as possible. Kranz, following my instructions, after traveling at a slow gait to enable us to pick up the trail, suddenly put on speed, only slowing down to round a corner.

"Easy, now, Greg, easy!" Brooke cautioned. "Let's not get too close to the fellow. Better put your lights on now. We'd be in a pretty mess if a motor-cycle cop decided to pick us up."

He lapsed into silence and I continued to wonder what his game might be? Whom were we trailing? What had happened in the darkened study? And what was the role that Evelyn Halloway was playing—or the absent Claire?

"Are we after Mitchell Gilbert?" I finally ventured.

Brooke laughed softly. "No, Greg—not young Gilbert. He is quite innocent—the story he told us was the truth. He is the one who unwittingly involved Claire Demoset. They went to the studio together and she waited for him in the reception room. Later, she thought something was up and came onto the stage and concealed herself in that Chinese street. When she saw Mitchell come out she feared the worst and that was why she refused to speak—to say anything. When the boy's father arrived she was unable to get away and that very nearly made matters worse. Claire finally told me the whole thing, and I tell you, boy, I was glad to hear it!"

"Then who—"

"Well, it's time I told you that the man in that taxicab is Carleton Dazian. Tonight's social event, with the aid of the goldfish globe, convinces me that Dazian is going to open our eyes to something rather amazing."

"But, what—"

"Ah—he's turning another corner," Brooke interrupted. "Watch now—slowly! Cross this street, Greg, then we'll turn around and pick up his trail again. Dazian may be watching from the rear seat. Now I'd better tell you what we're apt to encounter so that you'll be able to assist me and not get your instructions at the last minute. In the first place, I have no idea where Dazian is going, but it's plain enough that he's in a devilish hurry to get somewhere. Wherever it is, we've got to get there first and meet him when he steps out of the taxi. There's a slight chance that he'll go to his hotel, but I rather doubt it. Still—I'm prepared in case he does, so I'll tell you my plan.

"Assuming that Dazian goes to his hotel, Kranz is to wait for him till he comes out—he'll probably ask Kranz to wait anyway. Now he's got to come out, but if he doesn't, I've a subtle way of making him, which I'll tell you later. Anyway, should he alight at the hotel, we'll whizz by so fast that he won't see us. Then we'll park your car around the corner, get a cab, and drive to a corner across from the hotel. Kranz will be waiting there with his cab. I'll perform my stunt and Dazian will come out, re-enter Kranz's car and tell him where to drive. Kranz will pretend he doesn't know how to get to the address and will come over to our driver to ask. Then he'll tell our man what his destination is. While he's returning to his cab our driver will be under way so that we'll arrive at the address just ahead of Dazian and can nab him there. Is that all clear? You're to get the cab for us and give the instructions to Kranz. In the event that Dazian doesn't go to the hotel, but to this unknown address, we'll have to speed up and get him as he steps out of his taxi. H'm, we seem to be getting into town."

"Yes," I agreed. "Dazian must be heading for the hotel, unless he's cutting through town to get to this strange address you mention."

Clay Brooke chuckled to himself. "You're still pretty much in the dark, aren't you, Greg? Well, it won't be for much longer. I wonder—I wonder if Claire Demoset is still working at the studio? I had no idea that your hard-hearted.old producers made the darlings of the screen stay after school and work nights. Oh, well, I suppose it's this curse called 'efficiency', or else it has something to do with a quota. Well, I'm hoping we'll get this unpleasantness over soon and can return to your party in time to greet the lovely Claire."

"Say, Brooke!" I cut in. "Dazian is heading for the hotel, all right! It's right around the next corner! See, Kranz is slowing down for the traffic!"

"Good! Now, Greg—swing into that private driveway on the right! That's it! As soon as Dazian's taxi gets around the corner, we'll come out again and park. Now, if Dazian happened to be watching us, I'll wager we've given him a feeling of relief by turning in. Here comes a cab—I'll hail it while you're parking your car."

Clay Brooke sprang out swiftly, hurried down the drive and signaled for the approaching taxicab. It stopped as I swung out of the driveway, and after parking my coupe down the street I rejoined Brooke, who was standing by the door of the cab.

"I've given this fellow the instruction," he told me, "and I've also told him to listen well to Kranz's directions. Now you pile in and drive around to the corner across the street from the hotel. Then find Kranz and tell him what he's to do—not to accept any fare but Dazian, and to be sure and give the address of Dazian's destination to our driver. After you've done this, get back in this taxi and wait for me. I'm going to run into the hotel and make sure that Dazian obliges us by coming out. See you in a moment."

The criminologist disappeared around the corner and I followed in the taxicab, making sure that the driver stopped at the corner that Clay Brooke indicated. Kranz's taxi was stationed near the entrance, and I lost no time in acquainting him with the events which were to follow. The cab driver repeated my instructions carefully and glanced across, where our taxi was standing.

"I got you," he nodded when I finished. "What is this thing—are you tryin' to get the goods on a bum bootlegger? This bird I had in the cab is the most nervous guy I ever see."

"How do you mean?"

"Oh, I dunno—just naturally nervous. Didn't know where in hell he wanted to go. First he gave me an address in Los Angeles, then he decided on this hotel. Then he changed his mind, and finally I landed him here."

"What was the Los Angeles address?"

"Out by Temple Street, near Main."

"Well, we may get there before the night's over," I said. "I'd better be getting back to the other cab. You're sure you understand everything?"

"Okay," Kranz nodded.

I crossed the street and climbed into the cab to wait for Brooke. A few minutes later, the criminologist came hastily out of the hotel, dodged through the passing traffic and joined me in the taxicab.

"What luck?" I asked him.

"Everything's going according to schedule," Brooke announced. "He was in his room, but he ought to be out any minute. Do these cab drivers understand what they're to do?"

"Yes. By the way, Kranz said that Dazian first directed him to drive to Temple Street—that's an address in Los Angeles—then he changed his mind and told him to drive to this hotel. On the way he changed his mind again, but wound up by coming here."

"H'm," Brooke murmured. "That place in Los Angeles—that's probably where we'll be going. Dazian ought to be down in a minute. I wonder what's keeping him this long?"

"Are you sure he'll be down?"

"Absolutely! There he comes! Don't let him see you, Greg!"

We watched in silence as Carleton Dazian approached Kranz's cab, gave directions and stepped in. Brooke chuckled to himself as the driver immediately registered bewilderment. Dazian started to leave the cab and Brooke swore under his breath, but Kranz apparently assured his fare that it would only be the matter of a moment, and as Dazian sank back into his seat, Kranz approached our taxi.

"Boarding house on Temple near Main," we heard him murmur to our driver, giving the number of the house.

Then, as Kranz started back across the street, Brooke gave the signal to our driver and we were off through the traffic.

"Slower!" the criminologist shouted. "You can speed it up after we get clear of this traffic!" Brooke glanced out of the rear window. Then: "Yes, he's coming, all right! You can step on it now, Bill," he shouted, leaning forward.

The nervous tension of the affair was beginning to get me and I tossed my cigaret stub away and lighted another. Brooke continued to stare blankly into the darkness, becoming alert now and then and peering out of the rear window. Then he lighted a cigaret himself, and leaned back against the springless cushion of the cab.

"What's going to happen next?" I asked, breaking a long silence.

Clay Brooke appeared not to hear me. Then:

"What's that? Oh—what's going to happen next? I'm blessed if I know, Greg. One thing, I'm pretty certain, you're going to get the surprise of your life. But if you're hinting for future instructions, I can't give them to you. It's every man for himself from now on, so stay close to me."

"You—you mean we're apt to have some trouble?"

"Perhaps. Let's see, I ought to have a good word to use to bring you into action if it's necessary. How about 'sock'? That's one of the most descriptive words I know. 'Sock'—

you know, you 'sock' someone? Well, should I happen to say 'sock,' you're to haul off and 'sock' the nearest person—excepting me, of course!"

Clay Brooke paused for a moment to look through the small window in the rear of the cab.

"Can you step on it some more?" he called to the driver. Then turning to me, he added, "I can see a pair of headlights way down the stretch—I don't think he's gaining on us, but it's better to play safe. This is an odd thing, you know—instead of chasing our man, we're actually being chased!"

The criminologist lapsed into silence again as we sped to our mysterious destination. As I looked out of the window, I could see we were over the celluloid border and already in Los Angeles.

"We're getting close to Temple Street," I told Brooke. "It's only a few blocks more."

"Good!" he ejaculated. Then, leaning forward, he spoke to our driver. "When you get to this address drive slowly so that we can both jump. Then, keep going down the street and wait for us around the next corner. We'll try not to keep you waiting long. I'll whistle when I want you."

The driver nodded mechanically and in the next moment we whizzed around a corner and struck a bump in the road that nearly threw us both to the floor of the car.

"We must be here!" Brooke exclaimed. "Say, isn't this a dingy old street? Just the place for a strange assignation. I'll wager these old houses belonged to fashionable people at one time. Isn't it a pity to see them fall into decay?"

"This joint you're goin' to is half-way down the block," the driver said, turning slightly. "Better get ready to do your Brodie."

"All right, Greg!" Brooke said, opening the door. Then, as the driver indicated the house, Brooke sprang from the car and I followed, slamming the door after me. The cab continued down the street and Brooke drew me into the shadows as the headlights of another car came around the corner.

The house before us had evidently been the home of an old family of the better class, as Brooke had observed of the others in the row, but it now showed signs of dilapidation, and a card announcing rooms for rent was prominently displayed near the door. Few lights were visible, giving it an especially gloomy and forbidding look.

"There's a palm tree that was put here just for us," Brooke murmured? and keeping under cover he drew me to a dark spot in the small front yard. "Don't forget to 'sock', Greg, if it's necessary."

In the next moment the other car drew up and stopped. Carleton Dazian alighted, paid his fare, and dismissed the cab. Then, looking carefully about, he approached the house.

"Carleton Dazian, as I live!" Brooke exclaimed, stepping out from our hiding place. "Fancy meeting you here!"

"Why—why, Mr. Brooke!" Dazian stammered, staring as though he had seen an apparition.

"I had an idea you were going to make a late call when you left so hurriedly," the criminologist blandly continued, "so we thought we'd come along. You've no objection, I hope?"

"B—but there must be some mistake, Mr. Brooke. You see, I have a sick aunt who lives here and I promised to drop in and see her tonight."

"Seeing sick aunts is one of my favorite indoor sports," Brooke smiled. "I hope she's well enough to receive company."

"The fact is—she isn't! She's very ill, Mr. Brooke. I'm sorry I can't ask you to come in."

"Oh, but you will!" the criminologist replied coolly. "We're either going in with you, or you're going to police headquarters with us!"

"What for!"

"Charged with the murder of James Taylor! Now look here, Dazian, I'm on to your game and I won't waste words with you. If you don't want to talk to me I'll let you tell your story to John Rawson or to Captain Carling. I'm not fussy—you can take your choice."

Dazian looked decidedly uncomfortable. "You—you can't prove anything!" he blustered.

"Really, Dazian, I didn't expect you to be so unreasonable! I can recall a time a few days ago when you came before us and asked to help solve the murder of Berylyn Bovary. Since then, Barbatti has been murdered and something has happened to the studio detective."

"Well, what do you want me to do?" Dazian asked, regaining some of his composure.

"I want to know what happened to Taylor!" Brooke demanded. "And I want you to lead me into this house to the room where you were going—the ailing aunt's room, if you prefer to put it that way. And no funny business! Come, be a good fellow—let's waste no more time!"

Carleton Dazian hesitated and then appeared to come to the conclusion that it would be best for him to do as Brooke demanded.

"All right—come on!" he said with a shrug.

We followed him up the steps of the old house, then Clay Brooke stepped ahead and tried the handle of the door. It was unlocked, so he pushed it open.

"I'm relieved at that!" Brooke remarked. "I have a horror of ringing strange door-bells at this hour of the night unless—unless it's Hallowe'en. You'd better lead the way, Dazian."

A single light glowed in the hallway, at the bottom of an ornate old staircase. Dazian kept to the right of the stairs and led the way to a door at the rear of the narrow hall on the first floor. As he approached it, Clay Brooke stepped ahead of him and, stooping, peered through the keyhole. Then he tried the handle of the door.

"Your sick aunt seems to be locked in a dark room," the criminologist remarked humorously. "How are we going to get in there?"

In answer, Dazian bent down, and feeling under the corner of the well-worn red carpet drew out a key. This he inserted in the lock and opened the door for us to enter.

"Just a moment," Brooke said, "as this is a snap lock, I see no reason why we can't return the key to its hiding-place."

Dazian reluctantly did as the criminologist suggested, then pressed a light switch in the room and we entered. Brooke closed the door after him and glanced searchingly about the room. In one corner was a large wooden bed covered with a faded quilt, and between two open windows stood an oak bureau with a large, old-fashioned white china bowl and water pitcher. A green-cushioned morris chair, a table, and several wooden chairs completed the furnishings. No personal belongings were visible except two closed valises which stood by the bureau. Clay Brooke ignored the latter, his gaze falling on the two open windows, and walking toward them he closed each one.

"A person hesitates much longer about going through a closed window than an open one," he remarked. "You see, we're pretty close to the ground. Hence my precaution."

Brooke gazed in an amused manner at Dazian, who shifted nervously and then dropped into a chair.

"What do you really want of me tonight, Mr. Brooke?" he demanded.

"Your assistance—your assistance which you once generously offered."

"Then when you accused me of the murder of Taylor, you did so as a threat—to gain admittance to this place?"

"We're here, aren't we?" Brooke smiled. "Really, Dazian, I don't like to have you think ill of me, but—may I smoke? I'm sure your dear old aunt won't object."

Clay Brooke eyed the man before him narrowly as' he applied the flame of his lighter to his cigaret. Dazian shifted 'his gaze and looked nervously in the direction of the door.

"Oh, pardon me!" Brooke said, drawing his cigaret case from his pocket again. "I didn't mean to be rude. Won't you have one of these?"

Dazian shrugged his shoulders, then rose from his chair and accepted a cigaret. The criminologist handed the man his lighter, and just as Dazian snapped on the flame, Brooke clapped both of his hands on the man's hips, then came up with his right hand quick as a flash and drew an automatic out from under the gigolo's coat.

"Just a precaution," Brooke smiled. "I'm sure you don't mind."

"That's why I was carrying it—just as a precaution."

Dazian turned sulkily and walked back to his chair. He took to rocking his chair nervously, and a squeaky board in the floor seemed to annoy him; so he moved toward the bureau.

"A little nervous, Dazian?" Brooke asked.

"No—not much." He began rocking again. Then: "Well, what's going to happen next?"

"I think we'll turn out the lights," Brooke said. "Then we'll wait and see what's going to happen. Dazian, you stay where you are. Greg, you better get over in that far corner. I'll stay here, it's nearest to the light switch. Now, I want absolute silence, and when a key is fitted into that door I don't want any one to move. When our expected party enters and the door closes behind him, I'm going to switch on the lights. And, Gregory, don't forget that word of mine—'sock,' you know."

As Clay Brooke finished his instructions, he extinguished his cigaret in an ash tray, passed the tray to Dazian, who sullenly did the same, then stepped to the light switch and plunged the room in darkness.

"Greg," he said, after a few moments of silence, "your white shirt-front stands out like a light-house. Close up the front of your coat and I'll do the same. You, too, Dazian."

Suddenly a door slammed outside and a hush came over the room as we waited expectantly for approaching footsteps. I glanced at Carleton Dazian and noticed that he had shifted nervously in his chair. A steady tread on the creaking staircase informed us that the footsteps did not belong to the person we were awaiting.

Ten or fifteen minutes passed and nothing happened. The only sound in the darkened room was the harsh ticking of an alarm clock on the bureau. Clay Brooke stifled a nervous cough and I fancied he was about to speak when the silence was again broken by the opening of the front door. Then it slammed loudly and footsteps could be faintly heard coming down the hall, in the direction of the door to the room we were in!

It seemed that there must be two people approaching, for I could hear a hushed conversation outside. Then there was a fumbling under the carpet, and in the next moment a key was thrust in the door. As it slowly swung open, two forms came to view—a man and a woman— silhouetted by the light in the hall. They entered quietly, almost ghostly—then something happened that made my heart leap to my throat!

There was a sound like the opening of a bureau drawer, and something glistened in Dazian's hand.

"Damn you, Taylor!" he screamed. "You killed Berylyn—and you killed Barbatti!"

Then, before Clay Brooke or I could make a move, a streak of fire split the darkness and an explosion like the roar of a ship's big gun filled the room with a deafening noise. The man swayed and staggered, and the woman rushed to a corner as Dazian's revolver talked again. The intruder pitched forward with a crash upon the floor; then, seeming momentarily to recover himself, his hand sought something, and a bright object roared, then dropped clattering to the floor like iron.

"He—he got me—the damned murderer!" Dazian gasped in agony. "He—" Then he fell headlong and lay in a crumpled heap as Clay Brooke snapped on the lights.

It had all happened in a second or so, and blinking to accustom my eyes to the sudden glare of the lights I saw that the intruder lying in a pool of blood near the door was James Taylor, while the woman trembling with fright in the corner was Margaret Hagney. Dazian lay quite still where he had fallen.

"Grab those guns, Greg!" Brooke snapped. "Now I know why Dazian picked that traveling rocking-chair! I should have searched that bureau! Looks like he's done for! You!" he shouted in the direction of the Hagney woman, "Get some water—pronto! That pitcher will do!"

The criminologist hastened to the side of Carleton Dazian and bent over to see if the man's heart was still beating. He rose, shaking his head; then he stepped over to Taylor and raised him gently. The studio-detective's coat was thrown open and a large, crimson blood-stain was becoming visible on the left side of his shirt.

"Bring that water!" Brooke repeated sharply, turning to Margaret Hagney, who was staring dumbly in his direction. "Taylor's not quite done for. At least, he didn't have to chop up a chicken this time to furnish evidence of his own tragedy. But we're wasting time—Greg, you'd better run and 'phone for an ambulance—and make it snappy!"

XXIII. THE CASE ENDS

Clay Brooke nervously paced the corridor outside of the operating room of St. Margaret's Hospital. I was decidedly wrought-up myself, and wished that a small sign on the wall did not forbid smoking. The nerve-racking experience of scarcely fifteen minutes ago had shattered our sensibilities, and neither of us had spoken on the way to the hospital.

Suddenly the door of the operating room opened and Dr. Eberhardt appeared.

"How is he?" Brooke asked.

Dr. Eberhardt slowly shook his head. "It will be a miracle if he pulls through," he said. "I am very much afraid that death will come while we are probing for the bullet." He paused for a moment, then: "He has asked to speak with you, Mr. Brooke."

The criminologist mechanically reached for his cigaret case; then, remembering that smoking was forbidden, thrust it back into his pocket.

"All right," he murmured. "Greg, do you think you can stand it? I'd like to have you hear what he has to say."

The surgeon led us into the operating room. A nurse hovered over the operating table where James Taylor lay, the light overhead falling on his ghastly white face. As we drew closer, he opened his eyes and they lighted up with a wan smile of recognition.

"The Doc thinks I'm done for, Mr. Brooke," he said, in an almost inaudible voice, "but I'll fool 'em, even if I do have to do a stretch at San Quentin. They—they want to dig for the bullet, but I wanted to see you first, in case of—an accident."

"You're going to be all right, Taylor," Brooke said, "and I'm going to see that they do everything they can for you."

"You're a real guy, Mr. Brooke," Taylor murmured. "I knew it from the first—that's why I wanted to see you—to sorta set you right about things. But I guess maybe you know about everything."

"Not quite everything, Taylor."

"You—you sorta had an idea that first night, didn't you?"

"Just an idea," Brooke replied. "Your actions rather aroused my curiosity—when you showed me around the studio, and when you helped lift the murdered girl to the couch. You and Margaret Hagney made a bad mistake when you invented the mysterious stranger. That was very bad judgment. It excited my suspicions immediately."

"But even then you weren't sure, were you?"

"Not absolutely. I was a little surer when we visited Bovary's bungalow together and found Barbatti's Monte Cristo stock which you sold the girl. But it was when we re-enacted the crime that I was rather more convinced. You were a little too sure of yourself, Taylor. Then, when young Gilbert named Greg as the man who had deposited the body in the wardrobe—well, I observed that your trousers were of almost the same material. But I was fully convinced of your hand in the affair when I visited your rooms. I investigated your quarters at the time you came to Greg's house in answer to my message. There I found the solution to the star design which was on the blood-stained slip of paper containing Barbatti's initials. I found this same design on a memorandum pad and on a magazine, and I concluded that, like many people, you toy with a pencil—that you always scribble that particular design when you have a pencil in your hand."

Taylor regarded Brooke intently. "When—when did you connect me with Dazian?"

"On the night of the murder of Barbatti. You both planned alibis for that night. You had a telegram sent to yourself from San Bernardino, and Dazian went out of his way to tell me that he had tried to see me that night. An odd pair, you and Dazian."

"Yes—an odd pair," Taylor repeated feebly. "I—I'd like to tell you about it from the beginning. Doc, can I have some water?"

Dr. Eberhardt stepped quickly to the stand near the door, and returning, held the glass to Taylor's lips. After a moment the dying man began his story.

"It started when I left the bank, Mr. Brooke. I had a good job there, and I should have stuck. The—the people around the studios figured I must know about stocks and good things to pick up, and they gave me their money to invest. For a while I played square, then I began to spend some of the money and—and that was the beginning. When dividends were wanted, I paid it from the capital I got from new chumps. If I'd had any sense I would have known that sometime all of the jack must be returned. But I—"

A fit of coughing interrupted him and he was unable to continue. Dr. Eberhardt hovered over him anxiously, but Taylor rallied after sipping from the glass held out to him. The recital was obviously taxing his strength, but he persisted in going on with it.

"I've—got to—finish," he murmured. Then he seemed to be trying to remember where he had left off.

"The—the wop, Barbatti, was one of the suckers," he finally went on, "and it was in his place that I ran into Dazian. He was having plenty trouble—the Bovary dame, and everything else. I wish to God I'd never seen him! We—we got together and I got wise how he was selling bum stock to the dame. I sold her that Monte Cristo stuff. Well, we knew a show-down was coming, so we decided to crack the safe at the studio, then clean out. We'd got away with it, if it hadn't been for the dame. First we got Margaret Hagney a job as Bovary's maid. She got the combination of the safe and tipped us off when there'd be a stack of dough on hand. If I'd known Dazian was trying to get the girl to run away with him, I wouldn't have had anything to do with it. She fooled him into thinking she'd ditch old Gilbert, then skip to Canada and work back to New York. As if she'd gone through with it! Then—"

Taylor struggled for strength to go on. His speech thickened. Life and death seemed to be haggling over the man.

"Some brandy, Miss Morris!" the surgeon snapped, and, as the nurse rushed to his side, he managed to pour a few drops down Taylor's throat. For a moment the dying man's eyes seemed transfixed, then they turned to Clay Brooke, as if with the criminologist rested all his hopes.

"Suppose I go on from there," Brooke said soothingly. Then, after a moment: "On the night of the murder, Dazian visited Bovary to assure himself that she would go with him. Then he looked about to see if the coast was clear. The studio was empty—Barney was got out of the way; and Miss Hagney, on her way for the aspirin, had given the signal to you, outside. When you entered, Dazian was in the telephone booth, and you went to the prop room to get the gloves to prevent finger-prints. Wagner came in, got his coat, and went his way. Then you left the prop room and entered the office where you began work on the safe."

Brooke paused, and Taylor nodded feebly in confirmation.

"You were about to open the safe," Brooke continued, "when Dazian entered and asked you to wait. Then he brought Bovary in and told her what was up and that the time had come for them to skip. When the girl saw to what lengths Dazian was going for cold cash, she rebelled, telling him he was crazy, threatening to call out. At this point, Dazian saw red. He realized the risk he was running—and all for her! Well, he grabbed her, she struggled, and in a fury he picked up the first thing that came into his hand. Then it happened.

"At this time, Mitchell Gilbert entered the studio bound for the dressing-room. He heard sounds which terrified him and he hid in the wardrobe where you thrust the body of the murdered girl fairly on top of him. Then, Taylor, you picked up the jewels to make the crime appear to be a murder for robbery and ran blindly for the property room to gather your wits. When you were in the prop room, Gilbert got out of the studio—and all of the time there was a woman paralyzed with fear concealed in the Chinese street 'set'. She didn't see you go, Taylor. If you hadn't used that piece of paper to wipe the blood from your hands, it might have ended differently. And if you hadn't gone to Barbatti's to silence him—"

"I—I didn't silence Barbatti!" Taylor interrupted, attempting to raise himself from the pillow. "It was Dazian—damn him! He hurled himself on Barbatti and gave him the shove that caused his death!"

"But I knew you were there, Taylor," Brooke cut in quietly, "for you left the same clue that I found when you planned that curious murder of yourself—rubber heel marks. Very elemental, of course, but I had reached a point where I was ready to grasp at anything. Regarding your own private murder, Taylor, you probably do not know that there is a great difference between blood-stains from a human and blood-stains from a fowl. Dazian was the clever one—even suggesting that you carry the body into the dressing-room while he made his getaway, and hoping you'd be caught. Dazian—"

"God damn Dazian!" Taylor suddenly screamed, startling each one of us. "God damn Dazian and that woman of his! But I killed—"

His voice trailed off; he fell back still and ashen-hued. Dr. Eberhardt bent over and listened for heart beats.

"He's holding on," he murmured. "I'm going to probe for the bullet now. There's just a chance—a mighty slim chance."

"I don't think we'll be needed any longer, doctor," Brooke said, starting for the door.

Dr. Eberhardt shook his head in silence.

As we reached the corridor outside, John Rawson came in in a state of suppressed excitement. When he saw us he breathed a sigh of relief.

"Thank God—thank God, you're safe!" he exclaimed. "The message I received was considerably botched and I feared the worst. Brooke, what in the devil has happened!"

"Dazian is dead," Brooke announced calmly, "and Taylor is in pretty bad shape. The surgeon is preparing to probe for the bullet. The Hagney woman is in the custody of the police."

The criminologist then proceeded to relate the dramatic events which took place in the house on Temple Street and ended in the shooting fray.

"You see, Rawson," he finished, "Dazian got the sudden idea to accuse Taylor of both murders, then blazed away with his gun figuring he'd silence the man and nobody'd be the wiser. Thought he'd enter a plea of self-defense, likely, and get out of the mess. I took one gun away from him, but he snatched another from the bureau drawer just as Taylor entered. Taylor finished him. It was most exciting!"

"Good God!" Rawson exclaimed, half incredulously. "How did you get the goods on Dazian? This isn't all very clear to me, but I gather that Dazian killed Bovary and Barbatti, did he not?"

Brooke nodded. "It was the matter of my decision to use the inductive method, combined with a bit of clairvoyancy. I decided that Carleton Dazian was the murderer, then set out to prove it. I pulled a bluff on him by means of a crystal globe, having my fair seeress, Evelyn Halloway, tell him that she saw his business partner seeking him anxiously on a matter of the utmost importance. I had sized Dazian up as a superstitious type. It worked. He was bewildered, but convinced, and he scurried to Taylor's hiding place. But I'll tell you all about it in the morning, old fellow. I'm rather done up."

"I should think so—I should think so! Well, Brooke, I'll see you sometime in the morning. I'd run along with you now, but I'm interested in Dr. Eberhardt's report."

We left the District Attorney and stepped out into the freshness of the night—a night so lovely and peaceful that it seemed incongruous after the hair-raising experience we both had been through. Clay Brooke sniffed the cool air, then looked up at the cloudless sky.

"Just look at those stars—how they twinkle, Greg!" he said slowly. "Which reminds me—I wonder if it's too late to reach that loveliest of stars—Claire Demoset? I'd like to tell her—many things. I wonder if she'd listen? Greg, do you think I'd be known as Mr. Claire Demoset?"

THE END

Resurrected Press Books in *The Chief Inspector Pointer Mystery* Series

RESURRECTED PRESS BOOKS IN H. ASHBOOK'S
DETECTIVE SPIKE TRACY MYSTERY SERIES

RESURRECTED PRESS BOOKS FROM *THE
ETHEL THOMAS DETECTIVE STORY*
SERIES BY CORTLAND FITZSIMMON'S

The Whispering Window

The Moving Finger

Mystery at Hidden Harbor

The Evil Men Do

RESURRECTED PRESS BOOKS FROM *THE JAMES "BONNIE" DUNDEE MYSTERY* SERIES BY ANNE AUSTIN

The Black Pigeon

The Avenging Parrot

Murder Backstairs

Murder at Bridge

One Drop of Blood

Murdered, But Not Dead

AVAILABLE FROM RESURRECTED PRESS!

JOURNEYS INTO MYSTERY

A collection of three novels of travel and mystery from some of the best known writers of the Edwardian Age

A man is mysteriously murdered on the night express from Rome to Paris. Which one of the passengers is the murderer. The Countess? The General? The clergyman? The maid who disappeared?

A sapphire necklace stolen from a cab in the London fog. A ship's steward who is either more or less than he appears to be. A jewel thief who criss-crosses the Atlantic in search of victims.

A grand London hotel. A missing German prince. A murdered man whose body disappears from the hotel. These are the challenges facing an American millionaire and his daughter after he buys The Grand Babylon Hotel.

- **The Rome Express – Arthur Griffiths**

- **The Voice in the Fog – Harold MacGrath**

- **The Grand Babylon Hotel – Arnold Bennett**

AVAILABLE FROM RESURRECTED PRESS!

THE EDWARDIAN DETECTIVES
LITERARY SLEUTHS OF THE EDWARDIAN ERA

The exploits of the great Victorian Detectives, Poe's C. Auguste Dupin, Gaboriau's Lecoq, and most famously, Arthur Conan Doyle's Sherlock Holmes, are well known. But what of those fictional detectives that came after, those of the Edwardian Age? The period between the death of Queen Victoria and the First World War had been called the Golden Age of the detective short story, but how familiar is the modern reader with the sleuths of this era? And such an extraordinary group they were, including in their numbers an unassuming English priest, a blind man, a master of disguises, a lecturer in medical jurisprudence, a noble woman working for Scotland Yard, and a savant so brilliant he was known as "The Thinking Machine."

To introduce readers to these detectives, Resurrected Press has assembled a collection of stories featuring these and other remarkable sleuths in The Edwardian Detectives.

- The Case of Laker, Absconded by Arthur Morrison
- The Fenchurch Street Mystery by Baroness Orczy
- The Crime of the French Café by Nick Carter
- The Man with Nailed Shoes by R Austin Freeman
- The Blue Cross by G. K. Chesterton
- The Case of the Pocket Diary Found in the Snow by Augusta Groner
- The Ninescore Mystery by Baroness Orczy
- The Riddle of the Ninth Finger by Thomas W. Hanshew

- The Knight's Cross Signal Problem by Ernest Bramah
- The Problem of Cell 13 by Jacques Futrelle
- The Conundrum of the Golf Links by Percy James Brebner
- The Silkworms of Florence by Clifford Ashdown
- The Gateway of the Monster by William Hope Hodgson
- The Affair at the Semiramis Hotel by A. E. W. Mason
- The Affair of the Avalanche Bicycle & Tyre Co., LTD by Arthur Morrison

RESURRECTED PRESS CLASSIC MYSTERY CATALOGUE

Journeys into Mystery
Travel and Mystery in a More Elegant Time

The Edwardian Detectives
Literary Sleuths of the Edwardian Era

Gems of Mystery
Lost Jewels from a More Elegant Age

E. C. Bentley
Trent's Last Case: The Woman in Black

Ernest Bramah
Max Carrados Resurrected:
The Detective Stories of Max Carrados

Agatha Christie
The Secret Adversary
The Mysterious Affair at Styles

Octavus Roy Cohen
Midnight

Freeman Wills Croft
The Ponson Case
The Pit Prop Syndicate

J. S. Fletcher
The Herapath Property
The Rayner-Slade Amalgamation
The Chestermarke Instinct
The Paradise Mystery
Dead Men's Money

The Middle of Things
Ravensdene Court
Scarhaven Keep
The Orange-Yellow Diamond
The Middle Temple Murder
The Tallyrand Maxim
The Borough Treasurer
In the Mayor's Parlour
The Saftey Pin

R. Austin Freeman
*The Mystery of 31 New Inn from the Dr. Thorndyke
Series*
*John Thorndyke's Cases from the Dr. Thorndyke
Series*
The Red Thumb Mark from The Dr. Thorndyke Series
The Eye of Osiris from The Dr. Thorndyke Series
A Silent Witness from the Dr. John Thorndyke Series
The Cat's Eye from the Dr. John Thorndyke Series
*Helen Vardon's Confession: A Dr. John Thorndyke
Story*
As a Thief in the Night: A Dr. John Thorndyke Story
*Mr. Pottermack's Oversight: A Dr. John Thorndyke
Story*
*Dr. Thorndyke Intervenes: A Dr. John Thorndyke
Story*
The Singing Bone: The Adventures of Dr. Thorndyke
The Stoneware Monkey: A Dr. John Thorndyke Story
*The Great Portrait Mystery, and Other Stories: A
Collection of Dr. John Thorndyke and Other Stories*
The Penrose Mystery: A Dr. John Thorndyke Story
The Uttermost Farthing: A Savant's Vendetta

Arthur Griffiths
The Passenger From Calais
The Rome Express

Fergus Hume
The Mystery of a Hansom Cab
The Green Mummy
The Silent House
The Secret Passage

Edgar Jepson
The Loudwater Mystery

A. E. W. Mason
At the Villa Rose

A. A. Milne
The Red House Mystery
Baroness Emma Orczy
The Old Man in the Corner

Edgar Allan Poe
The Detective Stories of Edgar Allan Poe

Arthur J. Rees
The Hampstead Mystery
The Shrieking Pit
The Hand In The Dark
The Moon Rock
The Mystery of the Downs

Mary Roberts Rinehart
Sight Unseen and The Confession

Dorothy L. Sayers
Whose Body?

Sir William Magnay
The Hunt Ball Mystery

Mabel and Paul Thorne
The Sheridan Road Mystery

Louis Tracy
The Strange Case of Mortimer Fenley
The Albert Gate Mystery
The Bartlett Mystery
The Postmaster's Daughter
The House of Peril
The Sandling Case: What Would You Have Done?
Charles Edmonds Walk
The Paternoster Ruby

John R. Watson
The Mystery of the Downs
The Hampstead Mystery

Edgar Wallace
The Daffodil Mystery
The Crimson Circle

Carolyn Wells
Vicky Van
The Man Who Fell Through the Earth
In the Onyx Lobby
Raspberry Jam
The Clue
The Room with the Tassels
The Vanishing of Betty Varian
The Mystery Girl
The White Alley
The Curved Blades
Anybody but Anne
The Bride of a Moment
Faulkner's Folly
The Diamond Pin
The Gold Bag
The Mystery of the Sycamore
The Come Backy

Raoul Whitfield
Death in a Bowl

And much more!
Visit ResurrectedPress.com
for our complete catalogue

About Resurrected Press

A division of Intrepid Ink, LLC, Resurrected Press is dedicated to bringing high quality, vintage books back into publication. See our entire catalogue and find out more at www.ResurrectedPress.com.

For announcements and updates on upcoming publications, LIKE us on Facebook!

www.Facebook.com/ResurrectedPress